# Author's National Edition

---

### THE WRITINGS OF
## MARK TWAIN
### VOLUME XXIV

This is the authorized
Uniform Edition of all.
my books.

Mark Twain

MARK TWAIN ON HIS 70TH BIRTHDAY

# THE $30,000 BEQUEST

## AND OTHER STORIES

BY

## MARK TWAIN
(SAMUEL L. CLEMENS)

ILLUSTRATED

HARPER & BROTHERS, PUBLISHERS
NEW YORK AND LONDON

# CONTENTS

# ILLUSTRATIONS

# THE $30,000 BEQUEST

# THE $30,000 BEQUEST

## I

LAKESIDE was a pleasant little town of five or six thousand inhabitants, and a rather pretty one, too, as towns go in the Far West. It had church accommodations for 35,000, which is the way of the Far West and the South, where everybody is religious, and where each of the Protestant sects is represented and has a plant of its own. Rank was unknown in Lakeside — unconfessed, anyway; everybody knew everybody and his dog, and a sociable friendliness was the prevailing atmosphere.

Saladin Foster was book-keeper in the principal store, and the only high-salaried man of his profession in Lakeside. He was thirty-five years old, now; he had served that store for fourteen years; he had begun in his marriage-week at four hundred dollars a year, and had climbed steadily up, a hundred dollars a year, for four years; from that time forth his wage had remained eight hundred — a handsome figure indeed, and everybody conceded that he was worth it.

His wife, Electra, was a capable helpmeet, although
—like himself—a dreamer of dreams and a private
dabbler in romance. The first thing she did, after
her marriage—child as she was, aged only nineteen—
was to buy an acre of ground on the edge of the town,
and pay down the cash for it—twenty-five dollars, all
her fortune. Saladin had less, by fifteen. She instituted a vegetable garden there, got it farmed on shares
by the nearest neighbor, and made it pay her a hundred per cent. a year. Out of Saladin's first year's wage
she put thirty dollars in the savings-bank, sixty out
of his second, a hundred out of his third, a hundred
and fifty out of his fourth. His wage went to eight
hundred a year, then, and meantime two children had
arrived and increased the expenses, but she banked
two hundred a year from the salary, nevertheless,
thenceforth. When she had been married seven years
she built and furnished a pretty and comfortable two-
thousand-dollar house in the midst of her garden-acre,
paid half of the money down and moved her family
in. Seven years later she was out of debt and had
several hundred dollars out earning its living.

Earning it by the rise in landed estate; for she had
long ago bought another acre or two and sold the
most of it at a profit to pleasant people who were willing to build, and would be good neighbors and furnish
a general comradeship for herself and her growing
family. She had an independent income from safe
investments of about a hundred dollars a year; her
children were growing in years and grace; and she

was a pleased and happy woman. Happy in her husband, happy in her children, and the husband and the children were happy in her. It is at this point that this history begins.

The youngest girl, Clytemnestra—called Clytie for short—was eleven; her sister, Gwendolen—called Gwen for short—was thirteen; nice girls, and comely. The names betray the latent romance-tinge in the parental blood, the parents' names indicate that the tinge was an inheritance. It was an affectionate family, hence all four of its members had pet names. Saladin's was a curious and unsexing one—Sally; and so was Electra's—Aleck. All day long Sally was a good and diligent book-keeper and salesman; all day long Aleck was a good and faithful mother and house-wife, and thoughtful and calculating business-woman; but in the cosey living-room at night they put the plodding world away, and lived in another and a fairer, reading romances to each other, dreaming dreams, comrading with kings and princes and stately lords and ladies in the flash and stir and splendor of noble palaces and grim and ancient castles.

## II

Now came great news! Stunning news — joyous news, in fact. It came from a neighboring State, where the family's only surviving relative lived. It was Sally's relative—a sort of vague and indefinite uncle or second or third cousin by the name of Tilbury Foster, seventy and a bachelor, reputed well-off and correspondingly sour and crusty. Sally had tried to make up to him once, by letter, in a by-gone time, and had not made that mistake again. Tilbury now wrote to Sally, saying he should shortly die, and should leave him thirty thousand dollars, cash; not for love, but because money had given him most of his troubles and exasperations, and he wished to place it where there was good hope that it would continue its malignant work. The bequest would be found in his will, and would be paid over. *Provided*, that Sally should be able to prove to the executors that he had *taken no notice of the gift by spoken word or by letter, had made no inquiries concerning the moribund's progress towards the everlasting tropics, and had not attended the funeral.*

As soon as Aleck had partially recovered from the tremendous emotions created by the letter, she sent to the relative's habitat and subscribed for the local paper.

Man and wife entered into a solemn compact, now, to never mention the great news to any one while the relative lived, lest some ignorant person carry the fact to the death-bed and distort it and make it appear that they were disobediently thankful for the bequest, and just the same as confessing it and publishing it, right in the face of the prohibition.

For the rest of the day Sally made havoc and confusion with his books, and Aleck could not keep her mind on her affairs, nor even take up a flower-pot or book or a stick of wood without forgetting what she had intended to do with it. For both were dreaming.

"Thir-ty thousand dollars!"

All day long the music of those inspiring words sang through those people's heads.

From his marriage-day forth, Aleck's grip had been upon the purse, and Sally had seldom known what it was to be privileged to squander a dime on non-necessities.

"Thir-ty thousand dollars!" the song went on and on. A vast sum, an unthinkable sum!

All day long Aleck was absorbed in planning how to invest it, Sally in planning how to spend it.

There was no romance-reading that night. The children took themselves away early, for the parents were silent, distraught, and strangely unentertaining. The good-night kisses might as well have been impressed upon vacancy, for all the response they got; the parents were not aware of the kisses, and the

children had been gone an hour before their absence
was noticed.  Two pencils had been busy during that
hour — note-making; in the way of plans.  It was
Sally who broke the stillness at last.  He said, with
exultation—

"Ah, it 'll be grand, Aleck!  Out of the first thousand we'll have a horse and a buggy for summer, and
a cutter and a skin lap-robe for winter."

Aleck responded with decision and composure—

"Out of the *capital?*  Nothing of the kind.  Not
if it was a million!"

Sally was deeply disappointed; the glow went out
of his face.

"Oh, Aleck!" he said, reproachfully.  "We've always worked so hard and been so scrimped; and now
that we are rich, it does seem—"

He did not finish, for he saw her eye soften; his
supplication had touched her.  She said, with gentle
persuasiveness—

"We must not spend the capital, dear, it would not
be wise.  Out of the income from it—"

"That will answer, that will answer, Aleck!  How
dear and good you are!  There will be a noble income,
and if we can spend that—"

"Not *all* of it, dear, not all of it, but you can spend
a part of it.  That is, a reasonable part.  But the
whole of the capital — every penny of it — must be put
right to work, and kept at it.  You see the reasona-
bleness of that, don't you?"

"Why, ye-s.  Yes, of course.  But we'll have to

wait so long. Six months before the first interest falls due."

"Yes—maybe longer."

"Longer, Aleck? Why? Don't they pay half-yearly?"

"*That* kind of an investment—yes; but I sha'n't invest in that way."

"What way then?"

"For big returns."

"Big. That's good. Go on, Aleck. What is it?"

"Coal. The new mines. Cannel. I mean to put in ten thousand. Ground floor. When we organize, we'll get three shares for one."

"By George, but it sounds good, Aleck! Then the shares will be worth—how much? And when?"

"About a year. They'll pay ten per cent. half-yearly, and be worth thirty thousand. I know all about it; the advertisement is in the Cincinnati paper here."

"Land, thirty thousand for ten—in a year! Let's jam in the whole capital and pull out ninety! I'll write and subscribe right now—to-morrow it may be too late."

He was flying to the writing-desk, but Aleck stopped him and put him back in his chair. She said:

"Don't lose your head so. We mustn't subscribe till we've got the money; don't you know that?"

Sally's excitement went down a degree or two, but he was not wholly appeased.

"Why, Aleck, we'll *have* it, you know—and so soon,

too. He's probably out of his troubles before this, it's a hundred to nothing he's selecting his brimstone-shovel this very minute. Now, I think—"

Aleck shuddered, and said:

"How *can* you, Sally! Don't talk in that way, it is perfectly scandalous."

"Oh well, make it a halo, if you like, *I* don't care for his outfit, I was only just talking. Can't you let a person talk?"

"But why should you *want* to talk in that dreadful way? How would you like to have people talk so about *you*, and you not cold yet?"

"Not likely to be, for *one* while, I reckon, if my last act was giving away money for the sake of doing somebody a harm with it. But never mind about Tilbury, Aleck, let's talk about something worldly. It does seem to me that that mine is the place for the whole thirty. What's the objection?"

"All the eggs in one basket—that's the objection."

"All right, if you say so. What about the other twenty? What do you mean to do with that?"

"There is no hurry; I am going to look around before I do anything with it."

"All right, if your mind's made up," sighed Sally. He was deep in thought awhile, then he said:

"There'll be twenty thousand profit coming from the ten a year from now. We can spend that, can't we, Aleck?"

Aleck shook her head.

"No, dear," she said, "it won't sell high till we've

had the first semi-annual dividend. You can spend part of that."

"Shucks, only *that*—and a whole year to wait! Confound it, I—"

"Oh, do be patient! It might even be declared in three months—it's quite within the possibilities."

"Oh, jolly! oh, thanks!" and Sally jumped up and kissed his wife in gratitude. "It 'll be three thousand —three whole thousand! how much of it can we spend, Aleck? Make it liberal—do, dear, that's a good fellow."

Aleck was pleased; so pleased that she yielded to the pressure and conceded a sum which her judgment told her was a foolish extravagance—a thousand dollars. Sally kissed her half a dozen times and even in that way could not express all his joy and thankfulness. This new access of gratitude and affection carried Aleck quite beyond the bounds of prudence, and before she could restrain herself she had made her darling another grant—a couple of thousand out of the fifty or sixty which she meant to clear within a year out of the twenty which still remained of the bequest. The happy tears sprang to Sally's eyes, and he said:

"Oh, I want to hug you!" And he did it. Then he got his notes and sat down and began to check off, for first purchase, the luxuries which he should earliest wish to secure. "Horse—buggy—cutter—lap-robe— patent-leathers—dog—plug hat—church-pew—stem- winder—new teeth—*say*, Aleck!"

"Well?"

"Ciphering away, aren't you? That's right. Have you got the twenty thousand invested yet?"

"No, there's no hurry about that; I must look around first, and think."

"But you are ciphering; what's it about?"

"Why, I have to find work for the thirty thousand that comes out of the coal, haven't I?"

"Scott, what a head! I never thought of that. How are you getting along? Where have you arrived?"

"Not very far—two years or three. I've turned it over twice; once in oil and once in wheat."

"Why, Aleck, it's splendid! How does it aggregate?"

"I think—well, to be on the safe side, about a hundred and eighty thousand clear, though it will probably be more."

"My! isn't it wonderful? By gracious! luck has come our way at last, after all the hard sledding. Aleck!"

"Well?"

"I'm going to cash-in a whole three hundred on the missionaries—what real right have we to care for expenses!"

"You couldn't do a nobler thing, dear; and it's just like your generous nature, you unselfish boy."

The praise made Sally poignantly happy, but he was fair and just enough to say it was rightfully due to Aleck rather than to himself, since but for her he should never have had the money.

Then they went up to bed, and in their delirium of bliss they forgot and left the candle burning in the parlor. They did not remember until they were undressed; then Sally was for letting it burn; he said they could afford it, if it was a thousand. But Aleck went down and put it out.

A good job, too; for on her way back she hit on a scheme that would turn the hundred and eighty thousand into half a million before it had had time to get cold.

# III

THE little newspaper which Aleck had subscribe
for was a Thursday sheet; it would make the trip
of five hundred miles from Tilbury's village and arrive
on Saturday. Tilbury's letter had started on Friday,
more than a day too late for the benefactor to die and
get into that week's issue, but in plenty of time to
make connection for the next output. Thus the Fosters had to wait almost a complete week to find out
whether anything of a satisfactory nature had happened to him or not. It was a long, long week, and
the strain was a heavy one. The pair could hardly
have borne it if their minds had not had the relief of
wholesome diversion. We have seen that they had
that. The woman was piling up fortunes right along,
the man was spending them—spending all his wife
would give him a chance at, at any rate.

At last the Saturday came, and the *Weekly Sagamore* arrived. Mrs. Eversly Bennett was present.
She was the Presbyterian parson's wife, and was working the Fosters for a charity. Talk now died a sudden
death—on the Foster side. Mrs. Bennett presently
discovered that her hosts were not hearing a word she
was saying; so she got up, wondering and indignant,
and went away. The moment she was out of the

house, Aleck eagerly tore the wrapper from the paper, and her eyes and Sally's swept the columns for the death notices. Disappointment! Tilbury was not anywhere mentioned. Aleck was a Christian from the cradle, and duty and the force of habit required her to go through the motions. She pulled herself together and said, with a pious two-per-cent. trade joyousness:

"Let us be humbly thankful that he has been spared; and—"

"Damn his treacherous hide, I wish—"

"Sally! For shame!"

"I don't care!" retorted the angry man. "It's the way *you* feel, and if you weren't so immorally pious you'd be honest and say so."

Aleck said, with wounded dignity:

"I do not see how you can say such unkind and unjust things. There is no such thing as immoral piety."

Sally felt a pang, but tried to conceal it under a shuffling attempt to save his case by changing the form of it—as if changing the form while retaining the juice could deceive the expert he was trying to placate. He said:

"I didn't mean so bad as that, Aleck; I didn't really mean immoral piety, I only meant — meant — well, conventional piety, you know; er—shop piety; the— the—why, *you* know what I mean, Aleck—the—well, where you put up the plated article and play it for solid, you know, without intending anything improper but just out of trade habit, ancient policy, petrified custom, loyalty to—to—hang it, I can't find the right words, but *you* know what I mean, Aleck, and that there isn't any harm in it. I'll try again. You see, it's this way. If a person—"

"You have said quite enough," said Aleck, coldly; let the subject be dropped."

"*I'm* willing," fervently responded Sally, wiping the sweat from his forehead and looking the thankfulness he had no words for. Then, musingly, he apologized to himself. "I certainly held threes—I *know* it—but I drew and didn't fill. That's where I'm so often weak in the game. If I had stood pat—but I didn't. I never do. I don't know enough."

Confessedly defeated, he was properly tame now and subdued. Aleck forgave him with her eyes.

The grand interest, the supreme interest, came instantly to the front again; nothing could keep it in the background many minutes on a stretch. The couple took up the puzzle of the absence of Tilbury's death notice. They discussed it every which way, more or less hopefully, but they had to finish where they began, and concede that the only really sane explanation of the absence of the notice must be— and without doubt was—that Tilbury was not dead. There was something sad about it, something even a little unfair, maybe, but there it was, and had to be put up with. They were agreed as to that. To Sally it seemed a strangely inscrutable dispensation; more inscrutable than usual, he thought; one of the most

unnecessarily inscrutable he could call to mind, in
fact—and said so, with some feeling; but if he was
hoping to draw Aleck he failed; she reserved her
opinion, if she had one; she had not the habit of taking injudicious risks in any market, worldly or other.

The pair must wait for next week's paper—Tilbury
had evidently postponed. That was their thought
and their decision. So they put the subject away,
and went about their affairs again with as good heart
as they could.

Now, if they had but known it, they had been
wronging Tilbury all the time. Tilbury had kept
faith, kept it to the letter; he was dead, he had died
to schedule. He was dead more than four days now
and used to it; entirely dead, perfectly dead, as dead
as any other new person in the cemetery; dead in
abundant time to get into that week's *Sagamore*, too,
and only shut out by an accident; an accident which
could not happen to a metropolitan journal, but which
happens easily to a poor little village rag like the
*Sagamore*. On this occasion, just as the editorial page
was being locked up, a gratis quart of strawberry
water-ice arrived from Hostetter's Ladies' and Gents'
Ice-Cream Parlors, and the stickful of rather chilly
regret over Tilbury's translation got crowded out to
make room for the editor's frantic gratitude.

On its way to the standing-galley Tilbury's notice
got pied. Otherwise it would have gone into some
future edition, for *Weekly Sagamores* do not waste

"live" matter, and in their galleys "live" matter is immortal, unless a pi accident intervenes. But a thing that gets pied is dead, and for such there is no resurrection; its chance of seeing print is gone, forever and ever. And so, let Tilbury like it or not, let him rave in his grave to his fill, no matter—no mention of his death would ever see the light in the *Weekly Sagamore*.

## IV

FIVE weeks drifted tediously along. The *Sagamore* arrived regularly on the Saturdays, but never once contained a mention of Tilbury Foster. Sally's patience broke down at this point, and he said, resentfully:

"Damn his livers, he's immortal!"

Aleck gave him a very severe rebuke, and added, with icy solemnity:

"How would you feel if you were suddenly cut off just after such an awful remark had escaped out of you?"

Without sufficient reflection Sally responded:

"I'd feel I was lucky I hadn't got caught with it *in* me."

Pride had forced him to say something, and as he could not think of any rational thing to say he flung that out. Then he stole a base—as he called it—that is, slipped from the presence, to keep from getting brayed in his wife's discussion-mortar.

Six months came and went. The *Sagamore* was still silent about Tilbury. Meantime, Sally had several times thrown out a feeler—that is, a hint that he would like to know. Aleck had ignored the hints. Sally now resolved to brace up and risk a frontal attack. So he squarely proposed to disguise himself and go to Tilbury's village and surreptitiously find out as to the prospects. Aleck put her foot on the dangerous project with energy and decision. She said:

"What can you be thinking of? You do keep my hands full! You have to be watched all the time, like a little child, to keep you from walking into the fire. You'll stay right were you are!"

"Why, Aleck, I could do it and not be found out— I'm certain of it."

"Sally Foster, don't you know you would have to inquire around?"

"Of course, but what of it? Nobody would suspect who I was."

"Oh, listen to the man! Some day you've got to prove to the executors that you never inquired. What then?"

He had forgotten that detail. He didn't reply; there wasn't anything to say. Aleck added:

"Now then, drop that notion out of your mind, and don't ever meddle with it again. Tilbury set that trap for you. Don't you know it's a trap? He is on the watch, and fully expecting you to blunder into it. Well, he is going to be disappointed—at least while I am on deck. Sally!"

"Well?"

"As long as you live, if it's a hundred years, don't you ever make an inquiry. Promise!"

"All right," with a sigh and reluctantly.

Then Aleck softened and said:

"Don't be impatient. We are prospering; we can wait; there is no hurry. Our small dead-certain income increases all the time; and as to futures, I have not made a mistake yet—they are piling up by the thousands and the tens of thousands. There is not another family in the State with such prospects as ours. Already we are beginning to roll in eventual wealth. You know that, don't you?"

"Yes, Aleck, it's certainly so."

"Then be grateful for what God is doing for us, and stop worrying. You do not believe we could have achieved these prodigious results without His special help and guidance, do you?"

Hesitatingly, "N-no, I suppose not." Then, with feeling and admiration, "And yet, when it comes to judiciousness in watering a stock or putting up a hand to skin Wall Street I don't give in that *you* need any outside amateur help, if I do I wish I—"

"Oh, *do* shut up! I know you do not mean any harm or any irreverence, poor boy, but you can't seem to open your mouth without letting out things to make a person shudder. You keep me in constant dread. For you and for all of us. Once I had no fear of the thunder, but now when I hear it I—"

Her voice broke, and she began to cry, and could not finish. The sight of this smote Sally to the heart and he took her in his arms and petted her and comforted her and promised better conduct, and upbraided himself and remorsefully pleaded for forgiveness.

And he was in earnest, and sorry for what he had done and ready for any sacrifice that could make up for it.

And so, in privacy, he thought long and deeply over the matter, resolving to do what should seem best. It was easy to *promise* reform; indeed he had already promised it. But would that do any real good, any permanent good? No, it would be but temporary— he knew his weakness, and confessed it to himself with sorrow—he could not keep the promise. Something surer and better must be devised: and he devised it. At cost of precious money which he had long been saving up, shilling by shilling, he put a lightning-rod on the house.

At a subsequent time he relapsed.

What miracles habit can do! and how quickly and how easily habits are acquired—both trifling habits and habits which profoundly change us. If by accident we wake at two in the morning a couple of nights in succession, we have need to be uneasy, for another repetition can turn the accident into a habit; and a month's dallying with whiskey—but we all know these commonplace facts.

The castle-building habit, the day-dreaming habit —how it grows! what a luxury it becomes; how we fly to its enchantments at every idle moment, how we revel in them, steep our souls in them, intoxicate ourselves with their beguiling fantasies—oh yes, and how soon and how easily our dream-life and our material life become so intermingled and so fused

together that we can't quite tell which is which, any
more.

By-and-by Aleck subscribed for a Chicago daily
and for the *Wall Street Pointer*. With an eye single
to finance she studied these as diligently all the week
as she studied her Bible Sundays. Sally was lost in
admiration, to note with what swift and sure strides
her genius and judgment developed and expanded in
the forecasting and handling of the securities of both
the material and spiritual markets. He was proud
of her nerve and daring in exploiting worldly stocks,
and just as proud of her conservative caution in working her spiritual deals. He noted that she never lost
her head in either case; that with a splendid courage
she often went short on worldly futures, but heedfully
drew the line there—she was always long on the
others. Her policy was quite sane and simple, as
she explained it to him: what she put into earthly
futures was for speculation, what she put into spiritual futures was for investment; she was willing to
go into the one on a margin, and take chances, but
in the case of the other, "margin her no margins"
—she wanted to cash-in a hundred cents per dollar's-worth, and have the stock transferred on the
books.

It took but a very few months to educate Aleck's
imagination and Sally's. Each day's training added
something to the spread and effectiveness of the two
machines. As a consequence, Aleck made imaginary
money much faster than at first she had dreamed of

making it, and Sally's competency in spending the
overflow of it kept pace with the strain put upon it,
right along. In the beginning, Aleck had given the
coal speculation a twelvemonth in which to material-
ize, and had been loath to grant that this term might
possibly be shortened by nine months. But that was
the feeble work, the nursery work, of a financial fancy
that had had no teaching, no experience, no practice.
These aids soon came, then that nine months vanished, and the imaginary ten-thousand-dollar investment came marching home with three hundred per
cent. profit on its back!

It was a great day for the pair of Fosters. They
were speechless for joy. Also speechless for another
reason: after much watching of the market, Aleck
had lately, with fear and trembling, made her first
flyer on a "margin," using the remaining twenty thousand of the bequest in this risk. In her mind's eye
she had seen it climb, point by point—always with a
chance that the market would break—until at last
her anxieties were too great for further endurance—
she being new to the margin-business and unhard-
ened, as yet—and she gave her imaginary broker an
imaginary order by imaginary telegraph to sell. She
said forty thousand dollars profit was enough. The
sale was made on the very day that the coal-venture
had returned with its rich freight. As I have said,
the couple were speechless. They sat dazed and bliss-
ful that night, trying to realize the immense fact, the
overwhelming fact, that they were actually worth a

hundred thousand dollars in clean, imaginary cash. Yet so it was.

It was the last time that ever Aleck was afraid of a margin; at least afraid enough to let it break her sleep and pale her cheek to the extent that this first experience in that line had done.

Indeed it was a memorable night. Gradually the realization that they were rich sank securely home into the souls of the pair, then they began to place the money. If we could have looked out through the eyes of these dreamers, we should have seen their tidy little wooden house disappear, and a two-story brick with a cast-iron fence in front of it take its place; we should have seen a three-globed gas-chandelier grow down from the parlor ceiling; we should have seen the homely rag carpet turn to noble Brussels, a dollar and a half a yard; we should have seen the plebeian fireplace vanish away and a recherché, big base-burner with isinglass windows take position and spread awe around. And we should have seen other things, too; among them the buggy, the lap-robe, the stove-pipe hat, and so on.

From that time forth, although the daughters and the neighbors saw only the same old wooden house there, it was a two-story brick to Aleck and Sally; and not a night went by that Aleck did not worry about the imaginary gas-bills, and get for all comfort Sally's reckless retort, "What of it? we can afford it."

Before the couple went to bed, that first night that

they were rich, they had decided that they must celebrate. They must give a party—that was the idea.
But how to explain it—to the daughters and the
neighbors? They could not expose the fact that they
were rich. Sally was willing, even anxious, to do it;
but Aleck kept her head and would not allow it. She
said that although the money was as good as in, it
would be as well to wait until it was actually in. On
that policy she took her stand, and would not budge.
The great secret must be kept, she said—kept from
the daughters and everybody else.

The pair were puzzled. They must celebrate, they
were determined to celebrate, but since the secret
must be kept, what could they celebrate? No birth-
days were due for three months. Tilbury wasn't
available, evidently he was going to live forever;
what the nation *could* they celebrate? That was
Sally's way of putting it; and he was getting impatient, too, and harassed. But at last he hit it—just
by sheer inspiration, as it seemed to him—and all
their troubles were gone in a moment; they would
celebrate the Discovery of America. A splendid idea!

Aleck was almost too proud of Sally for words—
she said *she* never would have thought of it. But
Sally, although he was bursting with delight in the
compliment and with wonder at himself, tried not to
let on, and said it wasn't really anything, anybody
could have done it. Whereat Aleck, with a prideful
toss of her happy head, said:

"Oh, certainly! Anybody could—oh, anybody!

Hosannah Dilkins, for instance! Or maybe Adelbert Peanut—oh, *dear*—yes! Well, I'd like to see them try it, that's all. Dear-me-suz, if they could think of the discovery of a forty-acre island it's more than *I* believe they could; and as for a whole continent, why, Sally Foster, you know perfectly well it would strain the livers and lights out of them and *then* they couldn't!"

The dear woman, she knew he had talent; and if affection made her over-estimate the size of it a little, surely it was a sweet and gentle crime, and forgive-able for its source's sake.

3

## V

THE celebration went off well. The friends were all present, both the young and the old. Among the young were Flossie and Gracie Peanut and their brother Adelbert, who was a rising young journeyman tinner, also Hosannah Dilkins, Jr., journeyman plasterer, just out of his apprenticeship. For many months Adelbert and Hosannah had been showing interest in Gwendolen and Clytemnestra Foster, and the parents of the girls had noticed this with private satisfaction. But they suddenly realized now that that feeling had passed. They recognized that the changed financial conditions had raised up a social bar between their daughters and the young mechanics. The daughters could now look higher—and must. Yes, must. They need marry nothing below the grade of lawyer or merchant; poppa and momma would take care of this; there must be no mésalliances.

However, these thinkings and projects of theirs were private, and did not show on the surface, and therefore threw no shadow upon the celebration. What showed upon the surface was a serene and lofty contentment and a dignity of carriage and gravity of deportment which compelled the admiration and likewise the wonder of the company. All noticed it, all commented upon it, but none was able to divine the secret of it. It was a marvel and a mystery. Three several persons remarked, without suspecting what clever shots they were making:

"It's as if they'd come into property."

That was just it, indeed.

Most mothers would have taken hold of the matrimonial matter in the old regulation way; they would have given the girls a talking to, of a solemn sort and untactful—a lecture calculated to defeat its own purpose, by producing tears and secret rebellion; and the said mothers would have further damaged the business by requesting the young mechanics to discontinue their attentions. But this mother was different. She was practical. She said nothing to any of the young people concerned, nor to any one else except Sally. He listened to her and understood; understood and admired. He said:

"I get the idea. Instead of finding fault with the samples on view, thus hurting feelings and obstructing trade without occasion, you merely offer a higher class of goods for the money, and leave nature to take her course. It's wisdom, Aleck, solid wisdom, and sound as a nut. Who's your fish? Have you nominated him yet?"

"No, she hadn't. They must look the market over—which they did. To start with, they considered and discussed Bradish, rising young lawyer, and Fulton, rising young dentist. Sally must invite them to dinner. But not right away; there was no hurry, Aleck said. Keep an eye on the pair, and wait; nothing would be lost by going slowly in so important a matter.

It turned out that this was wisdom, too; for inside of three weeks Aleck made a wonderful strike which swelled her imaginary hundred thousand to four hundred thousand of the same quality. She and Sally were in the clouds that evening. For the first time they introduced champagne at dinner. Not real champagne, but plenty real enough for the amount of imagination expended on it. It was Sally that did it, and Aleck weakly submitted. At bottom both were troubled and ashamed, for he was a high-up Son of Temperance, and at funerals wore an apron which no dog could look upon and retain his reason and his opinion; and she was a W. C. T. U., with all that that implies of boiler-iron virtue and unendurable holiness. But there it was; the pride of riches was beginning its disintegrating work. They had lived to prove, once more, a sad truth which had been proven many times before in the world: that whereas principle is a great and noble protection against showy and degrading vanities and vices, poverty is worth six of it. More than four hundred thousand dollars to the good! They took up the matrimonial matter again. Neither the dentist nor the lawyer was mentioned; there was no occasion, they were out of the running. Disqualified. They discussed the son of the pork-packer and the son of the village banker. But finally, as in the

previous case, they concluded to wait and think, and
go cautiously and sure.

Luck came their way again. Aleck, ever watchful,
saw a great and risky chance, and took a daring flyer.
A time of trembling, of doubt, of awful uneasiness followed, for non-success meant absolute ruin and nothing short of it. Then came the result, and Aleck, faint
with joy, could hardly control her voice when she
said:

"The suspense is over, Sally—and we are worth a
cold million!"

Sally wept for gratitude, and said:

"Oh, Electra, jewel of women, darling of my heart,
we are free at last, we roll in wealth, we need never
scrimp again. It's a case for Veuve Cliquot!" and he
got out a pint of spruce-beer and made sacrifice, he
saying "Damn the expense," and she rebuking him
gently with reproachful but humid and happy eyes.

They shelved the pork-packer's son and the banker's
son, and sat down to consider the Governor's son and
the son of the Congressman.

## VI

It were a weariness to follow in detail the leaps and bounds the Foster fictitious finances took from this time forth. It was marvellous, it was dizzying, it was dazzling. Everything Aleck touched turned to fairy gold, and heaped itself glittering towards the firmament. Millions upon millions poured in, and still the mighty stream flowed thundering along, still its vast volume increased. Five millions—ten millions—twenty—thirty—was there never to be an end?

Two years swept by in a splendid delirium, the intoxicated Fosters scarcely noticing the flight of time. They were now worth three hundred million dollars; they were in every board of directors of every prodigious combine in the country; and still, as time drifted along, the millions went on piling up, five at a time, ten at a time, as fast as they could tally them off, almost. The three hundred doubled itself —then doubled again—and yet again—and yet once more.

Twenty-four hundred millions!

The business was getting a little confused. It was necessary to take an account of stock, and straighten it out. The Fosters knew it, they felt it, they realized that it was imperative; but they also knew that to do

it properly and perfectly the task must be carried to
a finish without a break when once it was begun. A
ten-hours' job; and where could *they* find ten leisure
hours in a bunch? Sally was selling pins and sugar
and calico all day and every day; Aleck was cooking
and washing dishes and sweeping and making beds
all day and every day, with none to help, for the
daughters were being saved up for high society. The
Fosters knew there was one way to get the ten hours
and only one. Both were ashamed to name it; each
waited for the other to do it. Finally Sally said:

"Somebody's got to give in. It's up to me. Consider that I've named it—never mind pronouncing it
out loud."

Aleck colored, but was grateful. Without further
remark, they fell. Fell, and—broke the Sabbath.
For that was their only free ten-hour stretch. It was
but another step in the downward path. Others
would follow. Vast wealth has temptations which
fatally and surely undermine the moral structure of
persons not habituated to its possession.

They pulled down the shades and broke the Sabbath. With hard and patient labor they overhauled
their holdings and listed them. And a long-drawn
procession of formidable names it was! Starting
with the Railway Systems, Steamer Lines, Standard
Oil, Ocean Cables, Diluted Telegraph, and all the rest,
and winding up with Klondike, De Beers, Tammany
Graft, and Shady Privileges in the Post-office De-
partment.

Twenty-four hundred millions, and all safely planted in Good Things, gilt-edged and interest-bearing.
Income, $120,000 000 a year.  Aleck fetched a long
purr of soft delight, and said:

"Is it enough?"

"It is, Aleck."

"What shall we do?"

"Stand pat."

"Retire from business?"

"That's it."

"I am agreed.  The good work is finished; we will
take a long rest and enjoy the money."

"Good!  Aleck!"

"Yes, dear?"

"How much of the income can we spend?"

"The whole of it."

It seemed to her husband that a ton of chains fell
from his limbs.  He did not say a word; he was
happy beyond the power of speech.

After that, they broke the Sabbaths right along,
as fast as they turned up.  It is the first wrong steps
that count.  Every Sunday they put in the whole
day, after morning service, on inventions—inventions of ways to spend the money.  They got to con-
tinuing this delicious dissipation until past midnight;
and at every séance Aleck lavished millions upon
great charities and religious enterprises, and Sally
lavished like sums upon matters to which (at first)
he gave definite names.  Only at first.  Later the
names gradually lost sharpness of outline, and

eventually faded into "sundries," thus becoming entirely—but safely—undescriptive. For Sally was crumbling. The placing of these millions added seriously and most uncomfortably to the family expenses—in tallow candles. For a while Aleck was worried. Then, after a little, she ceased to worry, for the occasion of it was gone. She was pained, she was grieved, she was ashamed; but she said nothing, and so became an accessory. Sally was taking candles; he was robbing the store. It is ever thus. Vast wealth, to the person unaccustomed to it, is a bane; it eats into the flesh and bone of his morals. When the Fosters were poor, they could have been trusted with untold candles. But now they—but let us not dwell upon it. From candles to apples is but a step: Sally got to taking apples; then soap; then maple - sugar; then canned - goods; then crockery. How easy it is to go from bad to worse, when once we have started upon a downward course!

Meantime, other effects had been milestoning the course of the Fosters' splendid financial march. The fictitious brick - dwelling had given place to an imaginary granite one with a checker-board mansard roof; in time this one disappeared and gave place to a still grander home—and so on and so on. Mansion after mansion, made of air, rose, higher, broader, finer, and each in its turn vanished away; until now, in these latter great days, our dreamers were in fancy housed, in a distant region, in a sumptuous vast palace which looked out from a leafy summit

upon a noble prospect of vale and river and receding
hills steeped in tinted mists—and all private, all the
property of the dreamers; a palace swarming with
liveried servants, and populous with guests of fame
and power, hailing from all the world's capitals,
foreign and domestic.

This palace was far, far away towards the rising
sun, immeasurably remote, astronomically remote,
in Newport, Rhode Island, Holy Land of High Society, ineffable Domain of the American Aristocracy.
As a rule, they spent a part of every Sabbath—after
morning service—in this sumptuous home, the rest
of it they spent in Europe, or in dawdling around in
their private yacht. Six days of sordid and plodding
Fact-life at home on the ragged edge of Lakeside
and straitened means, the seventh in Fairyland—
such had become their programme and their habit.

In their sternly restricted Fact-life they remained
as of old — plodding, diligent, careful, practical,
economical. They stuck loyally to the little Presbyterian Church, and labored faithfully in its interests
and stood by its high and tough doctrines with all
their mental and spiritual energies. But in their
Dream-life they obeyed the invitations of their
fancies, whatever they might be, and howsoever the
fancies might change. Aleck's fancies were not very
capricious, and not frequent, but Sally's scattered a
good deal. Aleck, in her dream-life, went over to
the Episcopal camp, on account of its large official
titles; next she became High-church on account of

the candles and shows; and next she naturally changed to Rome, where there were cardinals and more candles. But these excursions were as nothing to Sally's. His Dream-life was a glowing and continuous and persistent excitement, and he kept every part of it fresh and sparkling by frequent changes, the religious part along with the rest. He worked his religions hard, and changed them with his shirt.

The liberal spendings of the Fosters upon their fancies began early in their prosperities, and grew in prodigality step by step with their advancing fortunes. In time they became truly enormous. Aleck built a university or two per Sunday; also a hospital or two; also a Rowton hotel or so; also a batch of churches; now and then a cathedral; and once, with untimely and ill-chosen playfulness, Sally said, "It was a cold day when she didn't ship a cargo of missionaries to persuade unreflecting Chinamen to trade off twenty-four carat Confucianism for counterfeit Christianity."

This rude and unfeeling language hurt Aleck to the heart, and she went from the presence crying. That spectacle went to his own heart, and in his pain and shame he would have given worlds to have those unkind words back. She had uttered no syllable of reproach—and that cut him. Not one suggestion that he look at his own record—and she could have made, oh, so many, and such blistering ones! Her generous silence brought a swift revenge, for it turned

his thoughts upon himself, it summoned before him
a spectral procession, a moving vision of his life as
he had been leading it these past few years of limit-
less prosperity, and as he sat there reviewing it his
cheeks burned and his soul was steeped in humiliation.   Look at her life—how fair it was, and tending
ever upward; and look at his own—how frivolous,
how charged with mean vanities, how selfish, how
empty, how ignoble!   And its trend—never upward,
but downward, ever downward!

He instituted comparisons between her record and
his own.   He had found fault with her—so he mused
—*he!*   And what could he say for himself?   When
she built her first church what was he doing?   Gathering other blasé multimillionaires into a Poker
Club; defiling his own palace with it; losing hundreds
of thousands to it at every sitting, and sillily vain of
the admiring notoriety it made for him.   When she
was building her first university, what was he doing?
Polluting himself with a gay and dissipated secret
life in the company of other fast bloods, multimillionaires in money and paupers in character.   When
she was building her first foundling asylum, what
was he doing?   Alas!   When she was projecting her
noble Society for the Purifying of the Sex, what was
he doing?   Ah, what, indeed!   When she and the
W. C. T. U. and the Woman with the Hatchet, moving with resistless march, were sweeping the fatal
bottle from the land, what was he doing?   Getting
drunk three times a day.   When she, builder of a

hundred cathedrals, was being gratefully welcomed and blest in papal Rome and decorated with the Golden Rose which she had so honorably earned, what was he doing? Breaking the bank at Monte Carlo.

He stopped. He could go no farther; he could not bear the rest. He rose up, with a great resolution upon his lips: this secret life should be revealed, and confessed; no longer would he live it clandestinely; he would go and tell her All.

And that is what he did. He told her All; and wept upon her bosom; wept, and moaned, and begged for her forgiveness. It was a profound shock, and she staggered under the blow, but he was her own, the core of her heart, the blessing of her eyes, her all in all, she could deny him nothing, and she forgave him. She felt that he could never again be quite to her what he had been before; she knew that he could only repent, and not reform; yet all morally defaced and decayed as he was, was he not her own, her very own, the idol of her deathless worship? She said she was his serf, his slave, and she opened her yearning heart and took him in.

# VII

ONE Sunday afternoon some time after this they were sailing the summer seas in their dream-yacht, and reclining in lazy luxury under the awning of the after-deck. There was silence, for each was busy with his own thoughts. These seasons of silence had insensibly been growing more and more frequent of late; the old nearness and cordiality were waning. Sally's terrible revelation had done its work; Aleck had tried hard to drive the memory of it out of her mind, but it would not go, and the shame and bitterness of it were poisoning her gracious dream-life. She could see now (on Sundays) that her husband was becoming a bloated and repulsive Thing. She could not close her eyes to this, and in these days she no longer looked at him, Sundays, when she could help it.

But she—was she herself without blemish? Alas, she knew she was not. She was keeping a secret from him, she was acting dishonorably towards him, and many a pang it was costing her. *She was breaking the compact, and concealing it from him.* Under strong temptation she had gone into business again; she had risked their whole fortune in a purchase of all the railway systems and coal and steel companies in the country on a margin, and she was now trembling, every Sabbath hour, lest through some chance word of hers he find it out. In her misery and remorse for this treachery she could not keep her heart from going out to him in pity; she was filled with compunctions to see him lying there, drunk and content, and never suspecting. Never suspecting—trusting her with a perfect and pathetic trust, and she holding over him by a thread a possible calamity of so devastating a—

"*Say*—Aleck?"

The interrupting words brought her suddenly to herself. She was grateful to have that persecuting subject from her thoughts, and she answered, with much of the old-time tenderness in her tone:

"Yes, dear."

"Do you know, Aleck, I think we are making a mistake—that is, you are. I mean about the marriage business." He sat up, fat and froggy and benevolent, like a bronze Buddha, and grew earnest. "Consider—it's more than five years. You've continued the same policy from the start: with every rise, always holding on for five points higher. Always when I think we are going to have some weddings, you see a bigger thing ahead, and I undergo another disappointment. *I* think you are too hard to please. Some day we'll get left. First, we turned down the dentist and the lawyer. That was all right—it was sound. Next, we turned down the banker's son and the pork-butcher's heir—right again, and sound. Next, we turned down the Congressman's son and the Governor's—right as a trivet, I confess it. Next, the Senator's son and the son of the Vice-President of the United States—perfectly right, there's no permanency about those little distinctions. Then you went for the aristocracy; and I thought we had struck oil at last—yes. We would make a plunge at the Four Hundred, and pull in some ancient lineage, venerable, holy, ineffable, mellow with the antiquity of a hundred and fifty years, disinfected of the ancestral odors of salt cod and pelts all of a century ago, and unsmirched by a day's work since; and then! why, then the marriages, of course. But no, along comes a pair of real aristocrats from Europe, and straightway you throw over the half-breeds. It was awfully discouraging, Aleck! Since then, what a procession! You turned down the baronets for a pair of barons; you turned down the barons for a pair of viscounts; the viscounts for a pair of earls; the earls for a pair of marquises; the marquises for a brace of dukes. *Now*, Aleck, cash-in!—you've played the limit. You've got a job lot of four dukes under the hammer; of four nationalities; all sound in wind and limb and pedigree, all bankrupt and in debt up to the ears. They come high, but we can afford it. Come, Aleck, don't delay any longer, don't keep up the suspense: take the whole lay-out, and leave the girls to choose!"

Aleck had been smiling blandly and contentedly all through this arraignment of her marriage-policy, a pleasant light, as of triumph with perhaps a nice surprise peeping out through it, rose in her eyes, and she said, as calmly as she could:

"Sally, what would you say to—*royalty?*"

Prodigious! Poor man, it knocked him silly, and he fell over the garboard-strake and barked his shin on the cat-heads. He was dizzy for a moment, then he gathered himself up and limped over and sat down by his wife and beamed his old-time admiration and affection upon her in floods, out of his bleary eyes.

"By George!" he said, fervently, "Aleck, you *are* great—the greatest woman in the whole earth! I can't ever learn the whole size of you. I can't ever learn the immeasurable deeps of you. Here I've been considering myself qualified to criticise your game. *I!* Why, if I had stopped to think, I'd have known you had a lone hand up your sleeve. Now, dear heart, I'm all red-hot impatience—tell me about it!"

The flattered and happy woman put her lips to his ear and whispered a princely name. It made him catch his breath, it lit his face with exultation.

"Land!" he said, "it's a stunning catch! He's got a gambling-hell, and a graveyard, and a bishop, and a cathedral—all his very own. And all gilt-edged five-hundred-per-cent. stock, every detail of it; the tidiest little property in Europe. And that graveyard—it's the selectest in the world: none but suicides admitted; *yes*, sir, and the free-list suspended,

4

too, *all* the time. There isn't much land in the
principality, but there's enough: eight hundred acres
in the graveyard and forty - two outside. It's a
*sovereignty*—that's the main thing; *land's* nothing.
There's plenty land, Sahara's drugged with it."

Aleck glowed; she was profoundly happy. She
said:

"Think of it, Sally—it is a family that has never
married outside the Royal and Imperial Houses of
Europe: our grandchildren will sit upon thrones!"

"True as you live, Aleck—and bear sceptres, too;
and handle them as naturally and nonchalantly as
I handle a yardstick. It's a grand catch, Aleck.
He's corralled, is he? Can't get away? You didn't
take him on a margin?"

"No. Trust me for that. He's not a liability,
he's an asset. So is the other one."

"Who is it, Aleck?"

"His Royal Highness Sigismund-Siegfried-Lauen-
feld-Dinkelspiel-Schwartzenberg Blutwurst, Heredi-
tary Grand Duke of Katzenyammer."

"No! You can't mean it!"

"It's as true as I'm sitting here, I give you my
word," she answered.

His cup was full, and he hugged her to his heart
with rapture, saying:

"How wonderful it all seems, and how beautiful!
It's one of the oldest and noblest of the three hundred and sixty-four ancient German principalities,
and one of the few that was allowed to retain its

royal estate when Bismarck got done trimming them.
I know that farm, I've been there. It's got a rope-
walk and a candle-factory and an army. Standing
army. Infantry and cavalry. Three soldiers and a
horse. Aleck, it's been a long wait, and full of
heartbreak and hope deferred, but God knows I am
happy now. Happy, and grateful to you, my own,
who have done it all. When is it to be?"

"Next Sunday."

"Good. And we'll want to do these weddings up
in the very regalest style that's going. It's properly
due to the royal quality of the parties of the first
part. Now as I understand it, there is only one
kind of marriage that is sacred to royalty, exclusive
to royalty: it's the morganatic."

"What do they call it that for, Sally?"

"I don't know; but anyway it's royal, and royal
only."

"Then we will insist upon it. More—I will com-
pel it. It is morganatic marriage or none."

"That settles it!" said Sally, rubbing his hands
with delight. "And it will be the very first in
America. Aleck, it will make Newport sick."

Then they fell silent, and drifted away upon their
dream-wings to the far regions of the earth to invite
all the crowned heads and their families and provide
gratis transportation for them.

## VIII

DURING three days the couple walked upon air, with their heads in the clouds. They were but vaguely conscious of their surroundings; they saw all things dimly, as through a veil; they were steeped in dreams, often they did not hear when they were spoken to; they often did not understand when they heard; they answered confusedly or at random; Sally sold molasses by weight, sugar by the yard, and furnished soap when asked for candles, and Aleck put the cat in the wash and fed milk to the soiled linen. Everybody was stunned and amazed, and went about muttering, "What *can* be the matter with the Fosters?"

Three days. Then came events! Things had taken a happy turn, and for forty-eight hours Aleck's imaginary corner had been booming. Up—up—still up! Cost-point was passed. Still up—and up—and up! Five points above cost—then ten—fifteen —twenty! Twenty points cold profit on the vast venture, now, and Aleck's imaginary brokers were shouting frantically by imaginary long-distance, "Sell! sell! for Heaven's sake *sell!*"

She broke the splendid news to Sally, and he, too, said, "Sell! sell—oh, don't make a blunder, now,

you own the earth!—sell, sell!" But she set her iron
will and lashed it amidships, and said she would hold
on for five points more if she died for it.

It was a fatal resolve. The very next day came
the historic crash, the record crash, the devastating
crash, when the bottom fell out of Wall Street, and
the whole body of gilt-edged stocks dropped ninety-
five points in five hours, and the multimillionaire
was seen begging his bread in the Bowery. Aleck
sternly held her grip and "put up" as long as she
could, but at last there came a call which she was
powerless to meet, and her imaginary brokers sold
her out. Then, and not till then, the man in her
was vanquished, and the woman in her resumed
sway. She put her arms about her husband's neck
and wept, saying:

"I am to blame, do not forgive me, I cannot bear
it. We are paupers! Paupers, and I am so miserable. The weddings will never come off; all that is
past; we could not even buy the dentist, now."

A bitter reproach was on Sally's tongue: "I *begged*
you to sell, but you—" He did not say it; he had
not the heart to add a hurt to that broken and re-
pentant spirit. A nobler thought came to him and
he said:

"Bear up, my Aleck, all is not lost! You really
never invested a penny of my uncle's bequest, but
only its unmaterialized future; what we have lost was
only the increment harvested from that future by
your incomparable financial judgment and sagacity.

Cheer up, banish these griefs; we still have the thirty thousand untouched; and with the experience which you have acquired, think what you will be able to do with it in a couple of years! The marriages are not off, they are only postponed."

These were blessed words. Aleck saw how true they were, and their influence was electric; her tears ceased to flow, and her great spirit rose to its full stature again. With flashing eye and grateful heart, and with hand uplifted in pledge and prophecy, she said:

"Now and here I proclaim—"

But she was interrupted by a visitor. It was the editor and proprietor of the *Sagamore*. He had happened into Lakeside to pay a duty-call upon an obscure grandmother of his who was nearing the end of her pilgrimage, and with the idea of combining business with grief he had looked up the Fosters, who had been so absorbed in other things for the past four years that they had neglected to pay up their subscription. Six dollars due. No visitor could have been more welcome. He would know all about Uncle Tilbury and what his chances might be getting to be, cemeterywards. They could, of course, ask no questions, for that would squelch the bequest, but they could nibble around on the edge of the subject and hope for results. The scheme did not work. The obtuse editor did not know he was being nibbled at; but at last, chance accomplished what art had failed in. In illustration of something under discus-

sion which required the help of metaphor, the editor
said:

"Land, it's as tough as Tilbury Foster!—as *we*
say."

It was sudden, and it made the Fosters jump.
The editor noticed it, and said, apologetically:

"No harm intended, I assure you. It's just a
saying; just a joke, you know—nothing in it. Re-
lation of yours?"

Sally crowded his burning eagerness down, and answered with all the indifference he could assume:

"I—well, not that I know of, but we've heard of
him." The editor was thankful, and resumed his
composure. Sally added: "Is he—is he—well?"

"Is he *well?* Why, bless you he's in Sheol these
five years!"

The Fosters were trembling with grief, though it
felt like joy. Sally said, non-committally — and
tentatively:

"Ah, well, such is life, and none can escape—not
even the rich are spared."

The editor laughed.

"If you are including Tilbury," said he, "it don't
apply. *He* hadn't a cent; the town had to bury him."

The Fosters sat petrified for two minutes; petrified
and cold. Then, white-faced and weak-voiced, Sally
asked:

"Is it true? Do you *know* it to be true?"

"Well, I should say! I was one of the executors.
He hadn't anything to leave but a wheelbarrow, and

he left that to me. It hadn't any wheel, and wasn't any good. Still, it was something, and so, to square up, I scribbled off a sort of a little obituarial send-off for him, but it got crowded out."

The Fosters were not listening—their cup was full, it could contain no more. They sat with bowed heads, dead to all things but the ache at their hearts.

An hour later. Still they sat there, bowed, motionless, silent, the visitor long ago gone, they unaware.

Then they stirred, and lifted their heads wearily, and gazed at each other wistfully, dreamily, dazed; then presently began to twaddle to each other in a wandering and childish way. At intervals they lapsed into silences, leaving a sentence unfinished, seemingly either unaware of it or losing their way. Sometimes, when they woke out of these silences they had a dim and transient consciousness that something had happened to their minds; then with a dumb and yearning solicitude they would softly caress each other's hands in mutual compassion and support, as if they would say: "I am near you, I will not forsake you, we will bear it together; somewhere there is release and forgetfulness, somewhere there is a grave and peace; be patient, it will not be long."

They lived yet two years, in mental night, always brooding, steeped in vague regrets and melancholy dreams, never speaking; then release came to both on the same day.

Towards the end the darkness lifted from Sally's ruined mind for a moment, and he said:

"Vast wealth, acquired by sudden and unwholesome means, is a snare. It did us no good, transient were its feverish pleasures; yet for its sake we threw away our sweet and simple and happy life—let others take warning by us."

He lay silent awhile, with closed eyes; then as the chill of death crept upward towards his heart, and consciousness was fading from his brain, he muttered:

"Money had brought him misery, and he took his revenge upon us, who had done him no harm. He had his desire: with base and cunning calculation he left us but thirty thousand, knowing we would try to increase it, and ruin our life and break our hearts. Without added expense he could have left us far above desire of increase, far above the temptation to speculate, and a kinder soul would have done it; but in him was no generous spirit, no pity, no—"

# A DOG'S TALE

## I

MY father was a St. Bernard, my mother was a collie, but I am a Presbyterian. This is what my mother told me; I do not know these nice distinctions myself. To me they are only fine large words meaning nothing. My mother had a fondness for such; she liked to say them, and see other dogs look surprised and envious, as wondering how she got so much education. But, indeed, it was not real education; it was only show: she got the words by listening in the dining-room and drawing-room when there was company, and by going with the children to Sunday-school and listening there; and whenever she heard a large word she said it over to herself many times, and so was able to keep it until there was a dogmatic gathering in the neighborhood, then she would get it off, and surprise and distress them all, from pocket-pup to mastiff, which rewarded her for all her trouble. If there was a stranger he was nearly sure to be suspicious, and when he got his breath again he would ask her what it meant. An

she always told him. He was never expecting this,
but thought he would catch her; so when she told
him, he was the one that looked ashamed, whereas
he had thought it was going to be she. The others
were always waiting for this, and glad of it and
proud of her, for they knew what was going to happen, because they had had experience. When she
told the meaning of a big word they were all so taken
up with admiration that it never occurred to any
dog to doubt if it was the right one; and that was
natural, because, for one thing, she answered up so
promptly that it seemed like a dictionary speaking,
and for another thing, where could they find out
whether it was right or not? for she was the only
cultivated dog there was. By-and-by, when I was
older, she brought home the word Unintellectual,
one time, and worked it pretty hard all the week at
different gatherings, making much unhappiness and
despondency; and it was at this time that I noticed
that during that week she was asked for the meaning
at eight different assemblages, and flashed out a
fresh definition every time, which showed me that
she had more presence of mind than culture, though
I said nothing, of course. She had one word which
she always kept on hand, and ready, like a life-pre-
server, a kind of emergency word to strap on when she
was likely to get washed overboard in a sudden way
—that was the word Synonymous. When she happened to fetch out a long word which had had its day
weeks before and its prepared meanings gone to her

dump-pile, if there was a stranger there of course it knocked him groggy for a couple of minutes, then he would come to, and by that time she would be away down the wind on another tack, and not expecting anything; so when he'd hail and ask her to cash in, I (the only dog on the inside of her game) could see her canvas flicker a moment—but only just a moment—then it would belly out taut and full, and she would say, as calm as a summer's day, "It's synonymous with supererogation," or some godless long reptile of a word like that, and go placidly about and skim away on the next tack, perfectly comfortable, you know, and leave that stranger looking profane and embarrassed, and the initiated slatting the floor with their tails in unison and their faces transfigured with a holy joy.

And it was the same with phrases. She would drag home a whole phrase, if it had a grand sound, and play it six nights and two matinées, and explain it a new way every time—which she had to, for all she cared for was the phrase; she wasn't interested in what it meant, and knew those dogs hadn't wit enough to catch her, anyway. Yes, she was a daisy! She got so she wasn't afraid of anything, she had such confidence in the ignorance of those creatures. She even brought anecdotes that she had heard the family and the dinner guests laugh and shout over; and as a rule she got the nub of one chestnut hitched onto another chestnut, where, of course, it didn't fit and hadn't any point; and when she delivered the nub she fell over and rolled on the floor and laughed and barked in the most insane way, while I could see that she was wondering to herself why it didn't seem as funny as it did when she first heard it. But no harm was done; the others rolled and barked too, privately ashamed of themselves for not seeing the point, and never suspecting that the fault was not with them and there wasn't any to see.

You can see by these things that she was of a rather vain and frivolous character; still, she had virtues, and enough to make up, I think. She had a kind heart and gentle ways, and never harbored resentments for injuries done her, but put them easily out of her mind and forgot them; and she taught her children her kindly way, and from her we learned also to be brave and prompt in time of danger, and not to run away, but face the peril that threatened friend or stranger, and help him the best we could without stopping to think what the cost might be to us. And she taught us not by words only, but by example, and that is the best way and the surest and the most lasting. Why, the brave things she did, the splendid things! she was just a soldier; and so modest about it—well, you couldn't help admiring her, and you couldn't help imitating her; not even a King Charles spaniel could remain entirely despicable in her society. So, as you see, there was more to her than her education.

WHEN I was well grown, at last, I was sold and taken away, and I never saw her again. She was broken-hearted, and so was I, and we cried; but she comforted me as well as she could, and said we were sent into this world for a wise and good purpose, and must do our duties without repining, take our life as we might find it, live it for the best good of others, and never mind about the results; they were not our affair. She said men who did like this would have a noble and beautiful reward by-and-by in another world, and although we animals would not go there, to do well and right without reward would give to our brief lives a worthiness and dignity which in itself would be a reward. She had gathered these things from time to time when she had gone to the Sunday-school with the children, and had laid them up in her memory more carefully than she had done with those other words and phrases; and she had studied them deeply, for her good and ours. One may see by this that she had a wise and thoughtful head, for all there was so much lightness and vanity in it.

So we said our farewells, and looked our last upon each other through our tears; and the last thing she said—keeping it for the last to make me remember it the better, I think—was, "In memory of me, when there is a time of danger to another do not think of yourself, think of your mother, and do as she would do."

Do you think I could forget that? No.

# III

It was such a charming home!—my new one; a fine great house, with pictures, and delicate decorations, and rich furniture, and no gloom anywhere, but all the wilderness of dainty colors lit up with flooding sunshine; and the spacious grounds around it, and the great garden—oh, greensward, and noble trees, and flowers, no end!  And I was the same as a member of the family; and they loved me, and petted me, and did not give me a new name, but called me by my old one that was dear to me because my mother had given it me—Aileen Mavourneen. She got it out of a song; and the Grays knew that song, and said it was a beautiful name.

Mrs. Gray was thirty, and so sweet and so lovely, you cannot imagine it; and Sadie was ten, and just like her mother, just a darling slender little copy of her, with auburn tails down her back, and short frocks; and the baby was a year old, and plump and dimpled, and fond of me, and never could get enough of hauling on my tail, and hugging me, and laughing out its innocent happiness; and Mr. Gray was thirty-eight, and tall and slender and handsome, a little bald in front, alert, quick in his movements, business like, prompt, decided, unsentimental, and with that kind of trim-chiselled face that just seems to glint and sparkle with frosty intellectuality! He was a renowned scientist. I do not know what the word means, but my mother would know how to use it and get effects. She would know how to depress a rat-terrier with it and make a lap-dog look sorry he came. But that is not the best one; the best one was Laboratory. My mother could organize a Trust on that one that would skin the tax-collars off the whole herd. The laboratory was not a book, or a picture, or a place to wash your hands in, as the college president's dog said—no, that is the lavatory; the laboratory is quite different, and is filled with jars, and bottles, and electrics, and wires, and strange machines; and every week other scientists came there and sat in the place, and used the machines, and discussed, and made what they called experiments and discoveries; and often I came, too, and stood around and listened, and tried to learn, for the sake of my mother, and in loving memory of her, although it was a pain to me, as realizing what she was losing out of her life and I gaining nothing at all; for try as I might, I was never able to make anything out of it at all.

Other times I lay on the floor in the mistress's work-room and slept, she gently using me for a foot-stool, knowing it pleased me, for it was a caress; other times I spent an hour in the nursery, and got well tousled and made happy; other times I watched

5

by the crib there, when the baby was asleep and the
nurse out for a few minutes on the baby's affairs;
other times I romped and raced through the grounds
and the garden with Sadie till we were tired out,
then slumbered on the grass in the shade of a tree
while she read her book; other times I went visiting
among the neighbor dogs—for there were some most
pleasant ones not far away, and one very handsome
and courteous and graceful one, a curly-haired Irish
setter by the name of Robin Adair, who was a
Presbyterian like me, and belonged to the Scotch
minister.

The servants in our house were all kind to me and
were fond of me, and so, as you see, mine was a
pleasant life. There could not be a happier dog
than I was, nor a gratefuler one. I will say this for
myself, for it is only the truth: I tried in all ways to
do well and right, and honor my mother's memory
and her teachings, and earn the happiness that had
come to me, as best I could.

By-and-by came my little puppy, and then my
cup was full, my happiness was perfect. It was the
dearest little waddling thing, and so smooth and soft
and velvety, and had such cunning little awkward
paws, and such affectionate eyes, and such a sweet
and innocent face; and it made me so proud to see
how the children and their mother adored it, and
fondled it, and exclaimed over every little wonderful
thing it did. It did seem to me that life was just
too lovely to—

Then came the winter. One day I was standing a watch in the nursery. That is to say, I was asleep on the bed. The baby was asleep in the crib, which was alongside the bed, on the side next the fireplace. It was the kind of crib that has a lofty tent over it made of a gauzy stuff that you can see through. The nurse was out, and we two sleepers were alone. A spark from the wood-fire was shot out, and it lit on the slope of the tent. I suppose a quiet interval followed, then a scream from the baby woke me, and there was that tent flaming up towards the ceiling! Before I could think, I sprang to the floor in my fright, and in a second was half-way to the door; but in the next half - second my mother's farewell was sounding in my ears, and I was back on the bed again. I reached my head through the flames and dragged the baby out by the waistband, and tugged it along, and we fell to the floor together in a cloud of smoke; I snatched a new hold, and dragged the screaming little creature along and out at the door and around the bend of the hall, and was still tugging away, all excited and happy and proud, when the master's voice shouted:

"Begone, you cursed beast!" and I jumped to save myself; but he was wonderfully quick, and chased me up, striking furiously at me with his cane, I dodging this way and that, in terror, and at last a strong blow fell upon my left foreleg, which made me shriek and fall, for the moment, helpless; the cane went up for another blow, but never descended, for the nurse's voice rang wildly out, "The nursery's on fire!" and the master rushed away in that direction, and my other bones were saved.

The pain was cruel, but, no matter, I must not lose any time; he might come back at any moment; so I limped on three legs to the other end of the hall, where there was a dark little stairway leading up into a garret where old boxes and such things were kept, as I had heard say, and where people seldom went. I managed to climb up there, then I searched my way through the dark among the piles of things, and hid in the secretest place I could find. It was foolish to be afraid there, yet still I was; so afraid that I held in and hardly even whimpered, though it would have been such a comfort to whimper, because that eases the pain, you know. But I could lick my leg, and that did me some good.

For half an hour there was a commotion downstairs, and shoutings, and rushing footsteps, and then there was quiet again. Quiet for some minutes, and that was grateful to my spirit, for then my fears began to go down; and fears are worse than pains—oh, much worse. Then came a sound that froze me. They were calling me—calling me by name—hunting for me!

It was muffled by distance, but that could not take the terror out of it, and it was the most dreadful sound to me that I had ever heard. It went all about, everywhere, down there: along the halls, through all the rooms, in both stories, and in the basement and the cellar; then outside, and farther and farther away — then back, and all about the house again, and I thought it would never, never stop. But at last it did, hours and hours after the vague twilight of the garret had long ago been blotted out by black darkness.

Then in that blessed stillness my terrors fell little by little away, and I was at peace and slept. It was a good rest I had, but I woke before the twilight had come again. I was feeling fairly comfortable, and I could think out a plan now. I made a very good one; which was, to creep down, all the way down the back stairs, and hide behind the cellar door, and slip out and escape when the iceman came at dawn, while he was inside filling the refrigerator; then I would hide all day, and start on my journey when night came; my journey to—well, anywhere where they would not know me and betray me to the master. I was feeling almost cheerful now; then suddenly I thought: Why, what would life be without my puppy!

That was despair. There was no plan for me; I saw that; I must stay where I was; stay, and wait, and take what might come—it was not my affair; that was what life is—my mother had said it. Then —well, then the calling began again! All my sorrows came back. I said to myself, the master will never forgive. I did not know what I had done to make him so bitter and so unforgiving, yet I judged it was something a dog could not under-

stand, but which was clear to a man and dreadful.

They called and called—days and nights, it seemed
to me. So long that. the hunger and thirst near
drove me mad, and I recognized that I was getting
very weak. When you are this way you sleep a
great deal, and I did. Once I woke in an awful
fright—it seemed to me that the calling was right
there in the garret! And so it was: it was Sadie's
voice, and she was crying; my name was falling from
her lips all broken, poor thing, and I could not believe my ears for the joy of it when I heard her say:

"Come back to us—oh, come back to us, and forgive—it is all so sad without our—"

I broke in with *such* a grateful little yelp, and the
next moment Sadie was plunging and stumbling
through the darkness and the lumber and shouting
for the family to hear, "She's found, she's found!"

The days that followed—well, they were wonderful. The mother and Sadie and the servants—why,
they just seemed to worship me. They couldn't
seem to make me a bed that was fine enough; and
as for food, they couldn't be satisfied with anything
but game and delicacies that were out of season; and
every day the friends and neighbors flocked in to
hear about my heroism—that was the name they
called it by, and it means agriculture. I remember
my mother pulling it on a kennel once, and explaining it that way, but didn't say what agriculture was,

except that it was synonymous with intramural incandescence; and a dozen times a day Mrs. Gray and Sadie would tell the tale to new-comers, and say I risked my life to save the baby's, and both of us had burns to prove it, and then the company would pass me around and pet me and exclaim about me, and you could see the pride in the eyes of Sadie and her mother; and when the people wanted to know what made me limp, they looked ashamed and changed the subject, and sometimes when people hunted them this way and that way with questions about it, it looked to me as if they were going to cry.

And this was not all the glory; no, the master's friends came, a whole twenty of the most distinguished people, and had me in the laboratory, and discussed me as if I was a kind of discovery; and some of them said it was wonderful in a dumb beast, the finest exhibition of instinct they could call to mind; but the master said, with vehemence, "It's far above instinct; it's *reason*, and many a man, privileged to be saved and go with you and me to a better world by right of its possession, has less of it than this poor silly quadruped that's foreordained to perish;" and then he laughed, and said: "Why, look at me—I'm a sarcasm! bless you, with all my grand intelligence, the only thing I inferred was that the dog had gone mad and was destroying the child, whereas but for the beast's intelligence—it's *reason*, I tell you!—the child would have perished!"

They disputed and disputed, and *I* was the very

centre and subject of it all, and I wished my mother
could know that this grand honor had come to me;
it would have made her proud.

Then they discussed optics, as they called it, and
whether a certain injury to the brain would produce
blindness or not, but they could not agree about it,
and said they must test it by experiment by-and-by;
and next they discussed plants, and that interested
me, because in the summer Sadie and I had planted
seeds—I helped her dig the holes, you know—and
after days and days a little shrub or a flower came up
there, and it was a wonder how that could happen;
but it did, and I wished I could talk—I would have
told those people about it and shown them how
much I knew, and been all alive with the subject;
but I didn't care for the optics; it was dull, and
when they came back to it again it bored me, and I
went to sleep.

Pretty soon it was spring, and sunny and pleasant
and lovely, and the sweet mother and the children
patted me and the puppy good-bye, and went away
on a journey and a visit to their kin, and the master
wasn't any company for us, but we played together
and had good times, and the servants were kind and
friendly, so we got along quite happily and counted
the days and waited for the family.

And one day those men came again, and said, now
for the test, and they took the puppy to the laboratory, and I limped three-leggedly along, too, feeling
proud, for any attention shown the puppy was a

pleasure to me, of course. They discussed and experimented, and then suddenly the puppy shrieked, and they set him on the floor, and he went staggering around, with his head all bloody, and the master clapped his hands and shouted:

"There, I've won—confess it! He's as blind as a bat!"

And they all said:

"It's so—you've proved your theory, and suffering humanity owes you a great debt from henceforth," and they crowded around him, and wrung his hand cordially and thankfully, and praised him.

But I hardly saw or heard these things, for I ran at once to my little darling, and snuggled close to it where it lay, and licked the blood, and it put its head against mine, whimpering softly, and I knew in my heart it was a comfort to it in its pain and trouble to feel its mother's touch, though it could not see me. Then it dropped down, presently, and its little velvet nose rested upon the floor, and it was still, and did not move any more.

Soon the master stopped discussing a moment, and rang in the footman, and said, "Bury it in the far corner of the garden," and then went on with the discussion, and I trotted after the footman, very happy and grateful, for I knew the puppy was out of its pain now, because it was asleep. We went far down the garden to the farthest end, where the children and the nurse and the puppy and I used to play in the summer in the shade of a great elm, and there the footman dug a hole, and I saw he was going to plant the puppy, and I was glad, because it would grow and come up a fine handsome dog, like Robin Adair, and be a beautiful surprise for the family when they came home; so I tried to help him dig, but my lame leg was no good, being stiff, you know, and you have to have two, or it is no use. When the footman had finished and covered little Robin up, he patted my head, and there were tears in his eyes, and he said: "Poor little doggie, you SAVED *his* child."

I have watched two whole weeks, and he doesn't come up! This last week a fright has been stealing upon me. I think there is something terrible about this. I do not know what it is, but the fear makes me sick, and I cannot eat, though the servants bring me the best of food; and they pet me so, and even come in the night, and cry, and say, "Poor doggie—do give it up and ccme home; *don't* break our hearts!" and all this terrifies me the more, and makes me sure something has happened. And I am so weak; since yesterday I cannot stand on my feet any more. And within this hour the servants, looking towards the sun where it was sinking out of sight and the night chill coming on, said things I could not understand, but they carried something cold to my heart.

"Those poor creatures! They do not suspect. They will come home in the morning, and eagerly

"POOR LITTLE DOGGIE, YOU *SAVED HIS* CHILD"

ask for the little doggie that did the brave deed, and who of us will be strong enough to say the truth to them: 'The humble little friend is gone where go the beasts that perish.'"

# WAS IT HEAVEN? OR HELL?

## I

"YOU told a *lie?*"

"You confess it — you actually confess it — you told a lie!"

## II

THE family consisted of four persons: Margaret Lester, widow, aged thirty-six; Helen Lester, her daughter, aged sixteen; Mrs. Lester's maiden aunts, Hannah and Hester Gray, twins, aged sixty-seven. Waking and sleeping, the three women spent their days and nights in adoring the young girl; in watching the movements of her sweet spirit in the mirror of her face; in refreshing their souls with the vision of her bloom and beauty; in listening to the music of her voice; in gratefully recognizing how rich and fair for them was the world with this presence in it; in shuddering to think how desolate it would be with this light gone out of it.

By nature—and inside—the aged aunts were utterly dear and lovable and good, but in the matter of morals and conduct their training had been so uncompromisingly strict that it had made them exteriorly austere, not to say stern. Their influence was effective in the house; so effective that the mother and the daughter conformed to its moral and religious requirements cheerfully, contentedly, happily, unquestionably. To do this was become second nature to them. And so in this peaceful heaven there were no clashings, no irritations, no fault-findings, no heart-burnings.

In it a lie had no place. In it a lie was unthinkable. In it speech was restricted to absolute truth,
iron-bound truth, implacable and uncompromising
truth, let the resulting consequences be what they
might. At last, one day, under stress of circumstances, the darling of the house sullied her lips with
a lie—and confessed it, with tears and self-upbraid-
ings. There are not any words that can paint the
consternation of the aunts. It was as if the sky had
crumpled up and collapsed and the earth had tum-
bled to ruin with a crash. They sat side by side,
white and stern, gazing speechless upon the culprit,
who was on her knees before them with her face
buried first in one lap and then the other, moaning
and sobbing, and appealing for sympathy and forgiveness and getting no response, humbly kissing the
hand of the one, then of the other, only to see it with-
drawn as suffering defilement by those soiled lips.

Twice, at intervals, Aunt Hester said, in frozen
amazement:

"You told a *lie?*"

Twice, at intervals, Aunt Hannah followed with the
muttered and amazed ejaculation:

"You confess it—you actually confess it—you told
a lie!"

It was all they could say. The situation was new,
unheard-of, incredible; they could not understand it,
they did not know how to take hold of it, it approxi-
mately paralyzed speech.

At length it was decided that the erring child must

be taken to her mother, who was ill, and who ought to know what had happened. Helen begged, besought, implored that she might be spared this further disgrace, and that her mother might be spared the grief and pain of it; but this could not be: duty required this sacrifice, duty takes precedence of all things, nothing can absolve one from a duty, with a duty no compromise is possible.

Helen still begged, and said the sin was her own, her mother had had no hand in it—why must she be made to suffer for it?

But the aunts were obdurate in their righteousness, and said the law that visited the sins of the parent upon the child was by all right and reason reversible; and therefore it was but just that the innocent mother of a sinning child should suffer her rightful share of the grief and pain and shame which were the allotted wages of the sin.

The three moved towards the sick-room.

At this time the doctor was approaching the house. He was still a good distance away, however. He was a good doctor and a good man, and he had a good heart, but one had to know him a year to get over hating him, two years to learn to endure him, three to learn to like him, and four or five to learn to love him. It was a slow and trying education, but it paid. He was of great stature; he had a leonine head, a leonine face, a rough voice, and an eye which was sometimes a pirate's and sometimes a woman's, ac-

cording to the mood. He knew nothing about eti-
quette, and cared nothing about it; in speech, manner, carriage, and conduct he was the reverse of
conventional. He was frank, to the limit; he had
opinions on all subjects; they were always on tap
and ready for delivery, and he cared not a farthing
whether his listener liked them or didn't. Whom he
loved he loved, and manifested it; whom he didn't
love he hated, and published it from the house-tops.
In his young days he had been a sailor, and the salt
airs of all the seas blew from him yet. He was a
sturdy and loyal Christian, and believed he was the
best one in the land, and the only one whose Christianity was perfectly sound, healthy, full-charged
with common-sense, and had no decayed places in it.
People who had an axe to grind, or people who for
any reason wanted to get on the soft side of him,
called him The Christian—a phrase whose delicate
flattery was music to his ears, and whose capital T
was such an enchanting and vivid object to him that
he could *see* it when it fell out of a person's mouth
even in the dark. Many who were fond of him stood
on their consciences with both feet and brazenly
called him by that large title habitually, because it
was a pleasure to them to do anything that would
please him; and with eager and cordial malice his
extensive and diligently cultivated crop of enemies
gilded it, beflowered it, expanded it to "The *Only*
Christian." Of these two titles, the latter had the
wider currency; the enemy, being greatly in the

majority, attended to that. Whatever the doctor believed, he believed with all his heart, and would fight for it whenever he got the chance; and if the intervals between chances grew to be irksomely wide, he would invent ways of shortening them himself. He was severely conscientious, according to his rather independent lights, and whatever he took to be a duty he performed, no matter whether the judgment of the professional moralists agreed with his own or not. At sea, in his young days, he had used profanity freely, but as soon as he was converted he made a rule, which he rigidly stuck to ever afterwards, never to use it except on the rarest occasions, and then only when duty commanded. He had been a hard drinker at sea, but after his conversion he became a firm and outspoken teetotaler, in order to be an example to the young, and from that time forth he seldom drank; never, indeed, except when it seemed to him to be a duty—a condition which sometimes occurred a couple of times a year, but never as many as five times.

Necessarily, such a man is impressionable, impulsive, emotional. This one was, and had no gift at hiding his feelings; or if he had it he took no trouble to exercise it. He carried his soul's prevailing weather in his face, and when he entered a room the parasols or the umbrellas went up—figuratively speaking—according to the indications. When the soft light was in his eye it meant approval, and delivered a benediction; when he came with a frown he lowered the temperature ten degrees. He was a well-beloved man in the house of his friends, but sometimes a dreaded one.

He had a deep affection for the Lester household, and its several members returned this feeling with interest. They mourned over his kind of Christianity, and he frankly scoffed at theirs; but both parties went on loving each other just the same.

He was approaching the house—out of the distance; the aunts and the culprit were moving towards the sick-chamber.

## III

THE three last named stood by the bed; the aunts austere, the transgressor softly sobbing. The mother turned her head on the pillow; her tired eyes flamed up instantly with sympathy and passionate mother-love when they fell upon her child, and she opened the refuge and shelter of her arms.

"Wait!" said Aunt Hannah, and put out her hand and stayed the girl from leaping into them.

"Helen," said the other aunt, impressively, "tell your mother all. Purge your soul; leave nothing unconfessed."

Standing stricken and forlorn before her judges, the young girl mourned her sorrowful tale through to the end, then in a passion of appeal cried out:

"Oh, mother, can't you forgive me? won't you forgive me?—I am so desolate!"

"Forgive you, my darling? Oh, come to my arms! —there, lay your head upon my breast, and be at peace. If you had told a thousand lies—"

There was a sound—a warning—the clearing of a throat. The aunts glanced up, and withered in their clothes—there stood the doctor, his face a thunder-cloud. Mother and child knew nothing of his presence; they lay locked together, heart to heart, steeped in immeasurable content, dead to all things else. The physician stood many moments glaring and glooming upon the scene before him; studying it, analyzing it, searching out its genesis; then he put up his hand and beckoned to the aunts. They came trembling to him, and stood humbly before him and waited. He bent down and whispered:

"Didn't I tell you this patient must be protected from all excitement? What the hell have you been doing? Clear out of the place!"

They obeyed. Half an hour later he appeared in the parlor, serene, cheery, clothed in sunshine, conducting Helen, with his arm about her waist, petting her, and saying gentle and playful things to her; and she also was her sunny and happy self again.

"Now, then," he said, "good-bye, dear. Go to your room, and keep away from your mother, and behave yourself. But wait—put out your tongue. There, that will do—you're as sound as a nut!" He patted her cheek and added, "Run along now; I want to talk to these aunts."

She went from the presence. His face clouded over again at once; and as he sat down he said:

"You two have been doing a lot of damage—and maybe some good. Some good, yes—such as it is. That woman's disease is typhoid! You've brought it to a show-up, I think, with your insanities, and that's a service—such as it is. I hadn't been able to determine what it was before."

With one impulse the old ladies sprang to their feet, quaking with terror.

"Sit down!  What are you proposing to do?"

"Do?  We must fly to her.  We—"

"You'll do nothing of the kind; you've done enough harm for one day.  Do you want to squander all your capital of crimes and follies on a single deal?  Sit down, I tell you.  I have arranged for her to sleep; she needs it; if you disturb her without my orders, I'll brain you—if you've got the materials for it."

They sat down, distressed and indignant, but obedient, under compulsion.  He proceeded:

"Now, then, I want this case explained.  *They* wanted to explain it to me—as if there hadn't been emotion and excitement enough already.  You knew my orders; how did you dare to go in there and get up that riot?"

Hester looked appealingly at Hannah; Hannah returned a beseeching look at Hester—neither wanted to dance to this unsympathetic orchestra.  The doctor came to their help.  He said:

"Begin, Hester."

Fingering at the fringes of her shawl, and with lowered eyes, Hester said, timidly:

"We should not have disobeyed for any ordinary cause, but this was vital.  This was a duty.  With a duty one has no choice; one must put all lighter considerations aside and perform it.  We were obliged to arraign her before her mother.  She had told a lie."

The doctor glowered upon the woman a moment, and seemed to be trying to work up in his mind an understanding of a wholly incomprehensible proposition; then he stormed out:

"She told a lie! *Did* she? God bless my soul! I tell a million a day! And so does every doctor. And so does everybody—including you—for that matter. And *that* was the important thing that authorized you to venture to disobey my orders and imperil that woman's life! Look here, Hester Gray, this is pure lunacy; that girl *couldn't* tell a lie that was intended to injure a person. The thing is impossible —absolutely impossible. You know it yourselves— both of you; you know it perfectly well."

Hannah came to her sister's rescue:

"Hester didn't mean that it was that kind of a lie, and it wasn't. But it was a lie."

"Well, upon my word, I never heard such nonsense! Haven't you got sense enough to discriminate between lies? Don't you know the difference between a lie that helps and a lie that hurts?"

"*All* lies are sinful," said Hannah, setting her lips together like a vise; "all lies are forbidden."

The Only Christian fidgeted impatiently in his chair. He wanted to attack this proposition, but he did not quite know how or where to begin. Finally he made a venture:

"Hester, wouldn't you tell a lie to shield a person from an undeserved injury or shame?"

"No."

"Not even a friend?"

"No."

"Not even your dearest friend?"

"No. I would not."

The doctor struggled in silence awhile with this situation; then he asked:

"Not even to save him from bitter pain and misery and grief?"

"No. Not even to save his life."

Another pause. Then:

"Nor his soul."

There was a hush — a silence which endured a measurable interval — then Hester answered, in a low voice, but with decision:

"Nor his soul."

No one spoke for a while; then the doctor said:

"Is it with you the same, Hannah?"

"Yes," she answered.

"I ask you both—why?"

"Because to tell such a lie, or any lie, is a sin, and could cost us the loss of our own souls—*would*, indeed, if we died without time to repent."

"Strange . . . strange . . . it is past belief." Then he asked, roughly: "Is such a soul as that *worth* saving?" He rose up, mumbling and grumbling, and started for the door, stumping vigorously along. At the threshold he turned and rasped out an admonition: "Reform! Drop this mean and sordid and selfish devotion to the saving of your shabby little souls, and hunt up something to do that's got some dignity to it! *Risk* your souls! risk them in good causes; then if you lose them, why should you care? Reform!"

The good old gentlewomen sat paralyzed, pulverized, outraged, insulted, and brooded in bitterness and indignation over these blasphemies. They were hurt to the heart, poor old ladies, and said they could never forgive these injuries.

"Reform!"

They kept repeating that word resentfully. "Reform—and learn to tell lies!"

Time slipped along, and in due course a change came over their spirits. They had completed the human being's first duty—which is to think about himself until he has exhausted the subject, then he is in a condition to take up minor interests and think of other people. This changes the complexion of his spirits—generally wholesomely. The minds of the two old ladies reverted to their beloved niece and the fearful disease which had smitten her; instantly they forgot the hurts their self-love had received, and a passionate desire rose in their hearts to go to the help of the sufferer and comfort her with their love, and minister to her, and labor for her the best they could with their weak hands, and joyfully and affectionately wear out their poor old bodies in her dear service if only they might have the privilege.

"And we shall have it!" said Hester, with the tears running down her face. "There are no nurses comparable to us, for there are no others that will stand their watch by that bed till they drop and die, and God knows we would do that."

"Amen," said Hannah, smiling approval and endorsement through the mist of moisture that blurred her glasses. "The doctor knows us, and knows we will not disobey again; and he will call no others. He will not dare!"

"Dare?" said Hester, with temper, and dashing the water from her eyes; "he will dare anything—that Christian devil! But it will do no good for him to try it this time—but, laws! Hannah! after all's said and done, he is gifted and wise and good, and he would not think of such a thing. . . . It is surely time for one of us to go to that room. What is keeping him? Why doesn't he come and say so?"

They caught the sound of his approaching step. He entered, sat down, and began to talk.

"Margaret is a sick woman," he said. "She is still sleeping, but she will wake presently; then one of you must go to her. She will be worse before she is better. Pretty soon a night-and-day watch must be set. How much of it can you two undertake?"

"All of it!" burst from both ladies at once.

The doctor's eyes flashed, and he said, with energy:

"You *do* ring true, you brave old relics! And you *shall* do all of the nursing you can, for there's none to match you in that divine office in this town; but you can't do all of it, and it would be a crime to let you." It was grand praise, golden praise, coming

from such a source, and it took nearly all the resentment out of the aged twins' hearts. "Your Tilly
and my old Nancy shall do the rest—good nurses
both, white souls with black skins, watchful, loving,
tender—just perfect nurses!—and competent liars
from the cradle. . . . Look you! keep a little watch
on Helen; she is sick, and is going to be sicker."

The ladies looked a little surprised, and not credu-
lous; and Hester said:

"How is that? It isn't an hour since you said she
was as sound as a nut."

The doctor answered, tranquilly:

"It was a lie."

The ladies turned upon him indignantly, and
Hannah said:

"How can you make an odious confession like
that, in so indifferent a tone, when you know how
we feel about all forms of—"

"Hush! You are as ignorant as cats, both of you,
and you don't know what you are talking about.
You are like all the rest of the moral moles: you lie
from morning till night, but because you don't do it
with your mouths, but only with your lying eyes,
your lying inflections, your deceptively misplaced
emphasis, and your misleading gestures, you turn up
your complacent noses and parade before God and
the world as saintly and unsmirched Truth-Speakers,
in whose cold-storage souls a lie would freeze to
death if it got there! Why will you humbug yourselves with that foolish notion that no lie is a lie ex-

cept a spoken one? What is the difference between lying with your eyes and lying with your mouth? There is none; and if you would reflect a moment you would see that it is so. There isn't a human being that doesn't tell a gross of lies every day of his life; and you—why, between you, you tell thirty thousand; yet you flare up here in a lurid hypocritical horror because I tell that child a benevolent and sinless lie to protect her from her imagination, which would get to work and warm up her blood to a fever in an hour, if I were disloyal enough to my duty to let it. Which I should probably do if I were interested in saving my soul by such disreputable means.

"Come, let us reason together. Let us examine details. When you two were in the sick-room raising that riot, what would you have done if you had known I was coming?"

"Well, what?"

"You would have slipped out and carried Helen with you—wouldn't you?"

The ladies were silent.

"What would be your object and intention?"

"Well, what?"

"To keep me from finding out your guilt; to beguile me to infer that Margaret's excitement proceeded from some cause not known to you. In a word, to tell me a lie—a silent lie. Moreover, a possibly harmful one."

The twins colored, but did not speak.

"You not only tell myriads of silent lies, but you tell lies with your mouths—you two."

"*That* is not so!"

"It is so. But only harmless ones. You never dream of uttering a harmful one. Do you know that that is a concession—and a confession?"

"How do you mean?"

"It is an unconscious concession that harmless lies are not criminal; it is a confession that you constantly *make* that discrimination. For instance, you declined old Mrs. Foster's invitation last week to meet those odious Higbies at supper—in a polite note in which you expressed regret and said you were very sorry you could not go. It was a lie. It was as unmitigated a lie as was ever uttered. Deny it, Hester—with another lie."

Hester replied with a toss of her head.

"That will not do. Answer. Was it a lie, or wasn't it?"

The color stole into the cheeks of both women, and with a struggle and an effort they got out their confession:

"It was a lie."

"Good—the reform is beginning; there is hope for you yet; you will not tell a lie to save your dearest friend's soul, but you will spew out one without a scruple to save yourself the discomfort of telling an unpleasant truth."

He rose. Hester, speaking for both, said, coldly:

"We have lied; we perceive it; it will occur no

more.  To lie is a sin.  We shall never tell another one of any kind whatsoever, even lies of courtesy or benevolence, to save any one a pang or a sorrow decreed for him by God."

"Ah, how soon you will fall!  In fact, you have fallen already; for what you have just uttered is a lie.  Good-bye.  Reform!  One of you go to the sick-room now."

# IV

Twelve days later.

Mother and child were lingering in the grip of the hideous disease. Of hope for either there was little. The aged sisters looked white and worn, but they would not give up their posts. Their hearts were breaking, poor old things, but their grit was steadfast and indestructible. All the twelve days the mother had pined for the child, and the child for the mother, but both knew that the prayer of these longings could not be granted. When the mother was told—on the first day—that her disease was typhoid, she was frightened, and asked if there was danger that Helen could have contracted it the day before, when she was in the sick-chamber on that confession visit. Hester told her the doctor had poo-pooed the idea. It troubled Hester to say it, although it was true, for she had not believed the doctor; but when she saw the mother's joy in the news, the pain in her conscience lost something of its force—a result which made her ashamed of the constructive deception which she had practised, though not ashamed enough to make her distinctly and definitely wish she had refrained from it. From that moment the sick woman understood that her daughter must remain away, and she said she would reconcile herself to the separation the best she could, for she would rather suffer death than have her child's health imperilled. That afternoon Helen had to take to her bed, ill. She grew worse during the night. In the morning her mother asked after her:

"Is she well?"

Hester turned cold; she opened her lips, but the words refused to come. The mother lay languidly looking, musing, waiting; suddenly she turned white and gasped out:

"Oh, my God! what is it? is she sick?"

Then the poor aunt's tortured heart rose in rebellion, and words came:

"No—be comforted; she is well."

The sick woman put all her happy heart in her gratitude:

"Thank God for those dear words! Kiss me. How I worship you for saying them!"

Hester told this incident to Hannah, who received it with a rebuking look, and said, coldly:

"Sister, it was a lie."

Hester's lips trembled piteously; she choked down a sob, and said:

"Oh, Hannah, it was a sin, but I could not help it; I could not endure the fright and the misery that were in her face."

"No matter. It was a lie. God will hold you to account for it."

"Oh, I know it, I know it," cried Hester, wringing

her hands, "but even if it were now, I could not help it. I know I should do it again."

"Then take my place with Helen in the morning. I will make the report myself."

Hester clung to her sister, begging and imploring: "Don't, Hannah, oh, don't—you will kill her."

"I will at least speak the truth."

In the morning she had a cruel report to bear to the mother, and she braced herself for the trial. When she returned from her mission, Hester was waiting, pale and trembling, in the hall. She whispered:

"Oh, how did she take it—that poor, desolate mother?"

Hannah's eyes were swimming in tears. She said: "God forgive me, I told her the child was well!"

Hester gathered her to her heart, with a grateful "God bless you, Hannah!" and poured out her thankfulness in an inundation of worshipping praises.

After that, the two knew the limit of their strength, and accepted their fate. They surrendered humbly, and abandoned themselves to the hard requirements of the situation. Daily they told the morning lie, and confessed their sin in prayer; not asking forgiveness, as not being worthy of it, but only wishing to make record that they realized their wickedness and were not desiring to hide it or excuse it.

Daily, as the fair young idol of the house sank lower and lower, the sorrowful old aunts painted her glowing bloom and her fresh young beauty to the wan mother, and winced under the stabs her ecstasies of joy and gratitude gave them.

In the first days, while the child had strength to hold a pencil, she wrote fond little love-notes to her mother, in which she concealed her illness; and these the mother read and re-read through happy eyes wet with thankful tears, and kissed them over and over again, and treasured them as precious things under her pillow.

Then came a day when the strength was gone from the hand, and the mind wandered, and the tongue babbled pathetic incoherences. This was a sore di-lemma for the poor aunts. There were no love-notes for the mother. They did not know what to do. Hester began a carefully studied and plausible ex-planation, but lost the track of it and grew confused; suspicion began to show in the mother's face, then alarm. Hester saw it, recognized the imminence of the danger, and descended to the emergency, pulling herself resolutely together and plucking victory from the open jaws of defeat. In a placid and convincing voice she said:

"I thought it might distress you to know it, but Helen spent the night at the Sloanes'. There was a little party there, and although she did not want to go, and you so sick, we persuaded her, she being young and needing the innocent pastimes of youth, and we believing you would approve. Be sure she will write the moment she comes."

"How good you are, and how dear and thoughtful

for us both! Approve? Why, I thank you with all my heart. My poor little exile! Tell her I want her to have every pleasure she can—I would not rob her of one. Only let her keep her health, that is all I ask. Don't let that suffer; I could not bear it. How thankful I am that she escaped this infection—and what a narrow risk she ran, Aunt Hester! Think of that lovely face all dulled and burned with fever. I can't bear the thought of it. Keep her health. Keep her bloom! I can see her now, the dainty creature—with the big, blue, earnest eyes; and sweet, oh, so sweet and gentle and winning! Is she as beautiful as ever, dear Aunt Hester?"

"Oh, more beautiful and bright and charming than ever she was before, if such a thing can be"—and Hester turned away and fumbled with the medicine-bottles, to hide her shame and grief.

# V

AFTER a little, both aunts were laboring upon a difficult and baffling work in Helen's chamber. Patiently and earnestly, with their stiff old fingers, they were trying to forge the required note. They made failure after failure, but they improved little by little all the time. The pity of it all, the pathetic humor of it, there was none to see; they themselves were unconscious of it. Often their tears fell upon the notes and spoiled them; sometimes a single misformed word made a note risky which could have been ventured but for that; but at last Hannah produced one whose script was a good enough imitation of Helen's to pass any but a suspicious eye, and bountifully enriched it with the petting phrases and loving nicknames that had been familiar on the child's lips from her nursery days. She carried it to the mother, who took it with avidity, and kissed it, and fondled it, reading its precious words over and over again, and dwelling with deep contentment upon its closing paragraph:

"Mousie darling, if I could only see you, and kiss your eyes, and feel your arms about me! I am so glad my practising does not disturb you. Get well soon. Everybody is good to me, but I am so lonesome without you, dear mamma."

"The poor child, I know just how she feels. She cannot be quite happy without me; and I—oh, I live in the light of her eyes! Tell her she must practise all she pleases; and, Aunt Hannah—tell her I can't hear the piano this far, nor her dear voice when she sings: God knows I wish I could. No one knows how sweet that voice is to me; and to think—some day it will be silent! What are you crying for?"

"Only because—because—it was just a memory. When I came away she was singing, 'Loch Lomond.' The pathos of it! It always moves me so when she sings that."

"And me, too. How heart-breakingly beautiful it is when some youthful sorrow is brooding in her breast and she sings it for the mystic healing it brings. . . . Aunt Hannah?"

"Dear Margaret?"

"I am very ill. Sometimes it comes over me that I shall never hear that dear voice again."

"Oh, don't—don't, Margaret! I can't bear it!"

Margaret was moved and distressed, and said, gently:

"There—there—let me put my arms around you. Don't cry. There—put your cheek to mine. Be comforted. I wish to live. I will live if I can. Ah, what could she do without me! . . . Does she often speak of me?—but I know she does."

"Oh, all the time—all the time!"

"My sweet child! She wrote the note the moment she came home?"

"Yes—the first moment. She would not wait to take off her things."

"I knew it. It is her dear, impulsive, affectionate way. I knew it without asking, but I wanted to hear you say it. The petted wife knows she is loved, but she makes her husband tell her so every day, just for the joy of hearing it. . . . She used the pen this time. That is better; the pencil-marks could rub out, and I should grieve for that. Did you suggest that she use the pen?"

"Y-no—she—it was her own idea."

The mother looked her pleasure, and said:

"I was hoping you would say that. There was never such a dear and thoughtful child! . . . Aunt Hannah?"

"Dear Margaret?"

"Go and tell her I think of her all the time, and worship her. Why—you are crying again. Don't be so worried about me, dear; I think there is nothing to fear, yet."

The grieving messenger carried her message, and piously delivered it to unheeding ears. The girl babbled on unaware; looking up at her with wondering and startled eyes flaming with fever, eyes in which was no light of recognition:

"Are you—no, you are not my mother. I want her—oh, I want her! She was here a minute ago—I did not see her go. Will she come? will she come quickly? will she come now?... There are so many houses ... and they oppress me so ... and everything whirls and turns and whirls ... oh, my head, my head!"—and so she wandered on and on, in her pain, flitting from one torturing fancy to another, and tossing her arms about in a weary and ceaseless persecution of unrest.

Poor old Hannah wetted the parched lips and softly stroked the hot brow, murmuring endearing and pitying words, and thanking the Father of all that the mother was happy and did not know.

## VI

DAILY the child sank lower and steadily lower
towards the grave, and daily the sorrowing old
watchers carried gilded tidings of her radiant health
and loveliness to the happy mother, whose pilgrimage
was also now nearing its end. And daily they forged
loving and cheery notes in the child's hand, and stood
by with remorseful consciences and bleeding hearts,
and wept to see the grateful mother devour them and
adore them and treasure them away as things beyond
price, because of their sweet source, and sacred because her child's hand had touched them.

At last came that kindly friend who brings healing
and peace to all. The lights were burning low. In
the solemn hush which precedes the dawn vague
figures flitted soundless along the dim hall and gathered silent and awed in Helen's chamber, and grouped
themselves about her bed, for a warning had gone
forth, and they knew. The dying girl lay with closed
lids, and unconscious, the drapery upon her breast
faintly rising and falling as her wasting life ebbed
away. At intervals a sigh or a muffled sob broke
upon the stillness. The same haunting thought was
in all minds there: the pity of this death, the going

out into the great darkness, and the mother not here
to help and hearten and bless.

Helen stirred; her hands began to grope wistfully
about as if they sought something—she had been
blind some hours. The end was come; all knew it.
With a great sob Hester gathered her to her breast,
crying, "Oh, my child, my darling!" A rapturous
light broke in the dying girl's face, for it was merci-
fully vouchsafed her to mistake those sheltering arms
for another's; and she went to her rest murmuring,
"Oh, mamma, I am so happy—I so longed for you—
now I can die."

Two hours later Hester made her report. The
mother asked.

"How is it with the child?"

"She is well."

# VII

A SHEAF of white crape and black was hung upon
the door of the house, and there it swayed and
rustled in the wind and whispered its tidings. At
noon the preparation of the dead was finished, and
in the coffin lay the fair young form, beautiful, and
in the sweet face a great peace.  Two mourners sat
by it, grieving and worshipping—Hannah and the
black woman Tilly.  Hester came, and she was trembling, for a great trouble was upon her spirit. She
said:

"She asks for a note."

Hannah's face blanched.  She had not thought of
this; it had seemed that that pathetic service was
ended.  But she realized now that that could not be.
For a little while the two women stood looking into
each other's face, with vacant eyes; then Hannah
said:

"There is no way out of it—she must have it; she
will suspect, else."

"And she would find out."

"Yes.  It would break her heart."  She looked at
the dead face, and her eyes filled.  "I will write it,"
she said.

Hester carried it.  The closing line said:

"Darling Mousie, dear sweet mother, we shall soon be together again. Is not that good news? And it is true; they all say it is true."

The mother mourned, saying:

"Poor child, how will she bear it when she knows? I shall never see her again in life. It is hard, so hard. She does not suspect? You guard her from that?"

"She thinks you will soon be well."

"How good you are, and careful, dear Aunt Hester! None goes near her who could carry the infection?"

"It would be a crime."

"But you *see* her?"

"With a distance between—yes."

"That is so good. Others one could not trust; but you two guardian angels—steel is not so true as you. Others would be unfaithful; and many would deceive, and lie."

Hester's eyes fell, and her poor old lips trembled.

"Let me kiss you for her, Aunt Hester; and when I am gone, and the danger is past, place the kiss upon her dear lips some day, and say her mother sent it, and all her mother's broken heart is in it."

Within the hour, Hester, raining tears upon the dead face, performed her pathetic mission.

# VIII

ANOTHER day dawned, and grew, and spread its sunshine in the earth. Aunt Hannah brought comforting news to the failing mother, and a happy note, which said again, "We have but a little time to wait, darling mother, then we shall be together."

The deep note of a bell came moaning down the wind.

"Aunt Hannah, it is tolling. Some poor soul is at rest. As I shall be soon. You will not let her forget me?"

"Oh, God knows she never will!"

"Do not you hear strange noises, Aunt Hannah? It sounds like the shuffling of many feet."

"We hoped you would not hear it, dear. It is a little company gathering, for—for Helen's sake, poor little prisoner. There will be music—and she loves it so. We thought you would not mind."

"Mind? Oh no, no—oh, give her everything her dear heart can desire. How good you two are to her, and how good to me! God bless you both, always!"

After a listening pause:

"How lovely! It is her organ. Is she playing it herself, do you think?" Faint and rich and inspiring the chords floated to her ears on the still air. "Yes, it is her touch, dear heart, I recognize it. They are singing. Why—it is a hymn! and the sacredest of all, the most touching, the most consoling. . . . It seems to open the gates of paradise to me. . . . If I could die now. . . ."

Faint and far the words rose out of the stillness:

> Nearer, my God, to Thee,
> Nearer to Thee,
> E'en though it be a cross
> That raiseth me.

With the closing of the hymn another soul passed to its rest, and they that had been one in life were not sundered in death. The sisters, mourning and rejoicing, said:

"How blessed it was that she never knew!"

## IX

AT midnight they sat together, grieving, and the angel of the Lord appeared in the midst transfigured with a radiance not of earth; and speaking, said:

"For liars a place is appointed. There they burn in the fires of hell from everlasting unto everlasting. Repent!"

The bereaved fell upon their knees before him and clasped their hands and bowed their gray heads, adoring. But their tongues clove to the roof of their mouths, and they were dumb.

"Speak! that I may bear the message to the chancery of heaven and bring again the decree from which there is no appeal."

Then they bowed their heads yet lower, and one said:

"Our sin is great, and we suffer shame; but only perfect and final repentance can make us whole; and we are poor creatures who have learned our human weakness, and we know that if we were in those hard straits again our hearts would fail again, and we should sin as before. The strong could prevail, and so be saved, but we are lost."

They lifted their heads in supplication. The angel was gone. While they marvelled and wept he came again; and bending low, he whispered the decree.

## X

## Was it Heaven? Or Hell?

# THE CALIFORNIAN'S TALE

THIRTY-FIVE years ago I was out prospecting on the Stanislaus, tramping all day long with pick and pan and horn, and washing a hatful of dirt here and there, always expecting to make a rich strike, and never doing it. It was a lovely region, woodsy, balmy, delicious, and had once been populous, long years before, but now the people had vanished and the charming paradise was a solitude. They went away when the surface diggings gave out. In one place, where a busy little city with banks and newspapers and fire companies and a mayor and aldermen had been, was nothing but a wide expanse of emerald turf, with not even the faintest sign that human life had ever been present there. This was down towards Tuttletown. In the country neighborhood thereabouts, along the dusty roads, one found at intervals the prettiest little cottage homes, snug and cosey, and so cobwebbed with vines snowed thick with roses that the doors and windows were wholly hidden from sight — sign that these were deserted homes, forsaken years ago by defeated and disappointed families who could neither sell them nor give them away. Now and then, half an hour apart, one came across solitary log cabins of the earliest mining days, built by the first gold-miners, the predecessors of the cottage-builders. In some few cases these cabins were still occupied; and when this was so, you could depend upon it that the occupant was the very pioneer who had built the cabin; and you could depend on another thing, too—that he was there because he had once had his opportunity to go home to the States rich, and had not done it; had later lost his wealth, and had then in his humiliation resolved to sever all communication with his home relatives and friends, and be to them thenceforth as one dead. Round about California in that day were scattered a host of these living dead men—pride-smitten poor fellows, grizzled and old at forty, whose secret thoughts were made all of regrets and longings—regrets for their wasted lives, and longings to be out of the struggle and done with it all.

It was a lonesome land! Not a sound in all those peaceful expanses of grass and woods but the drowsy hum of insects; no glimpse of man or beast; nothing to keep up your spirits and make you glad to be alive. And so, at last, in the early part of the afternoon, when I caught sight of a human creature, I felt a most grateful uplift. This person was a man about forty-five years old, and he was standing at the gate of one of those cosey little rose-clad cottages of the sort already referred to. However, this one hadn't a deserted look; it had the look of being lived in and petted and cared for and looked after; and so had its front yard, which was a garden of flowers, abundant, gay, and flourishing. I was invited in, of course, and required to make myself at home—it was the custom of the country.

It was delightful to be in such a place, after long weeks of daily and nightly familiarity with miners' cabins — with all which this implies of dirt floor, never-made beds, tin plates and cups, bacon and beans and black coffee, and nothing of ornament but war pictures from the Eastern illustrated papers tacked to the log walls. That was all hard, cheerless, materialistic desolation, but here was a nest which had aspects to rest the tired eye and refresh that something in one's nature which, after long fasting, recognizes, when confronted by the belongings of art, howsoever cheap and modest they may be, that it has unconsciously been famishing and now has found nourishment. I could not have believed that a rag carpet could feast me so, and so content me; or that there could be such solace to the soul in wall-paper and framed lithographs, and bright-colored tidies and lamp-mats, and Windsor chairs, and varnished whatnots, with sea-shells and books and china vases on them, and the score of little unclassifiable tricks and touches that a woman's hand distributes about a home, which one sees without knowing he sees them, yet would miss in a moment if they were taken away. The delight that was in my heart showed in my face, and the man

saw it and was pleased; saw it so plainly that he answered it as if it had been spoken.

"All her work," he said, caressingly; "she did it
all herself—every bit," and he took the room in with
a glance which was full of affectionate worship. One
of those soft Japanese fabrics with which women
drape with careful negligence the upper part of a
picture-frame was out of adjustment. He noticed
it, and rearranged it with cautious pains, stepping
back several times to gauge the effect before he got
it to suit him. Then he gave it a light finishing pat
or two with his hand, and said: "She always does
that. You can't tell just what it lacks, but it does
lack something until you've done that—you can see
it yourself after it's done, but that is all you know;
you can't find out the law of it. It's like the finishing pats a mother gives the child's hair after she's
got it combed and brushed, I reckon. I've seen her
fix all these things so much that I can do them all
just her way, though I don't know the law of any of
them. But she knows the law. She knows the
why and the how both; but I don't know the why; I
only know the how."

He took me into a bedroom so that I might wash
my hands; such a bedroom as I had not seen for
years: white counterpane, white pillows, carpeted
floor, papered walls, pictures, dressing-table, with
mirror and pin-cushion and dainty toilet things; and
in the corner a wash-stand, with real china-ware
bowl and pitcher, and with soap in a china dish, and

on a rack more than a dozen towels—towels too clean and white for one out of practice to use without some vague sense of profanation. So my face spoke again, and he answered with gratified words:

"All her work; she did it all herself—every bit. Nothing here that hasn't felt the touch of her hand. Now you would think— But I mustn't talk so much."

By this time I was wiping my hands and glancing from detail to detail of the room's belongings, as one is apt to do when he is in a new place, where everything he sees is a comfort to his eye and his spirit; and I became conscious, in one of those unaccountable ways, you know, that there was something there somewhere that the man wanted me to discover for myself. I knew it perfectly, and I knew he was trying to help me by furtive indications with his eye, so I tried hard to get on the right track, being eager to gratify him. I failed several times, as I could see out of the corner of my eye without being told; but at last I knew I must be looking straight at the thing—knew it from the pleasure issuing in invisible waves from him. He broke into a happy laugh, and rubbed his hands together, and cried out:

"That's it! You've found it. I knew you would. It's her picture."

I went to the little black-walnut bracket on the farther wall, and did find there what I had not yet noticed—a daguerreotype-case. It contained the sweetest girlish face, and the most beautiful, as it seemed to me, that I had ever seen. The man drank the admiration from my face, and was fully satisfied.

"Nineteen her last birthday," he said, as he put the picture back; "and that was the day we were married. When you see her—ah, just wait till you see her!"

"Where is she? When will she be in?"

"Oh, she's away now. She's gone to see her people. They live forty or fifty miles from here. She's been gone two weeks to-day."

"When do you expect her back?"

"This is Wednesday. She'll be back Saturday, in the evening—about nine o'clock, likely."

I felt a sharp sense of disappointment.

"I'm sorry, because I'll be gone then," I said, regretfully.

"Gone? No—why should you go? Don't go. She'll be so disappointed."

She would be disappointed—that beautiful creature! If she had said the words herself they could hardly have blessed me more. I was feeling a deep, strong longing to see her—a longing so supplicating, so insistent, that it made me afraid. I said to myself: "I will go straight away from this place, for my peace of mind's sake."

"You see, she likes to have people come and stop with us—people who know things, and can talk—people like you. She delights in it; for she knows—oh, she knows nearly everything herself, and can talk, oh, like a bird—and the books she reads, why,

you would be astonished. Don't go; it's only a
little while, you know, and she'll be so disappointed."

I heard the words, but hardly noticed them, I was
so deep in my thinkings and strugglings. He left
me, but I didn't know it. Presently he was back,
with the picture-case in his hand, and he held it open
before me and said:

"There, now, tell her to her face you could have
stayed to see her, and you wouldn't."

That second glimpse broke down my good resolution. I would stay and take the risk. That night
we smoked the tranquil pipe, and talked till late
about various things, but mainly about her; and certainly I had had no such pleasant and restful time
for many a day. The Thursday followed and slipped
comfortably away. Towards twilight a big miner from
three miles away came—one of the grizzled, stranded
pioneers—and gave us warm salutation, clothed in
grave and sober speech. Then he said:

"I only just dropped over to ask about the little
madam, and when is she coming home. Any news
from her?"

"Oh yes, a letter. Would you like to hear it
Tom?"

"Well, I should think I would, if you don't mind,
Henry!"

Henry got the letter out of his wallet, and said he
would skip some of the private phrases, if we were
willing; then he went on and read the bulk of it—a
loving, sedate, and altogether charming and gracious

piece of handiwork, with a postscript full of affectionate regards and messages to Tom, and Joe, and
Charley, and other close friends and neighbors.

As the reader finished, he glanced at Tom, and
cried out:

"Oho, you're at it again! Take your hands
away, and let me see your eyes. You always do
that when I read a letter from her. I will write and
tell her."

"Oh no, you mustn't, Henry. I'm getting old,
you know, and any little disappointment makes me
want to cry. I thought she'd be here herself, and
now you've got only a letter."

"Well, now, what put that in your head? I
thought everybody knew she wasn't coming till
Saturday."

"Saturday! Why, come to think, I did know it.
I wonder what's the matter with me lately? Certainly I knew it. Ain't we all getting ready for her?
Well, I must be going now. But I'll be on hand
when she comes, old man!"

Late Friday afternoon another gray veteran
tramped over from his cabin a mile or so away, and
said the boys wanted to have a little gayety and a
good time Saturday night, if Henry thought she
wouldn't be too tired after her journey to be kept up.

"Tired? She tired! Oh, hear the man! Joe,
*you* know she'd sit up six weeks to please any one of
you!"

When Joe heard that there was a letter, he asked

to have it read, and the loving messages in it for him
broke the old fellow all up; but he said he was such
an old wreck that *that* would happen to him if she
only just mentioned his name. "Lord, we miss her
so!" he said.

Saturday afternoon I found I was taking out my
watch pretty often. Henry noticed it, and said,
with a startled look:

"You don't think she ought to be here so soon, do
you?"

I felt caught, and a little embarrassed; but I
laughed, and said it was a habit of mine when I was
in a state of expectancy. But he didn't seem quite
satisfied; and from that time on he began to show
uneasiness. Four times he walked me up the road
to a point whence we could see a long distance; and
there he would stand, shading his eyes with his
hand, and looking. Several times he said:

"I'm getting worried, I'm getting right down worried. I know she's not due till about nine o'clock,
and yet something seems to be trying to warn me
that something's happened. You don't think anything has happened, do you?"

I began to get pretty thoroughly ashamed of him
for his childishness; and at last, when he repeated
that imploring question still another time, I lost my
patience for the moment, and spoke pretty brutally
to him. It seemed to shrivel him up and cow him;
and he looked so wounded and so humble after that,
that I detested myself for having done the cruel and

unnecessary thing. And so I was glad when Charley, another veteran, arrived towards the edge of the evening, and nestled up to Henry to hear the letter read, and talked over the preparations for the welcome. Charley fetched out one hearty speech after another, and did his best to drive away his friend's bodings and apprehensions.

"Anything *happened* to her? Henry, that's pure nonsense. There isn't anything going to happen to her; just make your mind easy as to that. What did the letter say? Said she was well, didn't it? And said she'd be here by nine o'clock, didn't it? Did you ever know her to fail of her word? Why, you know you never did. Well, then, don't you fret; she'll *be* here, and that's absolutely certain, and as sure as you are born. Come, now, let's get to decorating—not much time left."

Pretty soon Tom and Joe arrived, and then all hands set about adorning the house with flowers. Towards nine the three miners said that as they had brought their instruments they might as well tune up, for the boys and girls would soon be arriving now, and hungry for a good, old-fashioned breakdown. A fiddle, a banjo, and a clarinet—these were the instruments. The trio took their places side by side, and began to play some rattling dance-music, and beat time with their big boots.

It was getting very close to nine. Henry was standing in the door with his eyes directed up the road, his body swaying to the torture of his mental distress. He had been made to drink his wife's health and safety several times, and now Tom shouted:

"All hands stand by! One more drink, and she's here!"

Joe brought the glasses on a waiter, and served the party. I reached for one of the two remaining glasses, but Joe growled, under his breath:

"Drop that! Take the other."

Which I did. Henry was served last. He had hardly swallowed his drink when the clock began to strike. He listened till it finished, his face growing pale and paler; then he said:

"Boys, I'm sick with fear. Help me—I want to lie down!"

They helped him to the sofa. He began to nestle and drowse, but presently spoke like one talking in his sleep, and said: "Did I hear horses' feet? Have they come?"

One of the veterans answered, close to his ear: "It was Jimmy Parrish come to say the party got delayed, but they're right up the road a piece, and coming along. Her horse is lame, but she'll be here in half an hour."

"Oh, I'm *so* thankful nothing has happened!"

He was asleep almost before the words were out of his mouth. In a moment those handy men had his clothes off, and had tucked him into his bed in the chamber where I had washed my hands. They closed the door and came back. Then they seemed preparing to leave; but I said: "Please don't go, gentlemen. She won't know me; I am a stranger."

They glanced at each other. Then Joe said:

"She? Poor thing, she's been dead nineteen years!"

"Dead?"

"That or worse. She went to see her folks half a year after she was married, and on her way back, on a Saturday evening, the Indians captured her within five miles of this place, and she's never been heard of since."

"And he lost his mind in consequence?"

"Never has been sane an hour since. But he only gets bad when that time of the year comes round. Then we begin to drop in here, three days before she's due, to encourage him up, and ask if he's heard from her, and Saturday we all come and fix up the house with flowers, and get everything ready for a dance. We've done it every year for nineteen years. The first Saturday there was twenty-seven of us, without counting the girls; there's only three of us now, and the girls are all gone. We drug him to sleep, or he would go wild; then he's all right for another year—thinks she's with him till the last three or four days come round; then he begins to look for her, and gets out his poor old letter, and we come and ask him to read it to us. Lord, she was a darling!"

# A HELPLESS SITUATION

ONCE or twice a year I get a letter of a certain
pattern, a pattern that never materially changes,
in form and substance, yet I cannot get used to that
letter—it always astonishes me.   It affects me as the
locomotive always affects me: I say to myself, "I
have seen you a thousand times, you always look
the same way, yet you are always a wonder, and you
are always impossible; to contrive you is clearly beyond human genius—you can't exist, you don't exist,
yet here you are!"

I have a letter of that kind by me, a very old one.
I yearn to print it, and where is the harm?  The
writer of it is dead years ago, no doubt, and if I conceal her name and address—her this-world address—
I am sure her shade will not mind.  And with it I
wish to print the answer which I wrote at the time
but probably did not send.  If it went—which is not
likely—it went in the form of a copy, for I find the
original still here, pigeon-holed with the said letter.
To that kind of letters we all write answers which we
do not send, fearing to hurt where we have no desire

to hurt; I have done it many a time, and this is
doubtless a case of the sort.


## THE LETTER

X——., CALIFORNIA, *June 3, 1879.*

*Mr. S. L. Clemens, Hartford, Conn.:*

DEAR SIR,—You will doubtless be surprised to
know who has presumed to write and ask a favor of
you. Let your memory go back to your days in the
Humboldt mines—'62–'63. You will remember, you
and Clagett and Oliver and the old blacksmith
Tillou lived in a lean-to which was half-way up the
gulch, and there were six log cabins in the camp—
strung pretty well separated up the gulch from its
mouth at the desert to where the last claim was, at
the divide. The lean-to you lived in was the one
with a canvas roof that the cow fell down through
one night, as told about by you in *Roughing It*—my
uncle Simmons remembers it very well. He lived in
the principal cabin, half-way up the divide, along
with Dixon and Parker and Smith. It had two
rooms, one for kitchen and the other for bunks, and
was the only one that had. You and your party
were there on the great night, the time they had
dried-apple-pie, Uncle Simmons often speaks of it.
It seems curious that dried-apple-pie should have
seemed such a great thing, but it was, and it shows
how far Humboldt was out of the world and difficult
to get to, and how slim the regular bill of fare was.

Sixteen years ago—it is a long time. I was a little girl then, only fourteen. I never saw you. I lived in Washoe. But Uncle Simmons ran across you every now and then, all during those weeks that you and party were there working your claim which was like the rest. The camp played out long and long ago, there wasn't silver enough in it to make a button. You never saw my husband, but he was there after you left, *and lived in that very lean-to*, a bachelor then but married to me now. He often wishes there had been a photographer there in those days, he would have taken the lean-to. He got hurt in the old Hal Clayton claim that was abandoned like the others, putting in a blast and not climbing out quick enough, though he scrambled the best he could. It landed him clear down on the trail and hit a Piute. For weeks they thought he would not get over it but he did, and is all right, now. Has been ever since. This is a long introduction but it is the only way I can make myself known. The favor I ask I feel assured your generous heart will grant: Give me some advice about a book I have written. I do not claim anything for it only it is mostly true and as interesting as most of the books of the times. I am unknown in the literary world and you know what that means unless one has some one of influence (like yourself) to help you by speaking a good word for you. I would like to place the book on royalty basis plan with any one you would suggest.

..his is a secret from my husband and family. I intend it as a surprise in case I get it published.

Feeling you will take an interest in this and if possible write me a letter to some publisher, or, better still, if you could see them for me and then let me hear.

I appeal to you to grant me this favor. With deepest gratitude I thank you for your attention.

One knows, without inquiring, that the twin of that embarrassing letter is forever and ever flying in this and that and the other direction across the continent in the mails, daily, nightly, hourly, unceasingly, unrestingly. It goes to every well-known merchant, and railway official, and manufacturer, and capitalist, and Mayor, and Congressman, and Governor, and editor, and publisher, and author, and broker, and banker—in a word, to every person who is supposed to have "influence." It always follows the one pattern: "You do not know me, *but you once knew a relative of mine*," etc., etc. We should all like to help the applicants, we should all be glad to do it, we should all like to return the sort of answer that is desired, but— Well, there is not a thing we can do that would be a help, for not in any instance does that letter ever come from any one who *can* be helped. The struggler whom you *could* help does his own helping; it would not occur to him to appeal to you, a stranger. He has talent and knows it, and he goes into his fight eagerly and with energy and

letermination — all alone, preferring to be alone.
That pathetic letter which comes to you from the
ncapable, the unhelpable—how do you who are
amiliar with it answer it? What do you find to
ay? You do not want to inflict a wound; you
unt ways to avoid that. What do you find? How
o you get out of your hard place with a contented
onscience? Do you try to explain? The old reply
f mine to such a letter shows that I tried that once.
Vas I satisfied with the result? Possibly; and pos-
bly not; probably not; almost certainly not. I
ave long ago forgotten all about it. But, anyway,
append my effort:


## THE REPLY

I know Mr. H., and I will go to him, dear madam,
upon reflection you find you still desire it. There
ll be a conversation. I know the form it will take.
will be like this:


*Mr. H.* How do her books strike you?
*Mr. Clemens.* I am not acquainted with them.
*H.* Who has been her publisher?
*C.* I don't know.
*H.* She *has* one, I suppose?
*C.* I—I think not.
*H.* Ah. You think this is her first book?
*C.* Yes—I suppose so. I think so.
*H.* What is it about? What is the character of it?

*C.* I believe I do not know.

*H.* Have you seen it?

*C.* Well—no, I haven't.

*H.* Ah-h. How long have you known her?

*C.* I don't know her.

*H.* Don't know her?

*C.* No.

*H.* Ah-h. How did you come to be interested i: her book, then?

*C.* Well, she—she wrote and asked me to find publisher for her, and mentioned you.

*H.* Why should she apply to you instead of to me

*C.* She wished me to use my influence.

*H.* Dear me, what has *influence* to do with such matter?

*C.* Well, I think she thought you would be mo likely to examine her book if you were influenced.

*H.* Why, what we are here *for* is to examine boo! —anybody's book that comes along. It's our *bus ness.* Why should we turn away a book unexan ined because it's a stranger's? It would be foolisl No publisher does it. On what ground did she r quest your influence, since you do not know he She must have thought you knew her literature ar could speak for it. Is that it?

*C.* No; she knew I didn't.

*H.* Well, what then? She had a reason of sor sort for believing you competent to recommend h literature, and also under obligations to do it?

*C.* Yes, I—I knew her uncle.

*H.* Knew her *uncle?*

*C.* Yes.

*H.* Upon my word! So, you knew her uncle; her uncle knows her literature; he endorses it to you; the chain is complete, nothing further needed; you are satisfied, and therefore—

*C.* No, that isn't all, there are other ties. I knew the cabin her uncle lived in, in the mines; I knew his partners, too; also I came near knowing her husband before she married him, and I *did* know the abandoned shaft where a premature blast went off and he went flying through the air and clear down to the trail and hit an Indian in the back with almost fatal consequences.

*H.* To *him*, or to the Indian?

*C.* She didn't say which it was.

*H.* (*With a sigh.*) It certainly beats the band! You don't know *her*, you don't know her literature. you don't know who got hurt when the blast went off, you don't know a single thing for us to build an estimate of her book upon, so far as I—

*C.* I knew her uncle. You are forgetting her uncle.

*H.* Oh, what use is *he?* Did you know him long? How long was it?

*C.* Well, I don't know that I really knew him, but I must have met him, anyway. I think it was that way; you can't tell about these things, you know, except when they are recent.

*H.* Recent? When was all this?

9

*C.* Sixteen years ago.

*H.* What a basis to judge a book upon! At first you said you knew him, and now you don't know whether you did or not.

*C.* Oh yes, I knew him; anyway, I think I thought I did; I'm perfectly certain of it.

*H.* What makes you think you thought you knew him?

*C.* Why, she says I did, herself.

*H. She* says so!

*C.* Yes, she does, and I *did* know him, too, though I don't remember it now.

*H.* Come—how can you know it when you don't remember it.

*C. I* don't know. That is, I don't know the process, but I *do* know lots of things that I don't remember, and remember lots of things that I don't know. It's so with every educated person.

*H.* (*After a pause.*) Is your time valuable?

*C.* No—well, not very.

*H.* Mine is.

So I came away then, because he was looking tired. Overwork, I reckon; I never do that; I have seen the evil effects of it. My mother was always afraid I would overwork myself, but I never did.

Dear madam, you see how it would happen if I went there. He would ask me those questions, and I would try to answer them to suit him, and he would hurt me here and there and yonder and get me embarrassed more and more all the time, and at last he would look tired on account of overwork, and there it would end and nothing done. I wish I could be useful to you, but, you see, they do not care for uncles or any of those things; it doesn't move them, it doesn't have the least effect, they don't care for anything but the literature itself, and they as good as despise influence. But they do care for books, and are eager to get them and examine them, no matter whence they come, nor from whose pen. If you will send yours to a publisher—any publisher —he will certainly examine it, I can assure you of that.

# A TELEPHONIC CONVERSATION

CONSIDER that a conversation by telephone—when you are simply sitting by and not taking any part in that conversation—is one of the solemnest curiosities of this modern life. Yesterday I was writing a deep article on a sublime philosophical subject while such a conversation was going on in the room. I notice that one can always write best when somebody is talking through a telephone close by. Well, the thing began in this way. A member of our household came in and asked me to have our house put into communication with Mr. Bagley's, down-town. I have observed, in many cities, that the sex always shrink from calling up the central office themselves. I don't know why, but they do. So I touched the bell, and this talk ensued:

*Central Office.* (*Gruffly.*) Hello!

*I.* Is it the Central Office?

*C. O.* Of course it is. What do you want?

*I.* Will you switch me on to the Bagleys, please?

*C. O.* All right. Just keep your ear to the telephone.

Then I heard, *k-look, k-look, k'look—klook-klook-klook-look-look!* then a horrible "gritting" of teeth, and finally a piping female voice: Y-e-s?   (*Rising inflection.*)   Did you wish to speak to me?

Without answering, I handed the telephone to the applicant, and sat down. Then followed that queerest of all the queer things in this world—a conversation with only one end to it. You hear questions asked; you don't hear the answer. You hear invitations given; you hear no thanks in return. You have listening pauses of dead silence, followed by apparently irrelevant and unjustifiable exclamations of glad surprise or sorrow or dismay. You can't make head or tail of the talk, because you never hear anything that the person at the other end of the wire says. Well, I heard the following remarkable series of observations, all from the one tongue, and all shouted—for you can't ever persuade the sex to speak gently into a telephone:

Yes? Why, how did *that* happen?

Pause.

What did you say?

Pause.

Oh no, I don't think it was.

Pause.

*No!* Oh no, I didn't mean *that*. I meant, put it in while it is still boiling—or just before it *comes* to a boil.

Pause.

WHAT?

Pause.

I turned it over with a backstitch on the selvage edge.

Pause.

Yes, I like that way, too; but I think it's better to baste it on with Valenciennes or bombazine, or something of that sort. It gives it such an air— and attracts so much notice.

Pause.

It's forty-ninth Deuteronomy, sixty-fourth to ninety-seventh inclusive. I think we ought all to read it often.

Pause.

Perhaps so; I generally use a hair-pin.

Pause.

What did you say? (*Aside.*) Children, do be quiet!

Pause.

*Oh! B flat!* Dear me, I thought you said it was the cat!

Pause.

Since *when?*

Pause.

Why, *I* never heard of it.

Pause.

You astound me! It seems utterly impossible*

Pause.

*Who* did?

Pause.

Good-ness gracious!

Pause.

Well, what *is* this world coming to? Was it right in *church?*

Pause.

And was her *mother* there?

Pause.

Why, Mrs. Bagley, I should have died of humiliation! What did they *do?*

Long pause.

I can't be perfectly sure, because I haven't the notes by me; but I think it goes something like this: te-rolly-loll-loll, loll lolly-loll-loll, O tolly-loll-loll-*lee-ly-li-i*-do! And then *repeat,* you know.

Pause.

Yes, I think it *is* very sweet—and very solemn and impressive, if you get the andantino and the pianissimo right.

Pause.

Oh, gum-drops, gum-drops! But I never allow them to eat striped candy. And of course they *can't,* till they get their teeth, anyway.

Pause.

*What?*

Pause.

Oh, not in the least—go right on. He's here writing—it doesn't bother *him.*

Pause.

Very well, I'll come if I can. (*Aside.*) Dear me, how it does tire a person's arm to hold this thing up so long! I wish she'd—

Pause.

Oh no, not at all; I *like* to talk—but I'm afraid I'm keeping you from your affairs.

Pause.

Visitors?

Pause.

No, we never use butter on them.

Pause.

Yes, that is a very good way; but all the cook-books say they are very unhealthy when they are out of season. And *he* doesn't like them, anyway—especially canned.

Pause.

Oh, I think that is too high for them; we have never paid over fifty cents a bunch.

Pause.

*Must* you go? Well, *good*-bye.

Pause.

Yes, I think so. *Good*-bye.

Pause.

Four o'clock, then—I'll be ready. *Good*-bye.

Pause.

Thank you ever so much. *Good*-bye.

Pause.

Oh, not at all!—just as fresh— *Which?* Oh, I'm glad to hear you say that. *Good*-bye.

(Hangs up the telephone and says, "Oh, it *does* tire a person's arm so!")

A man delivers a single brutal "Good-bye," and that is the end of it. Not so with the gentle sex—I say it in their praise; they cannot abide abruptness.

# EDWARD MILLS AND GEORGE BENTON: A TALE

THESE two were distantly related to each other — seventh cousins, or something of that sort. While still babies they became orphans, and were adopted by the Brants, a childless couple, who quickly grew very fond of them. The Brants were always saying: "Be pure, honest, sober, industrious, and considerate of others, and success in life is assured." The children heard this repeated some thousands of times before they understood it; they could repeat it themselves long before they could say the Lord's Prayer; it was painted over the nursery door, and was about the first thing they learned to read. It was destined to become the unswerving rule of Edward Mills's life. Sometimes the Brants changed the wording a little, and said: "Be pure, honest, sober, industrious, considerate, and you will never lack friends."

Baby Mills was a comfort to everybody about him. When he wanted candy and could not have it, he listened to reason, and contented himself without it. When Baby Benton wanted candy, he cried for it until he got it. Baby Mills took care of his toys; Baby Benton always destroyed his in a very brief time, and then made himself so insistently disagreeable that, in order to have peace in the house, little Edward was persuaded to yield up his playthings to him.

When the children were a little older, Georgie became a heavy expense in one respect: he took no care of his clothes; consequently, he shone frequently in new ones, which was not the case with Eddie. The boys grew apace. Eddie was an increasing comfort, Georgie an increasing solicitude. It was always sufficient to say, in answer to Eddie's petitions, "I would rather you would not do it"— meaning swimming, skating, picnicking, berrying, circusing, and all sorts of things which boys delight in. But *no* answer was sufficient for Georgie; he had to be humored in his desires, or he would carry them with a high hand. Naturally, no boy got more swimming, skating, berrying, and so forth than he; no boy ever had a better time. The good Brants did not allow the boys to play out after nine in summer evenings; they were sent to bed at that hour; Eddie honorably remained, but Georgie usually slipped out of the window towards ten, and enjoyed himself till midnight. It seemed impossible to break Georgie of this bad habit, but the Brants managed it at last by hiring him, with apples and marbles, to stay in. The good Brants gave all their time and attention to vain endeavors to regulate Georgie; they said, with grateful tears in their eyes, that Eddie needed no efforts of theirs, he was so good, so considerate, and in all ways so perfect.

By-and-by the boys were big enough to work, so they were apprenticed to a trade: Edward went voluntarily; George was coaxed and bribed. Edward worked hard and faithfully, and ceased to be an expense to the good Brants; they praised him, so did his master; but George ran away, and it cost Mr. Brant both money and trouble to hunt him up and get him back. By-and-by he ran away again—more money and more trouble. He ran away a third time — and stole a few little things to carry with him. Trouble and expense for Mr. Brant once more; and, besides, it was with the greatest difficulty that he succeeded in persuading the master to let the youth go unprosecuted for the theft.

Edward worked steadily along, and in time became a full partner in his master's business. George did not improve; he kept the loving hearts of his aged benefactors full of trouble, and their hands full of inventive activities to protect him from ruin. Edward, as a boy, had interested himself in Sunday-schools, debating societies, penny missionary affairs, anti-tobacco organizations, anti-profanity associations, and all such things; as a man, he was a quiet but steady and reliable helper in the church, the temperance societies, and in all movements looking to the aiding and uplifting of men. This excited no remark, attracted no attention — for it was his "natural bent."

Finally, the old people died. The will testified their loving pride in Edward, and left their little property to George—because he "needed it"; whereas, "owing to a bountiful Providence," such was not the case with Edward. The property was left to George conditionally: he must buy out Edward's partner with it; else it must go to a benevolent organization called the Prisoner's Friend Society. The old people left a letter, in which they begged their dear son Edward to take their place and watch over George, and help and shield him as they had done.

Edward dutifully acquiesced, and George became his partner in the business. He was not a valuable partner: he had been meddling with drink before; he soon developed into a constant tippler now, and his flesh and eyes showed the fact unpleasantly. Edward had been courting a sweet and kindly spirited girl for some time. They loved each other dearly, and— But about this period George began to haunt her tearfully and imploringly, and at last she went crying to Edward, and said her high and holy duty was plain before her—she must not let her own selfish desires interfere with it: she must marry "poor George" and "reform him." It would break her heart, she knew it would, and so on; but duty was duty. So she married George, and Edward's heart came very near breaking, as well as her own. How-

ever, Edward recovered, and married another girl—
a very excellent one she was, too.

Children came to both families. Mary did her
honest best to reform her husband, but the contract
was too large. George went on drinking, and by-
and-by he fell to misusing her and the little ones
sadly. A great many good people strove with
George—they were always at it, in fact—but he
calmly took such efforts as his due and their duty,
and did not mend his ways. He added a vice, presently—that of secret gambling. He got deeply in
debt; he borrowed money on the firm's credit, as
quietly as he could, and carried this system so far
and so successfully that one morning the sheriff took
possession of the establishment, and the two cousins
found themselves penniless.

Times were hard, now, and they grew worse. Edward moved his family into a garret, and walked the
streets day and night, seeking work. He begged for
it, but it was really not to be had. He was astonished to see how soon his face became unwelcome;
he was astonished and hurt to see how quickly the
ancient interest which people had had in him faded
out and disappeared. Still, he *must* get work; so he
swallowed his chagrin, and toiled on in search of it.
At last he got a job of carrying bricks up a ladder in
a hod, and was a grateful man in consequence; but
after that *nobody* knew him or cared anything about
him. He was not able to keep up his dues in the
various moral organizations to which he belonged,

and had to endure the sharp pain of seeing himself brought under the disgrace of suspension.

But the faster Edward died out of public knowledge and interest, the faster George rose in them. He was found lying, ragged and drunk, in the gutter one morning. A member of the Ladies' Temperance Refuge fished him out, took him in hand, got up a subscription for him, kept him sober a whole week, then got a situation for him. An account of it was published.

General attention was thus drawn to the poor fellow, and a great many people came forward, and helped him towards reform with their countenance and encouragement. He did not drink a drop for two months, and meantime was the pet of the good. Then he fell—in the gutter; and there was general sorrow and lamentation. But the noble sisterhood rescued him again. They cleaned him up, they fed him, they listened to the mournful music of his repentances, they got him his situation again. An account of this, also, was published, and the town was drowned in happy tears over the re-restoration of the poor beset and struggling victim of the fatal bowl. A grand temperance revival was got up, and after some rousing speeches had been made the chairman said, impressively: "We are now about to call for signers; and I think there is a spectacle in store for you which not many in this house will be able to view with dry eyes." There was an eloquent pause, and then George Benton, escorted by a red-sashed detachment of the Ladies of the Refuge, stepped forward upon the platform and signed the pledge. The air was rent with applause, and everybody cried for joy. Everybody wrung the hand of the new convert when the meeting was over; his salary was enlarged next day; he was the talk of the town, and its hero. An account of it was published.

George Benton fell, regularly, every three months, but was faithfully rescued and wrought with, every time, and good situations were found for him. Finally, he was taken around the country lecturing, as a reformed drunkard, and he had great houses an did an immense amount of good.

He was so popular at home, and so trusted—during his sober intervals—that he was enabled to use the name of a principal citizen, and get a large sum of money at the bank. A mighty pressure was brought to bear to save him from the consequences of his forgery, and it was partially successful—he was "sent up" for only two years. When, at the end of a year, the tireless efforts of the benevolent were crowned with success, and he emerged from the penitentiary with a pardon in his pocket, the Prisoner's Friend Society met him at the door with a situation and a comfortable salary, and all the other benevolent people came forward and gave him advice, encouragement, and help. Edward Mills had once applied to the Prisoner's Friend Society for a situation, when in dire need, but the question, "Have you been a prisoner?" made brief work of his case.

While all these things were going on, Edward Mills had been quietly making head against adversity. He was still poor, but was in receipt of a steady and sufficient salary, as the respected and trusted cashier of a bank. George Benton never came near him, and was never heard to inquire about him. George got to indulging in long absences from the town; there were ill reports about him, but nothing definite.

One winter's night some masked burglars forced their way into the bank, and found Edward Mills there alone. They commanded him to reveal the "combination," so that they could get into the safe. He refused. They threatened his life. He said his employers trusted him, and he could not be traitor to that trust. He could die, if he must, but while he lived he would be faithful; he would not yield up the "combination." The burglars killed him.

The detectives hunted down the criminals; the chief one proved to be George Benton. A wide sympathy was felt for the widow and orphans of the dead man, and all the newspapers in the land begged that all the banks in the land would testify their appreciation of the fidelity and heroism of the murdered cashier by coming forward with a generous contribution of money in aid of his family, now bereft of support. The result was a mass of solid cash amounting to upward of five hundred dollars—an average of nearly three-eighths of a cent for each bank in the Union. The cashier's own bank testified its gratitude by endeavoring to show (but humiliatingly failed in it) that the peerless servant's accounts were not square, and that he himself had knocked his brains out with a bludgeon to escape detection and punishment.

George Benton was arraigned for trial. Then everybody seemed to forget the widow and orphans in their solicitude for poor George. Everything that money and influence could do was done to save him, but it all failed; he was sentenced to death. Straightway the Governor was besieged with petitions for commutation or pardon; they were brought by tearful young girls; by sorrowful old maids; by deputations of pathetic widows; by shoals of impressive orphans. But no, the Governor—for once—would not yield.

Now George Benton experienced religion. The glad news flew all around. From that time forth his cell was always full of girls and women and fresh flowers; all the day long there was prayer, and hymn-singing, and thanksgivings, and homilies, and tears, with never an interruption, except an occasional five-minute intermission for refreshments.

This sort of thing continued up to the very gallows, and George Benton went proudly home, in the black cap, before a wailing audience of the sweetest and best that the region could produce. His grave had fresh flowers on it every day, for a while, and the head-stone bore these words, under a hand pointing aloft: "He has fought the good fight."

The brave cashier's head-stone has this inscrip-

10

tion: "Be pure, honest, sober, industrious, considerate, and you will never—"

Nobody knows who gave the order to leave it that
way, but it was so given.

The cashier's family are in stringent circumstances, now, it is said; but no matter; a lot of ap-
preciative people, who were not willing that an act
so brave and true as his should go unrewarded, have
collected forty-two thousand dollars—and built a
Memorial Church with it.

# SAINT JOAN OF ARC

## I

THE evidence furnished at the Trials and Rehabilitation sets forth Joan of Arc's strange and beautiful history in clear and minute detail. Among all the multitude of biographies that freight the shelves of the world's libraries, *this is the only one whose validity is confirmed to us by oath*. It gives us a vivid picture of a career and a personality of so extraordinary a character that we are helped to accept them as actualities by the very fact that both

NOTE.—The Official Record of the Trials and Rehabilitation of Joan of Arc is the most remarkable history that exists in any language; yet there are few people in the world who can say they have read it: in England and America it has hardly been heard of.

Three hundred years ago Shakespeare did not know the true story of Joan of Arc; in his day it was unknown even in France. For four hundred years it existed rather as a vaguely defined romance than as definite and authentic history. The true story remained buried in the official archives of France from the Rehabilitation of 1456 until Quicherat dug it out and gave it to the world two generations ago, in lucid and understandable modern French. It is a deeply fascinating story. But only in the Official Trials and Rehabilitation can it be found in its entirety.—M. T.

are beyond the inventive reach of fiction. The
public part of the career occupied only a mere
breath of time—it covered but two years; but what
a career it was! The personality which made it possible is one to be reverently studied, loved, and marvelled at, but not to be wholly understood and ac-
counted for by even the most searching analysis.

In Joan of Arc at the age of sixteen there was no
promise of a romance. She lived in a dull little village on the frontiers of civilization; she had been nowhere and had seen nothing; she knew none but
simple shepherd folk; she had never seen a person of
note; she hardly knew what a soldier looked like; she
had never ridden a horse, nor had a warlike weapon
in her hand; she could neither read nor write: she
could spin and sew; she knew her catechism and her
prayers and the fabulous histories of the saints, and
this was all her learning. That was Joan at sixteen.
What did she know of law? of evidence? of courts?
of the attorney's trade? of legal procedure? Nothing. Less than nothing. Thus exhaustively equipped with ignorance, she went before the court at
Toul to contest a false charge of breach of promise
of marriage; she conducted her cause herself, without any one's help or advice or any one's friendly
sympathy, and won it. She called no witnesses of
her own, but vanquished the prosecution by using
with deadly effectiveness its own testimony. The
astonished judge threw the case out of court, and
spoke of her as "this marvellous child."

She went to the veteran Commandant of Vaucouleurs and demanded an escort of soldiers, saying she
must march to the help of the King of France, since
she was commissioned of God to win back his lost
kingdom for him and set the crown upon his head.
The Commandant said, "What, you? you are only
a child." And he advised that she be taken back to
her village and have her ears boxed. But she said
she must obey God, and would come again, and
again, and yet again, and finally she would get the
soldiers. She said truly. In time he yielded, after
months of delay and refusal, and gave her the
soldiers; and took off his sword and gave her that,
and said, "Go—and let come what may." She made
her long and perilous journey through the enemy's
country, and spoke with the King, and convinced
him. Then she was summoned before the University of Poitiers to prove that she *was* commissioned of God and not of Satan, and daily during
three weeks she sat before that learned congress un-
afraid, and capably answered their deep questions
out of her ignorant but able head and her simple and
honest heart; and again she won her case, and with
it the wondering admiration of all that august company.

And now, aged seventeen, she was made Com-
mander-in-Chief, with a prince of the royal house
and the veteran generals of France for subordinates;
and at the head of the first army she had ever seen,
she marched to Orleans, carried the commanding

fortresses of the enemy by storm in three desperate assaults, and in ten days raised a siege which had defied the might of France for seven months.

After a tedious and insane delay caused by the King's instability of character and the treacherous counsels of his ministers, she got permission to take the field again. She took Jargeau by storm; then Meung; she forced Beaugency to surrender; then—in the open field—she won the memorable victory of Patay against Talbot, "the English lion," and broke the back of the Hundred Years' War. It was a campaign which cost but seven weeks of time; yet the political results would have been cheap if the time expended had been fifty years. Patay, that unsung and now long-forgotten battle, was the Moscow of the English power in France; from the blow struck that day it was destined never to recover. It was the beginning of the end of an alien dominion which had ridden France intermittently for three hundred years.

Then followed the great campaign of the Loire, the capture of Troyes by assault, and the triumphal march past surrendering towns and fortresses to Rheims, where Joan put the crown upon her King's head in the Cathedral, amid wild public rejoicings, and with her old peasant father there to see these things and believe his eyes if he could. She had restored the crown and the lost sovereignty; the King was grateful for once in his shabby poor life, and asked her to name her reward and have it. She

asked for nothing for herself, but begged that the
taxes of her native village might be remitted forever. The prayer was granted, and the promise
kept for three hundred and sixty years. Then it
was broken, and remains broken to-day. France
was very poor then, she is very rich now; but she
has been collecting those taxes for more than a
hundred years.

Joan asked one other favor: that now that her
mission was fulfilled she might be allowed to go
back to her village and take up her humble life
again with her mother and the friends of her childhood; for she had no pleasure in the cruelties of war,
and the sight of blood and suffering wrung her
heart. Sometimes in battle she did not draw her
sword, lest in the splendid madness of the onset she
might forget herself and take an enemy's life with it.
In the Rouen Trials, one of her quaintest speeches—
coming from the gentle and girlish source it did—
was her naïve remark that she had "never killed any
one." Her prayer for leave to go back to the rest
and peace of her village home was not granted.

Then she wanted to march at once upon Paris,
take it, and drive the English out of France. She
was hampered in all the ways that treachery and the
King's vacillation could devise, but she forced her
way to Paris at last, and fell badly wounded in a
successful assault upon one of the gates. Of course
her men lost heart at once—she was the only heart
they had. They fell back. She begged to be al-

lowed to remain at the front, saying victory was sure.
"I will take Paris now or die!" she said. But she
was removed from the field by force; the King or-
dered a retreat, and actually disbanded his army.
In accordance with a beautiful old military custom
Joan devoted her silver armor and hung it up in the
Cathedral of St. Denis. Its great days were over.

Then, by command, she followed the King and his
frivolous court and endured a gilded captivity for a
time, as well as her free spirit could; and whenever
inaction became unbearable she gathered some men
together and rode away and assaulted a stronghold
and captured it.

At last in a sortie against the enemy, from Com-
piègne, on the 24th of May (when she was turned
eighteen), she was herself captured, after a gallant
fight. It was her last battle. She was to follow the
drums no more.

Thus ended the briefest epoch-making military
career known to history. It lasted only a year and
a month, but it found France an English province,
and furnishes the reason that France is France to-
day and not an English province still. Thirteen
months! It was, indeed, a short career; but in the
centuries that have since elapsed five hundred millions of Frenchmen have lived and died blest by the
benefactions it conferred; and so long as France
shall endure, the mighty debt must grow. And
France is grateful; we often hear her say it. Also
thrifty: she collects the Domrémy taxes.

JOAN was fated to spend the rest of her life behind
bolts and bars. She was a prisoner of war, not a
criminal, therefore hers was recognized as an honorable captivity. By the rules of war she must be
held to ransom, and a fair price could not be refused
if offered. John of Luxembourg paid her the just
compliment of requiring a prince's ransom for her.
In that day that phrase represented a definite sum
—61,125 francs. It was, of course, supposable that
either the King or grateful France, or both, would
fly with the money and set their fair young benefactor free. But this did not happen. In five and
a half months neither King nor country stirred a
hand nor offered a penny. Twice Joan tried to escape. Once by a trick she succeeded for a moment,
and locked her jailer in behind her, but she was discovered and caught; in the other case she let herself
down from a tower sixty feet high, but her rope was
too short, and she got a fall that disabled her and
she could not get away.

Finally, Cauchon, Bishop of Beauvais, paid the
money and bought Joan—ostensibly for the Church,
to be tried for wearing male attire and for other im-
pieties, but really for the English, the enemy into

whose hands the poor girl was so piteously anxious not to fall. She was now shut up in the dungeons of the Castle of Rouen and kept in an iron cage, with her hands and feet and neck chained to a pillar; and from that time forth during all the months of her imprisonment, till the end, several rough English soldiers stood guard over her night and day— and not outside her room, but in it. It was a dreary and hideous captivity, but it did not conquer her: nothing could break that invincible spirit. From first to last she was a prisoner a year; and she spent the last three months of it on trial for her life before a formidable array of ecclesiastical judges, and disputing the ground with them foot by foot and inch by inch with brilliant generalship and dauntless pluck. The spectacle of that solitary girl, forlorn and friendless, without advocate or adviser, and without the help and guidance of any copy of the charges brought against her or rescript of the complex and voluminous daily proceedings of the court to modify the crushing strain upon her astonishing memory, fighting that long battle serene and undismayed against these colossal odds, stands alone in its pathos and its sublimity; it has nowhere its mate, either in the annals of fact or in the inventions of fiction.

And how fine and great were the things she daily said, how fresh and crisp—and she so worn in body, so starved, and tired, and harried! They run through the whole gamut of feeling and expression—

from scorn and defiance, uttered with soldierly fire and frankness, all down the scale to wounded dignity clothed in words of noble pathos; as, when her patience was exhausted by the pestering delvings and gropings and searchings of her persecutors to find out what kind of devil's witchcraft she had employed to rouse the war spirit in her timid soldiers, she burst out with, "What I said was, '*Ride these English down*'—and I did it myself!" and as, when insultingly asked why it was that *her* standard had place at the crowning of the King in the Cathedral of Rheims rather than the standards of the other captains, she uttered that touching speech, "*It had borne the burden, it had earned the honor*"—a phrase which fell from her lips without premeditation, yet whose moving beauty and simple grace it would bankrupt the arts of language to surpass.

Although she was on trial for her life, she was the only witness called on either side; the only witness summoned to testify before a packed jury commissioned with a definite task: to find her guilty, whether she was guilty or not. She must be convicted out of her own mouth, there being no other way to accomplish it. Every advantage that learning has over ignorance, age over youth, experience over inexperience, chicane over artlessness, every trick and trap and gin devisable by malice and the cunning of sharp intellects practised in setting snares for the unwary—all these were employed against her without shame; and when these arts were one by one de-

feated by the marvellous intuitions of her alert and
penetrating mind, Bishop Cauchon stooped to a final
baseness which it degrades human speech to describe: a priest who pretended to come from the
region of her own home and to be a pitying friend
and anxious to help her in her sore need was smuggled
into her cell, and he misused his sacred office to steal
her confidence; she confided to him the things sealed
from revealment by her Voices, and which her pros-
ecutors had tried so long in vain to trick her into be-
traying. A concealed confederate set it all down
and delivered it to Cauchon, who used Joan's secrets,
thus obtained, for her ruin.

Throughout the Trials, whatever the foredoomed
witness said was twisted from its true meaning when
possible, and made to tell against her; and whenever
an answer of hers was beyond the reach of twisting
it was not allowed to go upon the record. It was
upon one of these latter occasions that she uttered
that pathetic reproach—to Cauchon: "Ah, you set
down everything that is against me, but you will not
set down what is for me."

That this untrained young creature's genius for
war was wonderful, and her generalship worthy to
rank with the ripe products of a tried and trained
military experience, we have the sworn testimony of
two of her veteran subordinates — one, the Duc
d'Alençon, the other the greatest of the French generals of the time, Dunois, Bastard of Orleans; that
her genius was as great—possibly even greater—in

the subtle warfare of the forum we have for witness the records of the Rouen Trials, that protracted exhibition of intellectual fence maintained with credit against the master-minds of France; that her moral greatness was peer to her intellect we call the Rouen Trials again to witness, with their testimony to a fortitude which patiently and steadfastly endured during twelve weeks the wasting forces of captivity, chains, loneliness, sickness, darkness, hunger, thirst, cold, shame, insult, abuse, broken sleep, treachery, ingratitude, exhausting sieges of cross-examination, the threat of torture, with the rack before her and the executioner standing ready: yet never surrendering, never asking quarter, the frail wreck of her as unconquerable the last day as was her invincible spirit the first.

Great as she was in so many ways, she was perhaps even greatest of all in the lofty things just named— her patient endurance, her steadfastness, her granite fortitude. We may not hope to easily find her mate and twin in these majestic qualities; where we lift our eyes highest we find only a strange and curious contrast — there in the captive eagle beating his broken wings on the Rock of St. Helena.

## III

THE Trials ended with her condemnation. But
as she had conceded nothing, confessed nothing, this
was victory for her, defeat for Cauchon. But his
evil resources were not yet exhausted. She was persuaded to agree to sign a paper of slight import, then
by treachery a paper was substituted which contained a recantation and a detailed confession of
everything which had been charged against her during the Trials and denied and repudiated by her persistently during the three months; and this false
paper she ignorantly signed. This was a victory for
Cauchon. He followed it eagerly and pitilessly up
by at once setting a trap for her which she could not
escape. When she realized this she gave up the long
struggle, denounced the treason which had been
practised against her, repudiated the false confession, reasserted the truth of the testimony which she
had given in the Trials, and went to her martyrdom
with the peace of God in her tired heart, and on her
lips endearing words and loving prayers for the cur
she had crowned and the nation of ingrates she had
saved.

When the fires rose about her and she begged for
cross for her dying lips to kiss, it was not a frien

but an enemy, not a Frenchman but an alien, not a comrade in arms but an English soldier, that answered that pathetic prayer. He broke a stick across his knee, bound the pieces together in the form of the symbol she  loved, and gave it her; and his gentle deed is not forgotten, nor will be.

# IV

Twenty-five years afterwards the Process of Rehabilitation was instituted, there being a growing
doubt as to the validity of a sovereignty that had
been rescued and set upon its feet by a person who
had been proven by the Church to be a witch and a
familiar of evil spirits. Joan's old generals, her
secretary, several aged relations and other villagers
of Domrémy, surviving judges and secretaries of the
Rouen and Poitiers Processes—a cloud of witnesses
some of whom had been her enemies and persecutors
—came and made oath and testified; and what they
said was written down. In that sworn testimony
the moving and beautiful history of Joan of Arc is
laid bare, from her childhood to her martyrdom
From the verdict she rises stainlessly pure, in mind
and heart, in speech and deed and spirit, and will so
endure to the end of time.

She is the Wonder of the Ages. And when we
consider her origin, her early circumstances, her sex
and that she did all the things upon which her renown rests while she was still a young girl, we recognize that while our race continues she will be also
the *Riddle* of the Ages. When we set about ac-
counting for a Napoleon or a Shakespeare or

Raphael or a Wagner or an Edison or other extraordinary person, we understand that the measure of his talent will not explain the whole result, nor even the largest part of it; no, it is the atmosphere in which the talent was cradled that explains; it is the training which it received while it grew, the nurture it got from reading, study, example, the encouragement it gathered from self-recognition and recognition from the outside at each stage of its development: when we know all these details, then we know why the man was ready when his opportunity came. We should expect Edison's surroundings and atmosphere to have the largest share in discovering him to himself and to the world; and we should expect him to live and die undiscovered in a land where an inventor could find no comradeship, no sympathy, no ambition-rousing atmosphere of recognition and applause — Dahomey, for instance. Dahomey could not find an Edison out; in Dahomey an Edison could not find himself out. Broadly speaking, genius is not born with sight, but blind; and it is not itself that opens its eyes, but the subtle influences of a myriad of stimulating exterior circumstances.

We all know this to be not a guess, but a mere commonplace fact, a truism. Lorraine was Joan of Arc's Dahomey. And there the Riddle confronts us. We can understand how she could be born with military genius, with leonine courage, with incomparable fortitude, with a mind which was in several particulars a prodigy—a mind which included among its specialties the lawyer's gift of detecting traps laid by the adversary in cunning and treacherous arrangements of seemingly innocent words, the orator's gift of eloquence, the advocate's gift of presenting a case in clear and compact form, the judge's gift of sorting and weighing evidence, and finally, something recognizable as more than a mere trace of the statesman's gift of understanding a political situation and how to make profitable use of such opportunities as it offers; we can comprehend how she could be born with these great qualities, but we cannot comprehend how they became immediately usable and effective without the developing forces of a sympathetic atmosphere and the training which comes of teaching, study, practice—years of practice,—and the crowning and perfecting help of a thousand mistakes. We can understand how the possibilities of the future perfect peach are all lying hid in the humble bitter-almond, but we cannot conceive of the peach springing directly from the almond without the intervening long seasons of patient cultivation and development. Out of a cattle-pasturing peasant village lost in the remotenesses of an unvisited wilderness and atrophied with ages of stupefaction and ignorance we cannot see a Joan of Arc issue equipped to the last detail for her amazing career and hope to be able to explain the riddle of it, labor at it as we may.

It is beyond us. All the rules fail in this girl's

case. In the world's history she stands alone—quite alone. Others have been great in their first public exhibitions of generalship, valor, legal talent, diplomacy, fortitude; but always their previous years and associations had been in a larger or smaller degree a preparation for these things. There have been no exceptions to the rule. But Joan was competent in a law case at sixteen without ever having seen a law book or a court-house before; she had no training in soldiership and no associations with it, yet she was a competent general in her first campaign; she was brave in her first battle, yet her courage had had no education—not even the education which a boy's courage gets from never-ceasing reminders that it is not permissible in a boy to be a coward, but only in a girl; friendless, alone, ignorant, in the blossom of her youth, she sat week after week, a prisoner in chains, before her assemblage of judges, enemies hunting her to her death, the ablest minds in France, and answered them out of an untaught wisdom which overmatched their learning, baffled their tricks and treacheries with a native sagacity which compelled their wonder, and scored every day a victory against these incredible odds and camped unchallenged on the field. In the history of the human intellect, untrained, inexperienced, and using only its birthright equipment of untried capacities, there is nothing which approaches this. Joan of Arc stands alone, and must continue to stand alone, by reason of the unfellowed fact that in the things wherein she

was great she was so without shade or suggestion of
help from preparatory teaching, practice, environment, or experience. There is no one to compare
her with, none to measure her by; for all others
among the illustrious *grew* towards their high place
in an atmosphere and surroundings which discovered
their gift to them and nourished it and promoted it,
intentionally or unconsciously. There have been
other young generals, but they were not girls; young
generals, but they had been soldiers before they were
generals: she *began* as a general; she commanded the
first army she ever saw; she led it from victory to
victory, and never lost a battle with it; there have
been young commanders-in-chief, but none so young
as she: she is the only soldier in history who has
held the supreme command of a nation's armies at
the age of seventeen.

Her history has still another feature which sets her
apart and leaves her without fellow or competitor:
there have been many uninspired prophets, but she
was the only one who ever ventured the daring detail of naming, along with a foretold event, the
event's precise nature, the special time-limit within
which it would occur, and the place—*and scored ful-
filment*. At Vaucouleurs she said she must go to the
King and be made his general, and break the English power, and crown her sovereign—"at Rheims."
It all happened. It was all to happen "next year"
—and it did. She foretold her first wound and its
character and date a month in advance, and the

prophecy was recorded in a public record-book three weeks in advance. She repeated it the morning of the date named, and it was fulfilled before night. At Tours she foretold the limit of her military career —saying it would end in one year from the time of its utterance—and she was right. She foretold her martyrdom—using *that word*, and naming a time three months away—and again she was right. At a time when France seemed hopelessly and permanently in the hands of the English she twice asserted in her prison before her judges that within seven years the English would meet with a mightier disaster than had been the fall of Orleans: it happened within five—the fall of Paris. Other prophecies of hers came true, both as to the event named and the time-limit prescribed.

She was deeply religious, and believed that she had daily speech with angels; that she saw them face to face, and that they counselled her, comforted and heartened her, and brought commands to her direct from God. She had a childlike faith in the heavenly origin of her apparitions and her Voices, and not any threat of any form of death was able to frighten it out of her loyal heart. She was a beautiful and simple and lovable character. In the records of the Trials this comes out in clear and shining detail. She was gentle and winning and affectionate; she loved her home and friends and her village life; she was miserable in the presence of pain and suffering; she was full of compassion: on the field of her most splendid victory she forgot her triumphs to hold in her lap the head of a dying enemy and comfort his passing spirit with pitying words; in an age when it was common to slaughter prisoners she stood dauntless between hers and harm, and saved them alive; she was forgiving, generous, unselfish, magnanimous, she was pure from all spot or stain of baseness. And always she was a *girl;* and dear and worshipful, as is meet for that estate: when she fell wounded, the first time, she was frightened, and cried when she saw her blood gushing from her breast; but she was Joan of Arc! and when presently she found that her generals were sounding the retreat, she staggered to her feet and led the assault again and took that place by storm.

There is no blemish in that rounded and beautiful character.

How strange it is!—that almost invariably the artist remembers only one detail—one minor and meaningless detail of the personality of Joan of Arc: to wit, that she was a peasant girl—and forgets all the rest; and so he paints her as a strapping middle-aged fishwoman, with costume to match, and in her face the spirituality of a ham. He is slave to his one idea, and forgets to observe that the supremely great souls are never lodged in gross bodies. No brawn, no muscle, could endure the work that their bodies must do; they do their miracles by the spirit, which has fifty times the strength and staying power of brawn and muscle. The Napoleons are little, not big; and they work twenty hours in the twenty-four, and come up fresh, while the big soldiers with the little hearts faint around them with fatigue. We know what Joan of Arc was like, without asking—merely by what she did. The artist should paint her *spirit*—then he could not fail to paint her body aright. She would rise before us, then, a vision to win us, not repel: a lithe young slender figure, instinct with "the unbought grace of youth," dear and bonny and lovable, the face beautiful, and transfigured with the light of that lustrous intellect and the fires of that unquenchable spirit.

Taking into account, as I have suggested before, all the circumstances—her origin, youth, sex, illiteracy, early environment, and the obstructing conditions under which she exploited her high gifts and made her conquests in the field and before the courts that tried her for her life,—she is easily and by far the most extraordinary person the human race has ever produced.

# THE FIVE BOONS OF LIFE

## I

IN the morning of life came the good fairy with her basket, and said:

"Here are gifts. Take one, leave the others. And be wary, choose wisely; oh, choose wisely! for only one of them is valuable."

The gifts were five: Fame, Love, Riches, Pleasure, Death. The youth said, eagerly:

"There is no need to consider"; and he chose Pleasure.

He went out into the world and sought out the pleasures that youth delights in. But each in its turn was short-lived and disappointing, vain and empty; and each, departing, mocked him. In the end he said: "These years I have wasted. If I could but choose again, I would choose wisely."

## II

THE fairy appeared, and said:

"Four of the gifts remain. Choose once more; and oh, remember—time is flying, and only one of them is precious."

The man considered long, then chose Love; and did not mark the tears that rose in the fairy's eyes.

After many, many years the man sat by a coffin, in an empty home. And he communed with himself, saying: "One by one they have gone away and left me; and now she lies here, the dearest and the last. Desolation after desolation has swept over me; for each hour of happiness the treacherous trader, Love, has sold me I have paid a thousand hours of grief. Out of my heart of hearts I curse him."

# III

"Choose again." It was the fairy speaking. "The years have taught you wisdom—surely it must be so. Three gifts remain. Only one of them has any worth—remember it, and choose warily."

The man reflected long, then chose Fame; and the fairy, sighing, went her way.

Years went by and she came again, and stood behind the man where he sat solitary in the fading day, thinking. And she knew his thought:

"My name filled the world, and its praises were on every tongue, and it seemed well with me for a little while. How little a while it was! Then came envy; then detraction; then calumny; then hate; then persecution. Then derision, which is the beginning of the end. And last of all came pity, which is the funeral of fame. Oh, the bitterness and misery of renown! target for mud in its prime, for contempt and compassion in its decay."

## IV

"Choose yet again." It was the fairy's voice. "Two gifts remain. And do not despair. In the beginning there was but one that was precious, and it is still here."

"Wealth—which is power! How blind I was!" said the man. "Now, at last, life will be worth the living. I will spend, squander, dazzle. These mockers and despisers will crawl in the dirt before me, and I will feed my hungry heart with their envy. I will have all luxuries, all joys, all enchantments of the spirit, all contentments of the body that man holds dear. I will buy, buy, buy! deference, respect, esteem, worship — every pinchbeck grace of life the market of a trivial world can furnish forth. I have lost much time, and chosen badly heretofore, but let that pass; I was ignorant then, and could but take for best what seemed so."

Three short years went by, and a day came when the man sat shivering in a mean garret; and he was gaunt and wan and hollow-eyed, and clothed in rags; and he was gnawing a dry crust and mumbling:

"Curse all the world's gifts, for mockeries and gilded lies! And miscalled, every one. They are not gifts, but merely lendings. Pleasure, Love,

Fame, Riches: they are but temporary disguises for lasting realities—Pain, Grief, Shame, Poverty. The fairy said true; in all her store there was but one gift which was precious, only one that was not valueless. How poor and cheap and mean I know those others now to be, compared with that inestimable one, that dear and sweet and kindly one, that steeps in dreamless and enduring sleep the pains that persecute the body, and the shames and griefs that eat the mind and heart. Bring it! I am weary, I would rest."

# V

THE fairy came, bringing again four of the gifts, but Death was wanting.  She said:

"I gave it to a mother's pet, a little child.  It was ignorant, but trusted me, asking me to choose for it. You did not ask me to choose."

"Oh, miserable me!  What is there left for me?"

"What not even you have deserved: the wanton insult of Old Age."

# THE FIRST WRITING-MACHINES

SOME days ago a correspondent sent in an old type-written sheet, faded by age, containing the following letter over the signature of Mark Twain:

"HARTFORD, *March 19, 1875.*

"Please do not use my name in any way. Please do not even divulge the fact that I own a machine. I have entirely stopped using the type-writer, for the reason that I never could write a letter with it to anybody without receiving a request by return mail that I would not only describe the machine, but state what progress I had made in the use of it, etc., etc. I don't like to write letters, and so I don't want people to know I own this curiosity-breeding little joker."

A note was sent to Mr. Clemens asking him if the letter was genuine and whether he really had a type-writer as long ago as that. Mr. Clemens replied that his best answer is in the following chapter from his unpublished autobiography:

*1904. Villa Quarto, Florence, January.*

Dictating autobiography to a type-writer is a new experience for me, but it goes very well, and is going to save time and "language"—the kind of language that soothes vexation.

I have dictated to a type-writer before—but not autobiography. Between that experience and the present one there lies a mighty gap—more than thirty years! It is a sort of lifetime. In that wide interval much has happened—to the type-machine as well as to the rest of us. At the beginning of that interval a type-machine was a curiosity. The person who owned one was a curiosity, too. But now it is the other way about: the person who *doesn't* own one is a curiosity. I saw a type-machine for the first time in—what year? I suppose it was 1873—because Nasby was with me at the time, and it was in Boston. We must have been lecturing, or we could not have been in Boston, I take it. I quitted the platform that season.

But never mind about that, it is no matter. Nasby and I saw the machine through a window, and went in to look at it. The salesman explained it to us, showed us samples of its work, and said it could do fifty-seven words a minute—a statement which we frankly confessed that we did not believe. So he put his type-girl to work, and we timed her by the watch. She actually did the fifty-seven in sixty seconds. We were partly convinced, but said it probably couldn't happen again. But it did. We timed the girl over and over again—with the same result always: she won out. She did her work on narrow slips of paper, and we pocketed them as fast as she turned them out, to show as curiosities. The price of the machine was $125. I bought one, and we went away very much excited.

At the hotel we got out our slips and were a little disappointed to find that they all contained the same words. The girl had economized time and labor by using a formula which she knew by heart. However, we argued—safely enough—that the *first* type-girl must naturally take rank with the first billiard-player: neither of them could be expected to get out of the game any more than a third or a half of what was in it. If the machine survived—*if* it survived —experts would come to the front, by-and-by, who would double this girl's output without a doubt. They would do one hundred words a minute — my talking speed on the platform. That score has long ago been beaten.

At home I played with the toy, repeating and re-peating and repeating "The Boy stood on the Burn-ing Deck," until I could turn that boy's adventure out at the rate of twelve words a minute; then I re-sumed the pen, for business, and only worked the machine to astonish inquiring visitors. They car-ried off many reams of the boy and his burning deck

By-and-by I hired a young woman, and did my first dictating (letters, merely), and my last until now. The machine did not do both capitals and

lower case (as now), but only capitals. Gothic capitals they were, and sufficiently ugly. I remember
the first letter I dictated. It was to Edward Bok,
who was a boy then. I was not acquainted with
him at that time. His present enterprising spirit
is not new — he had it in that early day. He was
accumulating autographs, and was not content with
mere signatures, he wanted a whole autograph *letter*.
I furnished it—in type-machine capitals, *signature
and all*. It was long; it was a sermon; it contained
advice; also reproaches. I said writing was my
*trade*, my bread-and-butter; I said it was not fair to
ask a man to give away samples of his trade; would
he ask the blacksmith for a horseshoe? would he ask
the doctor for a corpse?

Now I come to an important matter—as I regard
it. In the year '74 the young woman copied a considerable part of a book of mine *on the machine*. In
a previous chapter of this Autobiography I have
claimed that I was the first person in the world that
ever had a telephone in his house for practical pur-
poses; I will now claim—until dispossessed—that I
was the first person in the world to *apply the type-
machine to literature*. That book must have been
*The Adventures of Tom Sawyer*. I wrote the first
half of it in '72, the rest of it in '74. My machinist
type-copied a book for me in '74, so I concluded it
was that one.

That early machine was full of caprices, full of de-
fects—devilish ones. It had as many immoralities

12

as the machines of to-day has virtues. After a year or two I found that it was degrading my character, so I thought I would give it to Howells. He was reluctant, for he was suspicious of novelties and unfriendly towards them, and he remains so to this day. But I persuaded him. He had great confidence in me, and I got him to believe things about the machine that I did not believe myself. He took it home to Boston, and my morals began to improve, but his have never recovered.

He kept it six months, and then returned it to me. I gave it away twice after that, but it wouldn't stay; it came back. Then I gave it to our coachman, Patrick McAleer, who was very grateful, because he did not know the animal, and thought I was trying to make him wiser and better. As soon as he got wiser and better he traded it to a heretic for a side-saddle which he could not use, and there my knowledge of its history ends.

# ITALIAN WITHOUT A MASTER

IT is almost a fortnight now that I am domiciled in a mediæval villa in the country, a mile or two from Florence. I cannot speak the language; I am too old now to learn how, also too busy when I am busy, and too indolent when I am not; wherefore some will imagine that I am having a dull time of it. But it is not so. The "help" are all natives; they talk Italian to me, I answer in English; I do not understand them, they do not understand me, consequently no harm is done, and everybody is satisfied. In order to be just and fair, I throw in an Italian word when I have one, and this has a good influence. I get the word out of the morning paper. I have to use it while it is fresh, for I find

that Italian words do not keep in this climate. They fade towards night, and next morning they are gone. But it is no matter; I get a new one out of the paper before breakfast, and thrill the domestics with it while it lasts. I have no dictionary, and I do not want one; I can select my words by the sound, or by orthographic aspect. Many of them have a French or German or English look, and these are the ones I enslave for the day's service. That is, as a rule. Not always. If I find a learnable phrase that has an imposing look and warbles musically along I do not care to know the meaning of it; I pay it out to the first applicant, knowing that if I pronounce it carefully *he* will understand it, and that's enough.

"SONO DISPIACENTISSIMO"

Yesterday's word was *avanti*. It sounds Shakespearian, and probably means Avaunt and quit my sight. To-day I have a whole phrase: *sono dispiacentissimo*. I do not know what it means, but it seems to fit in everywhere and give satisfaction. Although as a rule my words and phrases are good for one day and train only, I have several that stay

by me all the time, for some unknown reason, and
these come very handy when I get into a long conversation and need things to fire up with in monotonous stretches.   One of the best ones is *Dov' è il
gatto.*   It nearly always produces a pleasant surprise,
therefore I save it up for places where I want to express applause or admiration.   The fourth word has
a French sound, and I think the phrase means "that
takes the cake."

During my first week in the deep and dreamy stillness of this woodsy and flowery place I was without
news of the outside world, and was well content
without it.   It had been four weeks since I had seen
a newspaper, and this lack seemed to give life a
new charm and grace, and to saturate it with a
feeling verging upon actual delight.   Then came a
change that was to be expected: the appetite for
news began to rise again, after this invigorating rest.
I had to feed it, but I was not willing to let it make
me its helpless slave again; I determined to put it
on a diet, and a strict and limited one.   So I examined an Italian paper, with the idea of feeding it
on that, and on that exclusively.   On that exclusively, and without help of a dictionary.   In this way
I should surely be well protected against overloading
and indigestion.

A glance at the telegraphic page filled me with
encouragement.   There were no scare-heads.   That
was good—supremely good.   But there were headings—one-liners and two-liners—and that was good

too; for without these, one must do as one does with a German paper—pay out precious time in finding out what an article is about, only to discover, in many cases, that there is nothing in it of interest to you. The head-line is a valuable thing.

Necessarily we are all fond of murders, scandals, swindles, robberies, explosions, collisions, and all such things, when we know the people, and when they are neighbors and friends, but when they are strangers we do not get any great pleasure out of them, as a rule. Now the trouble with an American paper is that it has no discrimination; it rakes the whole earth for blood and garbage, and the result is that you are daily overfed and suffer a surfeit. By habit you stow this muck every day, but you come by-and-by to take no vital interest in it—indeed, you almost get tired of it. As a rule, forty-nine-fiftieths of it concerns strangers only—people away off yonder, a thousand miles, two thousand miles, ten thousand miles from where you are. Why, when you come to think of it, who cares what becomes of those people? I would not give the assassination of one personal friend for a whole massacre of those others. And, to my mind, one relative or neighbor mixed up in a scandal is more interesting than a whole Sodom and Gomorrah of outlanders gone rotten. Give me the home product every time.

Very well. I saw at a glance that the Florentine paper would suit me: five out of six of its scandals and tragedies were local; they were adventures of one's very neighbors, one might almost say one's friends. In the matter of world news there was not too much, but just about enough. I subscribed. I have had no occasion to regret it. Every morning I get all the news I need for the day; sometimes from the head-lines, sometimes from the text. I have never had to call for a dictionary yet. I read the paper with ease. Often I do not quite understand, often some of the details escape me, but no matter, I get the idea. I will cut out a passage or two, then you will see how limpid the language is:

The first line means that the Italian sovereigns are coming back—they have been to England. The second line seems to mean that they enlarged the King at the Italian hospital. With a banquet, I suppose. An English banquet has that effect. Further:

Return of the sovereigns to Rome, you see. Date of the telegram, Rome, November 24, ten minutes

"THEY ENLARGED THE KING"

before twenty-three o'clock.   The telegram seems to say, "The Sovereigns and the Royal Children expect themselves at Rome to-morrow at fifty-one minutes after fifteen o'clock."

I do not know about Italian time, but I judge it begins at midnight and runs through the twenty-four hours without breaking bulk.   In the following ad. the theatres open at half-past twenty.   If these are not matinées, 20.30 must mean 8.30 P.M., by my reckoning.

Spettacoli del dì 25

TEATRO DELLA PERGOLA — (Ore 20,30) — Opera : *Bohème.*
TEATRO ALFIERI. — Compagnia drammatica Drago — (Ore 20,30) — *La Legge.*
ALHAMBRA — (Ore 20,30) — Spettacolo variato.
SALA EDISON — Grandioso spettacolo Cinematografico: *Quo-Vadis?* — Inaugurazione della Chiesa Russa — In coda al Direttissimo — Vedute di Firenze con gran movimento — America: Trasporto tronchi giganteschi — I ladri in casa del Diavolo — Scene comiche.
CINEMATOGRAFO — Via Brunelleschi n. 4. — Programma straordinario, *Don Chisciotte* — Prezzi popolari.

The whole of that is intelligible to me—and sane and rational, too—except the remark about the Inauguration of a Russian Cheese.   That one oversizes my hand.   Gimme five cards.

This is a four-page paper; and as it is set in long primer leaded and has a page of advertisements, there is no room for the crimes, disasters, and general sweepings of the outside world—thanks be!   To-day I find only a single importation of the off-color sort:

> **Una principessa**
> che fugge con un cocchiere
> PARIGI, 24. - Il *Matin* ha da Berlino che la principessa Schovenbare-Waldenbure scomparve il 9 novembre. Sarebbe partita col suo cocchiere.
> La Principessa ha 27 anni.

Twenty-seven years old, and scomparve—scampered—on the 9th November.   You see by the added detail that she departed with her coachman.   I hope Sarebbe has not made a mistake, but I am afraid the chances are that she has.   *Sono dispiacentissimo.*

There are several fires: also a couple of accidents. This is one of them:

> **Grave disgrazia sul Ponte Vecchio**
> Stamattina, circa le 7,30, mentre Giuseppe Sciatti, di anni 55, di Casellina e Torri, passava dal Ponte Vecchio, stando seduto sopra un barroccio carico di verdura, perse l'equilibrio e cadde al suolo, rimanendo con la gamba destra sotto una ruota del veicolo.
> Lo Sciatti fu subito raccolto da alcuni cittadini, che, per mezzo della pubblica vettura n. 865, lo trasportarono a San Giovanni di Dio.
> Ivi il medico di guardia gli riscontrò la frattura della gamba destra e alcune lievi escoriazioni giudicandolo guaribile in 50 giorni salvo complicazioni.

"I HOPE SAREBBE HAS NOT MADE A MISTAKE"

What it seems to say is this: "Serious Disgrace on the Old Old Bridge.  This morning about 7.30, Mr. Joseph Sciatti, aged 55, of Casellina and Torri, while standing up in a sitting posture on top of a carico barrow of verdure (foliage? hay? vegetables?), lost his equilibrium and fell on himself, arriving with his left leg under one of the wheels of the vehicle.

"Said Sciatti was suddenly harvested (gathered in?) by several citizens, who by means of public cab No. 365 transported him to St. John of God."

Paragraph No. 3 is a little obscure, but I think it says that the medico set the broken left leg—right enough, since there was nothing the matter with the other one—and that several are encouraged to hope that fifty days will fetch him around in quite giudi-candolo-guaribile way, if no complications intervene.

I am sure I hope so myself.

There is a great and peculiar charm about reading news-scraps in a language which you are not ac-quainted with—the charm that always goes with the mysterious and the uncertain.  You can never be absolutely sure of the meaning of anything you read in such circumstances; you are chasing an alert and gamy riddle all the time, and the baffling turns and dodges of the prey make the life of the hunt.  A dictionary would spoil it.  Sometimes a single word of doubtful purport will cast a veil of dreamy and golden uncertainty over a whole paragraph of cold and practical certainties, and leave steeped in a haunting and adorable mystery an incident which

"'SERIOUS DISGRACE ON THE OLD OLD BRIDGE'"

had been vulgar and commonplace but for that bene-
faction.   Would you be wise to draw a dictionary on
that gracious word? would you be properly grateful?

After a couple of days' rest I now come back to my
subject and seek a case in point.   I find it without
trouble, in the morning paper; a cablegram from
Chicago and Indiana by way of Paris.   All the words
save one are guessable by a person ignorant of
Italian:

> **Revolverate in teatro**
>
> PARIGI, 27. - La *Patrie* ha da Chicago:
> Il guardiano del teatro dell'opera di Wal-
> lace (Indiana), avendo voluto espellere uno
> spettatore che continuava a fumare malgrado
> il divieto, questo spalleggiato dai suoi amici
> tirò diversi colpi di rivoltella. Il guardiano
> rispose. Nacque una scarica generale. Grande
> panico fra gli spettatori. Nessun ferito.

*Translation.* — "REVOLVERATION IN THEATRE.
*Paris, 27th.  La Patrie* has from Chicago: The cop
of the theatre of the opera of Wallace, Indiana, had
willed to expel a spectator which continued to smoke
in spite of the prohibition, who, spalleggiato by his
friends, tirò (Fr. *tiré*, Anglice *pulled*) manifold re-
volver-shots.  The cop responded.  Result, a general scare; great panic among the spectators.  Nobody hurt."

It is bettable that that harmless cataclysm in the
theatre of the opera of Wallace, Indiana, excited not
a person in Europe but me, and so came near to not

"'THE REVOLVERATION IN THEATRE'"

being worth cabling to Florence by way of France. But it does excite me. It excites me because I cannot make out, for sure, what it was that moved that spectator to resist the officer. I was gliding along smoothly and without obstruction or accident, until I came to that word spalleggiato, then the bottom fell out. You notice what a rich gloom, what a sombre and pervading mystery, that word sheds all over the whole Wallachian tragedy. That is the charm of the thing, that is the delight of it. This is where you begin, this is where you revel. You can guess and guess, and have all the fun you like; you need not be afraid there will be an end to it; none is possible, for no amount of guessing will ever furnish you a meaning for that word that you can be sure is the right one. All the other words give you hints, by their form, their sound, or their spelling—this one doesn't, this one throws out no hints, this one keeps its secret. If there is even the slightest slight shadow of a hint anywhere, it lies in the very meagrely suggestive fact that spalleggiato carries our word "egg" in its stomach. Well, make the most out of it, and then where are you at? You conjecture that the spectator which was smoking in spite of the prohibition and become reprohibited by the guardians, was "egged on" by his friends, and that it was owing to that evil influence that he initiated the revolveration in theatre that has galloped under the sea and come crashing through the European press without exciting anybody but me. But are you sure, are you dead sure, that that was the way of it? No. Then the uncertainty remains, the mystery abides, and with it the charm. Guess again.

If I had a phrase-book of a really satisfactoiy sort I would study it, and not give all my free time to un-dictionarial readings, but there is no such work on the market. The existing phrase-books are inade-quate. They are well enough as far as they go, bi t when you fall down and skin your leg they don c teil you what to say.

13

# ITALIAN WITH GRAMMAR

I FOUND that a person of large intelligence could read this beautiful language with considerable facility without a dictionary, but I presently found that to such a person a grammar could be of use at times. It is because, if he does not know the *Were's* and the *Was's* and the *May-be's* and the *Has-been's* apart, confusions and uncertainties can arise. He can get the idea that a thing is going to happen next week when the truth is that it has already happened week before last. Even more previously, sometimes. Examination and inquiry showed me that the adjectives and such things were frank and fair-minded and straightforward, and did not shuffle; it was the Verb that mixed the hands, it was the Verb that lacked stability, it was the Verb that had no permanent opinion about anything, it was the Verb that was always dodging the issue and putting out the light and making all the trouble.

Further examination, further inquiry, further reflection, confirmed this judgment, and established beyond peradventure the fact that the Verb was the storm-centre. This discovery made plain the right and wise course to pursue in order to acquire certainty and exactness in understanding the statements which the newspaper was daily endeavoring to convey to me: I must catch a Verb and tame it. I must find out its ways, I must spot its eccentricities, I must penetrate its disguises, I must intelligently foresee and forecast at least the commoner of the dodges it was likely to try upon a stranger in given circumstances, I must get in on its main shifts and head them off, I must learn its game and play the limit.

I had noticed, in other foreign languages, that verbs are bred in families, and that the members of each family have certain features or resemblances that are common to that family and distinguish it from the other families—the other kin, the cousins and what not. I had noticed that this family-mark is not usually the nose or the hair, so to speak, but the tail— the Termination,—and that these tails are quite definitely differentiated; insomuch that an expert can tell a Pluperfect from a Subjunctive by its tail as easily and as certainly as a cowboy can tell a cow from a horse by the like process, the result of observation and culture. I should explain that I am speaking of legitimate verbs, those verbs which in the slang of the grammar are called Regular. There are others—I am not meaning to conceal this; others called Irregulars, born out of wedlock, of unknown and uninteresting parentage, and naturally destitute of family resemblances, as regards all features, tails included. But of these pathetic outcasts I have nothing to say. I do not approve of them, I do not encourage them; I am prudishly delicate and sensitive, and I do not allow them to be used in my presence.

But, as I have said, I decided to catch one of the others and break it to harness. One is enough. Once familiar with its assortment of tails, you are immune; after that, no regular verb can conceal its specialty from you and make you think it is working the past or the future or the conditional or the unconditional when it is engaged in some other line of business—its tail will give it away. I found out all these things by myself, without a teacher.

I selected the verb *Amare*, *to love*. Not for any personal reason, for I am indifferent about verbs; I care no more for one verb than for another, and have little or no respect for any of them; but in foreign languages you always begin with that one. Why, I do not know. It is merely habit, I suppose; the first teacher chose it, Adam was satisfied, and there hasn't been a successor since with originality enough to start a fresh one. For they *are* a pretty limited lot, you will admit that? Originality is not in their line; they can't think up anything new, anything to freshen up the old moss-grown dulness of the language lesson and put life and "go" into it, and charm and grace and picturesqueness.

I knew I must look after those details myself; therefore I thought them out and wrote them down, and sent for the *facchino* and explained them to him, and said he must arrange a proper plant, and get together a good stock company among the *contadini*,

and design the costumes, and distribute the parts;
and drill the troupe, and be ready in three days to
begin on this Verb in a shipshape and workman-like
manner. I told him to put each grand division of
it under a foreman, and each subdivision under a
subordinate of the rank of sergeant or corporal or
something like that, and to have a different uniform
for each squad, so that I could tell a Pluperfect from
a Compound Future without looking at the book;
the whole battery to be under his own special and
particular command, with the rank of Brigadier, and
I to pay the freight.

I then inquired into the character and possibilities
of the selected verb, and was much disturbed to find
that it was over my size, it being chambered for fifty-
seven rounds—fifty-seven ways of saying *I love* without reloading; and yet none of them likely to con-
vince a girl that was laying for a title, or a title that
was laying for rocks.

It seemed to me that with my inexperience it
would be foolish to go into action with this mitrail-
leuse, so I ordered it to the rear and told the facchino
to provide something a little more primitive to start
with, something less elaborate, some gentle old-
fashioned flint-lock, smooth-bore, double-barrelled
thing, calculated to cripple at two hundred yards and
kill at forty—an arrangement suitable for a beginner
who could be satisfied with moderate results on the
offstart and did not wish to take the whole territory
in the first campaign.

But in vain.  He was not able to mend the matter, all the verbs being of the same build, all Gatlings, all of the same calibre and delivery, fifty-seven to the volley, and fatal at a mile and a half.  But he said the auxiliary verb AVERE, *to have*, was a tidy thing, and easy to handle in a seaway, and less likely to miss stays in going about than some of the others; so, upon his recommendation I chose that one, and told him to take it along and scrape its bottom and break out its spinnaker and get it ready for business.

I will explain that a facchino is a general-utility domestic.   Mine was a horse-doctor in his better days, and a very good one.

At the end of three days  the facchino-doctor-brigadier was ready.  I was also ready, with a ste-nographer.  We were in the room called the Rope-Walk.   This is a formidably long room, as is indicated by its facetious name, and is a good place for reviews. At 9.30 the F.-D.-B. took his place near me and gave the word of command; the drums began to rumble and thunder, the head of the forces appeared at an upper door, and the "march-past" was on.  Down they filed, a blaze of variegated color, each squad gaudy in a uniform of its own and bearing a banner inscribed with its verbal rank and quality: first the Present Tense in Mediterranean blue and old-gold, then the Past Definite in scarlet and black, then the Imperfect in green and yellow, then the Indicative Future in the stars and stripes, then the Old Red

Sandstone Subjunctive in purple and silver—and so
on and so on, fifty-seven privates and twenty commissioned and non-commissioned officers; certainly
one of the most fiery and dazzling and eloquent sights
I have ever beheld. I could not keep back the tears.
Presently—

"Halt!" commanded the Brigadier.

"Front—face!"

"Right dress!"

"Stand at ease!"

"One—two—three. In unison—*recite!*"

It was fine. In one noble volume of sound all the
fifty-seven Haves in the Italian language burst forth
in an exalting and splendid confusion. Then came
the commands—

"About—face! Eyes—front! Helm alee—hard
aport! Forward—march!" and the drums let go
again.

When the last Termination had disappeared, the
commander said the instruction drill would now begin, and asked for suggestions. I said:

"They say *I have, thou hast, he has,* and so on, but
they don't say *what.* It will be better, and more
definite, if they have something to have; just an
object, you know, a something—anything will do;
anything that will give the listener a sort of personal
as well as grammatical interest in their joys and com-
plaints, you see."

He said:

"It is a good point. Would a dog do?"

I said I did not know, but we could try a dog and see. So he sent out an aide-de-camp to give the order to add the dog.

The six privates of the Present Tense now filed in, in charge of Sergeant AVERE (*to have*), and displaying their banner. They formed in line of battle, and recited, one at a time, thus:

"*Io ho un cane*, I have a dog."

"*Tu hai un cane*, thou hast a dog."

"*Egli ha un cane*, he has a dog."

"*Noi abbiamo un cane*, we have a dog."

"*Voi avete un cane*, you have a dog."

"*Eglino hanno un cane*, they have a dog."

No comment followed. They returned to camp, and I reflected a while. The commander said:

"I fear you are disappointed."

"Yes," I said; "they are too monotonous, too singsong, too dead-and-alive; they have no expression, no elocution. It isn't natural; it could never happen in real life. A person who has just acquired a dog is either blame' glad or blame' sorry. He is not on the fence. I never saw a case. What the nation do you suppose is the matter with these people?"

He thought maybe the trouble was with the dog. He said:

"These are *contadini*, you know, and they have a prejudice against dogs—that is, against marimane. Marimana dogs stand guard over people's vines and

olives, you know, and are very savage, and thereby
a grief and an inconvenience to persons who want
other people's things at night. In my judgment they
have taken this dog for a marimana, and have soured
on him."

I saw that the dog was a mistake, and not function-
able: we must try something else; something, if possible, that could evoke sentiment, interest, feeling.

"What is cat, in Italian?" I asked.

"Gatto."

"Is it a gentleman cat, or a lady?"

"Gentleman cat."

"How are these people as regards that animal?"

"We-ll, they—they—"

"You hesitate: that is enough. How are they
about chickens?"

He tilted his eyes towards heaven in mute ecstasy.
I understood.

"What is chicken in Italian?" I asked.

"Pollo, *podere*." (Podere is Italian for master. It
is a title of courtesy, and conveys reverence and
admiration.) "Pollo is one chicken by itself; when
there are enough present to constitute a plural, it is
*polli*."

"Very well, polli will do. Which squad is detailed
for duty next?"

"The Past Definite."

"Send out and order it to the front—with chickens.
And let them understand that we don't want any
more of this cold indifference."

He gave the order to an aide, adding, with a haunt‑
ing tenderness in his tone and a watering mouth in
his aspect:

"Convey to them the conception that these are un‑
protected chickens." He turned to me, saluting with
his hand to his temple, and explained, "It will inflame
their interest in the poultry, sire."

A few minutes elapsed. Then the squad marched
in and formed up, their faces glowing with enthusiasm,
and the file-leader shouted:

"*Ebbi polli*, I had chickens!"

"Good!" I said. "Go on, the next."

"*Avesti polli*, thou hadst chickens!"

"Fine! Next!"

"*Ebbe polli*, he had chickens!"

"Moltimoltissimo! Go on, the next!"

"*Avemmo polli*, we had chickens!"

"Basta - basta aspettatto avanti — last man —
*charge!*"

"*Ebbero polli*, they had chickens!"

Then they formed in echelon, by column of fours,
refusing the left, and retired in great style on the
double-quick. I was enchanted, and said:

"Now, doctor, that is something *like!* Chickens
are the ticket, there is no doubt about it. What is
the next squad?"

"The Imperfect."

"How does it go?"

"*Io aveva*, I had, *tu avevi*, thou hadst, *egli aveva*,
he had, *noi av—*"

"Wait—we've just *had* the hads.   What are you giving me?"

"But this is another breed."

"What do we want of another breed?   Isn't one breed enough?   *Had* is HAD, and your tricking it out in a fresh way of spelling isn't going to make it any hadder than it was before; now you know that yourself."

"But there is a distinction—they are not just the same Hads."

"How do you make it out?"

"Well, you use that first Had when you are referring to something that happened at a named and sharp and perfectly definite moment; you use the other when the thing happened at a vaguely defined time and in a more prolonged and indefinitely continuous way."

"Why, doctor, it is pure nonsense; you know it yourself.   Look here: If I have had a had, or have wanted to have had a had, or was in a position right then and there to have had a had that hadn't had any chance to go out hadding on account of this foolish discrimination which lets one Had go hadding in any kind of indefinite grammatical weather but restricts the other one to definite and datable meteoric convulsions, and keeps it pining around and watching the barometer all the time, and liable to get sick through confinement and lack of exercise, and all that sort of thing, why—why, the inhumanity of it is enough, let alone the wanton superfluity and uselessness of any such a loafing consumptive hospital-bird of a Had taking up room and cumbering the place for nothing. These finical refinements revolt me; it is not right, it is not honorable; it is constructive nepotism to keep in office a Had that is so delicate it can't come out when the wind's in the nor'west—I won't have this dude on the pay-roll. Cancel his exequatur; and look here—"

"But you miss the point. It is like this. You see—"

"Never mind explaining, I don't care anything about it. Six Hads is enough for me; anybody that needs twelve, let him subscribe; I don't want any stock in a Had Trust. Knock out the Prolonged and Indefinitely Continuous; four-fifths of it is water, anyway."

"But I beg you, podere! It is often quite indispensable in cases where—"

"Pipe the next squad to the assault!"

But it was not to be; for at that moment the dull boom of the noon gun floated up out of far-off Florence, followed by the usual softened jangle of church-bells, Florentine and suburban, that bursts out in murmurous response; by labor-union law the *colazione* [1] must stop; stop promptly, stop instantly, stop definitely, like the chosen and best of the breed of Hads.

---

[1] Colazione is Italian for a collection, a meeting, a séance, a sitting.—M. T.

# A BURLESQUE BIOGRAPHY

TWO or three persons having at different times intimated that if I would write an autobiography they would read it when they got leisure, I yield at last to this frenzied public demand and herewith tender my history.

Ours is a noble old house, and stretches a long way back into antiquity. The earliest ancestor the Twains have any record of was a friend of the family by the name of Higgins. This was in the eleventh century, when our people were living in Aberdeen, county of Cork, England. Why it is that our long line has ever since borne the maternal name (except when one of them now and then took a playful refuge in an alias to avert foolishness), instead of Higgins, is a mystery which none of us has ever felt much desire to stir. It is a kind of vague, pretty romance, and we leave it alone. All the old families do that way.

Arthour Twain was a man of considerable note—a solicitor on the highway in William Rufus's time. At about the age of thirty he went to one of those fine old English places of resort called Newgate, to see about something, and never returned again. While there he died suddenly.

Augustus Twain seems to have made something of a stir about the year 1160. He was as full of fun as he could be, and used to take his old sabre and sharpen it up, and get in a convenient place on a dark night, and stick it through people as they went by, to see them jump. He was a born humorist. But he got to going too far with it; and the first time he was found stripping one of these parties, the authorities removed one end of him, and put it up on a nice high place on Temple Bar, where it could contemplate the people and have a good time. He never liked any situation so much or stuck to it so long.

Then for the next two hundred years the family tree shows a succession of soldiers—noble, high-spirit-  ed fellows, who always went into battle sing- ing, right behind the army, and always went out a-whooping, right ahead of it.

This is a scathing rebuke to old dead Froissart's poor witti- cism that our family tree never had but one limb to it, and that that one stuck out at right angles, and bore fruit winter and summer.

Early in the fifteenth century we have Beau Twain, called "the Scholar." He wrote a beautiful, beautiful hand. And he could imitate anybody's hand so closely that it was enough to make a person laugh his head off to see it. He had infinite sport with his talent. But by-and-by he took a contract to break stone for a road, and the roughness of the work spoiled his hand. Still, he enjoyed life all the time he was in the stone business, which, with inconsiderable intervals, was some forty-two years. In fact, he died in harness. During all those long years he gave such satisfaction that he never was through with one contract a week till the government gave him another. He was a perfect pet. And he was always a favorite with his fellow-artists, and was a conspicuous member of their benevolent secret society, called the Chain Gang. He always wore his hair short, had a preference for striped clothes, and died lamented by the government. He was a sore loss to his country. For he was so regular.

Some years later we have the illustrious John Morgan Twain. He came over to this country with Columbus in 1492 as a passenger. He appears to have been of a crusty, uncomfortable disposition. He complained of the food all the way over, and was always threatening to go ashore unless there was a change. He wanted fresh shad. Hardly a day passed over his head that he did not go idling about the ship with his nose in the air, sneering about the commander, and saying he did not believe Columbus knew where he was going to or had ever been there before. The memorable cry of "Land ho!" thrilled every heart in the ship but his. He gazed a while through a piece of smoked glass at the pencilled line lying on the distant water, and then said: "Land be hanged,—it's a raft!"

When this questionable passenger came on board the ship, he brought nothing with him but an old newspaper containing a handkerchief marked "B. G.," one cotton sock marked "L. W. C.," one woollen one marked "D. F.," and a night-shirt marked "O. M. R." And yet during the voyage he worried more about his "trunk," and gave himself more airs about it, than all the rest of the passengers put together. If the ship was "down by the head," and would not steer, he would go and move his "trunk" farther aft, and then watch the effect. If the ship was "by the stern," he would suggest to Columbus to detail some men to "shift that baggage." In storms he had to be gagged, because his wailings about his "trunk" made it impossible for the men to hear the orders. The man does not appear to have been openly charged with any gravely unbecoming thing, but it is noted in the ship's log as a "curious circumstance" that albeit he brought his baggage on board the ship in a newspaper, he took it ashore in four trunks, a queensware crate, and a couple of champagne baskets. But when he came back insinuating, in an insolent, swaggering way, that some of his things were missing, and was going to search the other passengers' baggage, it was too much, and they threw him overboard. They watched long and wonderingly for him to come up, but not even a bubble rose on the quietly ebbing tide. But while every one was most absorbed in gazing over the side, and the interest was momentarily increasing, it was observed with consternation that the vessel was adrift and the anchor-cable hanging limp from the bow. Then in the ship's dimmed and ancient log we find this quaint note:

"In time it was discouvered yt ye troblesome passenger hadde gonne downe and got ye anchor, and toke ye same and solde it to ye dam sauvages from ye interior, saying yt he hadde founde it, ye sonne of a ghun!"

Yet this ancestor had good and noble instincts, and it is with pride that we call to mind the fact that he was the first white person who ever interested himself in the work of elevating and civilizing our Indians. He built a commodious jail and put up a gallows, and to his dying day he claimed with satisfaction that he had had a more restraining and elevating influence on the Indians than any other reformer that ever labored among them. At this point the chronicle becomes less frank and chatty, and closes abruptly by saying that the old voyager went to see his gallows perform on the first white man ever hanged in America, and while there received injuries which terminated in his death.

The great-grandson of the "Reformer" flourished in sixteen hundred and something, and was known

in our annals as "the old Admiral," though in history
he had other titles. He was long in command of
fleets of swift vessels, well armed and manned, and
did great service in hurrying up merchantmen. Vessels which he followed and kept his eagle eye on,
always made good fair time across the ocean. But if
a ship still loitered in spite of all he could do, his
indignation would grow till he could contain himself
no longer—and then he would take that ship home
where he lived and keep it there carefully, expecting
the owners to come for it, but they never did. And
he would try to get the idleness and sloth out of the
sailors of that ship by compelling them to take invigorating exercise and a bath. He called it "walking a plank." All the pupils liked it. At any rate
they never found any fault with it after trying it.
When the owners were late coming for their ships, the
Admiral always burned them, so that the insurance
money should not be lost. At last this fine old tar
was cut down in the fulness of his years and honors.
And to her dying day, his poor heart-broken widow
believed that if he had been cut down fifteen minutes
sooner he might have been resuscitated.

Charles Henry Twain lived during the latter part
of the seventeenth century, and was a zealous and
distinguished missionary. He converted sixteen
thousand South Sea islanders, and taught them that
a dog-tooth necklace and a pair of spectacles was not
enough clothing to come to divine service in. His
poor flock loved him very, very dearly; and when his

funeral was over, they got up in a body (and came out of the restaurant) with tears in their eyes, and saying, one to another, that he was a good tender missionary, and they wished they had some more of him.

Pah-go-to-wah-wah-pukketekeewis (Mighty-Hunt-er-with-a-Hog-Eye-Twain) adorned the middle of the eighteenth century, and aided General Braddock with all his heart to resist the oppressor Washington. It was this ancestor who fired seventeen times at our Washington from behind a tree. So far the beautiful romantic narrative in the moral story-books is correct; but when that narrative goes on to say that at the seventeenth round the awe-stricken savage said solemnly that that man was being reserved by the Great Spirit for some mighty mission, and he dared not lift his sacrilegious rifle against him again, the narrative seriously impairs the integrity of history. What he did say was:

"It ain't no (hic) no use. 'At man's so drunk he can't stan' still long enough for a man to hit him. I (hic) I can't 'ford to fool away any more am'nition on him."

That was why he stopped at the seventeenth round, and it was a good, plain, matter-of-fact reason, too, and one that easily commends itself to us by the eloquent, persuasive flavor of probability there is about it.

I always enjoyed the story-book narrative, but I felt a marring misgiving that every Indian at Brad-

dock's Defeat who fired at a soldier a couple of times
(two easily grows to seventeen in a century), and
missed him, jumped to the conclusion that the Great
Spirit was reserving that soldier for so le grand
mission; and so I somehow feared that the only
reason why Washington's case is remembered and
the others forgotten is, that in his the prophecy came
true, and in that of the others it didn't. There are
not books enough on earth to contain the record of
the prophecies Indians and other unauthorized parties
have made; but one may carry in his overcoat-pockets
the record of all the prophecies that have been fulfilled.

I will remark here, in passing, that certain ancestors
of mine are so thoroughly well-known in history by
their aliases, that I have not felt it to be worth while
to dwell upon them, or even mention them in the
order of their birth. Among these may be mentioned
Richard Brinsley Twain, alias Guy Fawkes; John
Wentworth Twain, alias Sixteen-String Jack; William Hogarth Twain, alias Jack Sheppard; Ananias
Twain, alias Baron Munchausen; John George Twain,
alias Captain Kydd; and then there are George Francis
Train, Tom Pepper, Nebuchadnezzar, and Baalam's
Ass—they all belong to our family, but to a branch
of it somewhat distinctly removed from the honorable
direct line—in fact, a collateral branch, whose members chiefly differ from the ancient stock in that, in
order to acquire the notoriety we have always yearned
and hungered for, they have got into a low way of
going to jail instead of getting hanged.

It is not well, when writing an autobiography, to follow your ancestry down too close to your own time —it is safest to speak only vaguely of your great-grandfather, and then skip from there to yourself, which I now do.

I was born without teeth—and there Richard III. had the advantage of me; but I was born without a humpback, likewise, and there I had the advantage of him. My parents were neither very poor nor conspicuously honest.

But now a thought occurs to me. My own history would really seem so tame contrasted with that of my ancestors, that it is simply wisdom to leave it unwritten until I am hanged. If some other biographies I have read had stopped with the ancestry until a like event occurred, it would have been a felicitous thing for the reading public. How does it strike you?

# GENERAL WASHINGTON'S NEGRO BODY-SERVANT

## A BIOGRAPHICAL SKETCH

THE stirring part of this celebrated colored man's life properly began with his death — that is to say, the notable features of his biography begin with the first time he died. He had been little heard of up to that time, but since then we have never ceased to hear of him; we have never ceased to hear of him at stated, unfailing intervals. His was a most remarkable career, and I have thought that its history would make a valuable addition to our biographical literature. Therefore, I have carefully collated the materials for such a work, from authentic sources, and here present them to the public. I have rigidly excluded from these pages everything of a doubtful character, with the object in view of introducing my work into the schools for the instruction of the youth of my country.

The name of the famous body-servant of General Washington was George. After serving his illustrious master faithfully for half a century, and enjoying throughout this long term his high regard and confidence, it became his sorrowful duty at last to lay that beloved master to rest in his peaceful grave by the Potomac. Ten years afterwards—in 1809—full of years and honors, he died himself, mourned by all who knew him. The Boston *Gazette* of that date thus refers to the event:

"George, the favorite body-servant of the lamented Washington, died in Richmond, Va., last Tuesday, at the ripe age of 95 years. His intellect was unimpaired, and his memory tenacious, up to within a few minutes of his decease. He was present at the second installation of Washington as President, and also at his funeral, and distinctly remembered all the prominent incidents connected with those noted events."

From this period we hear no more of the favorite body-servant of General Washington until May, 1825, at which time he died again. A Philadelphia paper thus speaks of the sad occurrence:

"At Macon, Ga., last week, a colored man named George, who was the favorite body-servant of General Washington, died, at the advanced age of 95 years. Up to within a few hours of his dissolution he was in full possession of all his faculties, and could distinctly recollect the second installation of Washington, his death and burial, the surrender of Cornwallis, the battle of Trenton, the griefs and hardships of Valley Forge, etc. Deceased was followed to the grave by the entire population of Macon."

On the Fourth of July, 1830, and also of 1834 and 1836, the subject of this sketch was exhibited in great state upon the rostrum of the orator of the day, and

in November of 1840 he died again.  The St. Louis
*Republican* of the 25th of that month spoke as
follows:

## "ANOTHER RELIC OF THE REVOLUTION GONE

"George, once the favorite body-servant of General
Washington, died yesterday at the house of Mr. John
Leavenworth, in this city, at the venerable age of 95
years.  He was in the full possession of his faculties up
to the hour of his death, and distinctly recollected the
first and second installations and death of President
Washington, the surrender of Cornwallis, the battles
of Trenton and Monmouth, the sufferings of the patriot
army at Valley Forge, the proclamation of the Declaration of Independence, the speech of Patrick Henry in
the Virginia House of Delegates, and many other old-
time reminiscences of stirring interest.  Few white men
die lamented as was this aged negro.  The funeral was
very largely attended."

During the next ten or eleven years the subject of
this sketch appeared at intervals at Fourth-of-July
celebrations in various parts of the country, and was
exhibited upon the rostrum with flattering success.
But in the fall of 1855 he died again.  The California
papers thus speak of the event:

## "ANOTHER OLD HERO GONE

"Died, at Dutch Flat, on the 7th of March, George
(once the confidential body-servant of General Washington), at the great age of 95 years.  His memory, which
did not fail him till the last, was a wonderful storehouse

of interesting reminiscences. He could distinctly recollect the first and second installations and death of
President Washington, the surrender of Cornwallis, the
battles of Trenton and Monmouth, and Bunker Hill,
the proclamation of the Declaration of Independence,
and Braddock's Defeat. George was greatly respected
in Dutch Flat, and it is estimated that there were
10,000 people present at his funeral."

The last time the subject of this sketch died was
in June, 1864; and until we learn the contrary, it is
just to presume that he died permanently this time.
The Michigan papers thus refer to the sorrowful event:

## "ANOTHER CHERISHED REMNANT OF THE REVOLUTION GONE

"George, a colored man, and once the favorite body-
servant of General Washington, died in Detroit last
week, at the patriarchal age of 95 years. To the moment
of his death his intellect was unclouded, and he could
distinctly remember the first and second installations
and death of Washington, the surrender of Cornwallis,
the battles of Trenton and Monmouth, and Bunker Hill,
the proclamation of the Declaration of Independence,
Braddock's Defeat, the throwing over of the tea in Boston harbor, and the landing of the Pilgrims. He died
greatly respected, and was followed to the grave by a
vast concourse of people."

The faithful old servant is gone! We shall never
see him more until he turns up again. He has closed
his long and splendid career of dissolution, for the
present, and sleeps peacefully, as only they sleep who

have earned their rest. He was in all respects a
remarkable man. He held his age better than any
celebrity that has figured in history; and the longer
he lived the stronger and longer his memory grew.
If he lives to die again, he will distinctly recollect the
discovery of America.

The above résumé of his biography I believe to be
substantially correct, although it is possible that he
may have died once or twice in obscure places where
the event failed of newspaper notoriety. One fault I
find in all notices of his death which I have quoted,
and this ought to be corrected. In them he uniformly
and impartially died at the age of 95. This could not
have been. He might have done that once, or maybe
twice, but he could not have continued it indefinitely.
Allowing that when he first died, he died at the age
of 95, he was 151 years old when he died last, in 1864.
But his age did not keep pace with his recollections.
When he died the last time, he distinctly remembered
the landing of the Pilgrims, which took place in 1620.
He must have been about twenty years old when he
witnessed that event, wherefore it is safe to assert
that the body-servant of General Washington was in
the neighborhood of two hundred and sixty or seventy
years old when he departed this life finally.

Having waited a proper length of time, to see if the
subject of this sketch had gone from us reliably and
irrevocably, I now publish his biography with confidence, and respectfully offer it to a mourning
nation.

P. S.—I see by the papers that this infamous old fraud has just died again, in Arkansas. This makes six times that he is known to have died, and always in a new place. The death of Washington's body-servant has ceased to be a novelty; its charm is gone; the people are tired of it; let it cease. This well-meaning but misguided negro has now put six different communities to the expense of burying him in state, and has swindled tens of thousands of people into following him to the grave under the delusion that a select and peculiar distinction was being conferred upon them. Let him stay buried for good now; and let that newspaper suffer the severest censure that shall ever, in all future time, publish to the world that General Washington's favorite colored body-servant has died again.

# WIT INSPIRATIONS OF THE "TWO-YEAR-OLDS"

ALL infants appear to have an impertinent and disagreeable fashion nowadays of saying "smart" things on most occasions that offer, and especially on occasions when they ought not to be saying anything at all. Judging by the average published specimens of smart sayings, the rising generation of children are little better than idiots. And the parents must surely be but little better than the children, for in most cases they are the publishers of the sunbursts of infantile imbecility which dazzle us from the pages of our periodicals. I may seem to speak with some heat, not to say a suspicion of personal spite; and I do admit that it nettles me to hear about so many gifted infants in these days, and remember that I seldom said anything smart when I was a child. I tried it once or twice, but it was not popular. The family were not expecting brilliant remarks from me, and so they snubbed me sometimes and spanked me the rest. But it makes my flesh creep and my blood run cold to think what might have happened to me if I had dared to utter some of the smart things of this generation's "four-year-olds" where my father could hear me. To have simply skinned me alive and considered his duty at an end would have seemed to him criminal leniency towards one so sinning. He was a stern unsmiling man, and hated all forms of precocity. If I had said some of the things I have referred to, and said them in his hearing, he would have destroyed me. He would, indeed. He would, provided the opportunity remained with him. But it would not, for I would have had judgment enough to take some strychnine first and say my smart thing afterwards. The fair record of my life has been tarnished by just one pun. My father overheard that, and he hunted me over four or five townships seeking to take my life. If I had been full-grown, of course he would have been right; but, child as I was, I could not know how wicked a thing I had done.

I made one of those remarks ordinarily called "smart things" before that, but it was not a pun. Still, it came near causing a serious rupture between my father and myself. My father and mother, my uncle Ephraim and his wife, and one or two others were present, and the conversation turned on a name for me. I was lying there trying some India-rubber rings of various patterns, and endeavoring to make a selection, for I was tired of trying to cut my teeth on people's fingers, and wanted to get hold of something that would enable me to hurry the thing through and get something else. Did you ever notice what a nuisance it was cutting your teeth on your nurse's

finger, or how back-breaking and tiresome it was trying to cut them on your big toe? And did you never
get out of patience and wish your teeth were in
Jericho long before you got them half cut? To me
it seems as if these things happened yesterday. And
they did, to some children. But I digress. I was
lying there trying the India-rubber rings. I remember looking at the clock and noticing that in an hour
and twenty-five minutes I would be two weeks old,
and thinking how little I had done to merit the bless-
ings that were so unsparingly lavished upon me. My
father said:

"Abraham is a good name. My grandfather was
named Abraham."

My mother said:

"Abraham is a good name. Very well. Let us
have Abraham for one of his names."

I said:

"Abraham suits the subscriber."

My father frowned, my mother looked pleased;
my aunt said:

"What a little darling it is!"

My father said:

"Isaac is a good name, and Jacob is a good
name."

My mother assented, and said:

"No names are better. Let us add Isaac and
Jacob to his names."

I said:

"All right. Isaac and Jacob are good enough for

yours truly. Pass me that rattle, if you please. I can't chew India-rubber rings all day."

Not a soul made a memorandum of these sayings of mine, for publication. I saw that, and did it myself, else they would have been utterly lost. So far from meeting with a generous encouragement like other children when developing intellectually, I was now furiously scowled upon by my father; my mother looked grieved and anxious, and even my aunt had about her an expression of seeming to think that maybe I had gone too far. I took a vicious bite out of an India-rubber ring, and covertly broke the rattle over the kitten's head, but said nothing. Presently my father said:

"Samuel is a very excellent name."

I saw that trouble was coming. Nothing could prevent it. I laid down my rattle; over the side of the cradle I dropped my uncle's silver watch, the clothes-brush, the toy dog, my tin soldier, the nutmeg-grater, and other matters which I was accustomed to examine, and meditate upon and make pleasant noises with, and bang and batter and break when I needed wholesome entertainment. Then I put on my little frock and my little bonnet, and took my pygmy shoes in one hand and my licorice in the other, and climbed out on the floor. I said to myself, Now, if the worst comes to worst, I am ready. Then I said aloud, in a firm voice:

"Father, I cannot, cannot wear the name of Samuel."

"My son!"

"Father, I mean it. I cannot."

"Why?"

"Father, I have an invincible antipathy to that name."

"My son, this is unreasonable. Many great and good men have been named Samuel."

"Sir, I have yet to hear of the first instance."

"What! There was Samuel the prophet. Was not he great and good?"

"Not so very."

"My son! With His own voice the Lord called him."

"Yes, sir, and had to call him a couple of times before he would come!"

And then I sallied forth, and that stern old man sallied forth after me. He overtook me at noon the following day, and when the interview was over I had acquired the name of Samuel, and a thrashing, and other useful information; and by means of this compromise my father's wrath was appeased and a misunderstanding bridged over which might have become a permanent rupture if I had chosen to be unreasonable. But just judging by this episode, what would my father have done to me if I had ever uttered in his hearing one of the flat, sickly things these "two-year-olds" say in print nowadays? In my opinion there would have been a case of infanticide in our family.

# AN ENTERTAINING ARTICLE

I TAKE the following paragraph from an article in
the Boston *Advertiser*:

"AN ENGLISH CRITIC ON MARK TWAIN

"Perhaps the most successful flights of the humor of
Mark Twain have been descriptions of the persons who
did not appreciate his humor at all. We have become
familiar with the Californians who were thrilled with
terror by his burlesque of a newspaper reporter's way
of telling a story, and we have heard of the Pennsylvania
clergyman who sadly returned his *Innocents Abroad* to
the book-agent with the remark that 'the man who could
shed tears over the tomb of Adam must be an idiot.'
But Mark Twain may now add a much more glorious
instance to his string of trophies. The *Saturday Review*,
in its number of October 8th, reviews his book of travels,
which has been republished in England, and reviews it
seriously. We can imagine the delight of the humorist
in reading this tribute to his power; and indeed it is so
amusing in itself that he can hardly do better than re-
produce the article in full in his next monthly Memoranda."

(Publishing the above paragraph thus, gives me a
sort of authority for reproducing the *Saturday Review's* article in full in these pages. I dearly wanted

to do it, for I cannot write anything half so delicious myself. If I had a cast-iron dog that could read this English criticism and preserve his austerity, I would drive him off the door-step.)

## (From the London " Saturday Review.")

### "REVIEWS OF NEW BOOKS

"THE INNOCENTS ABROAD. A Book of Travels. By Mark Twain. London: Hotten, publisher. 1870.

"Lord Macaulay died too soon. We never felt this so deeply as when we finished the last chapter of the above-named extravagant work. Macaulay died too soon—for none but he could mete out complete and comprehensive justice to the insolence, the impertinence, the presumption, the mendacity, and, above all, the majestic ignorance of this author.

"To say that the *Innocents Abroad* is a curious book, would be to use the faintest language—would be to speak of the Matterhorn as a neat elevation or of Niagara as being 'nice' or 'pretty.' 'Curious' is too tame a word wherewith to describe the imposing insanity of this work. There is no word that is large enough or long enough. Let us, therefore, photograph a passing glimpse of book and author, and trust the rest to the reader. Let the cultivated English student of human nature picture to himself this Mark Twain as a person capable of doing the following-described things—and not only doing them, but with incredible innocence *printing them* calmly and tranquilly in a book. For instance:

"He states that he entered a hair-dresser's in Paris to get shaved, and the first '*rake*' the barber gave with his razor it *loosened his 'hide'* and *lifted him out of the chair*.

"This is unquestionably exaggerated. In Florence

he was so annoyed by beggars that he pretends to have seized and eaten one in a frantic spirit of revenge. There is, of course, no truth in this. He gives at full length a theatrical programme seventeen or eighteen hundred years old, which he professes to have found in the ruins of the Coliseum, among the dirt and mould and rubbish. It is a sufficient comment upon this statement to remark that even a cast-iron programme would not have lasted so long under such circumstances. In Greece he plainly betrays both fright and flight upon one occasion, but with frozen effrontery puts the latter in this falsely tame form: 'We *sidled* towards the Piræus.' 'Sidled,' indeed! He does not hesitate to intimate that at Ephesus, when his mule strayed from the proper course, he got down, took him under his arm, carried him to the road again, pointed him right, remounted, and went to sleep contentedly till it was time to restore the beast to the path once more. He states that a growing youth among his ship's passengers was in the constant habit of appeasing his hunger with soap and oakum between meals. In Palestine he tells of ants that came eleven miles to spend the summer in the desert and brought their provisions with them; yet he shows by his description of the country that the feat was an impossibility. He mentions, as if it were the most commonplace of matters, that he cut a Moslem in two in broad daylight in Jerusalem, with Godfrey de Bouillon's sword, and would have shed more blood *if he had had a graveyard of his own.* These statements are unworthy a moment's attention. Mr. Twain or any other foreigner who did such a thing in Jerusalem would be mobbed, and would infallibly lose his life. But why go on? Why repeat more of his audacious and exasperating falsehoods? Let us close fittingly with this one: he affirms that 'in the mosque of St. Sophia at Constantinople I got my feet so stuck up with a complication of gums, slime, and general impurity, that I wore out more than two thousand pair of bootjacks getting my boots off that night, and even then some Christian hide peeled off with them.' It is monstrous. Such statements are simply lies—there is no other name for them. Will the reader longer marvel at the brutal ignorance that pervades the American nation when we tell him that we are informed upon perfectly good authority that this extravagant compilation of falsehoods, this exhaustless mine of stupendous lies, this *Innocents Abroad*, has actually been adopted by the schools and colleges of several of the States as a text-book!

"But if his falsehoods are distressing, his innocence and his ignorance are enough to make one burn the book and despise the author. In one place he was so appalled at the sudden spectacle of a murdered man, unveiled by the moonlight, that he jumped out of the window, going through sash and all, and then remarks with the most childlike simplicity that he 'was not scared, but was considerably agitated.' It puts us out of patience to note that the simpleton is densely unconscious that Lucrezia Borgia ever existed off the stage. He is vulgarly ignorant of all foreign languages, but is frank enough to criticise the Italians' use of their own tongue. He says they spell the name of their great painter 'Vinci, but pronounce it Vinchy'—and then adds with a naïveté possible only to helpless ignorance, 'foreigners always spell better than they pronounce.' In another place he commits the bald absurdity of putting the phrase 'tare an ouns' into an Italian's mouth. In Rome he unhesitatingly believes the legend that St. Philip Neri's heart was so inflamed with divine love that it burst his ribs—believes it wholly because an author with a learned list of university degrees strung after his name endorses it—'otherwise,' says this gentle idiot, 'I should have felt a curiosity to know what Philip had for dinner.' Our author makes a long, fatiguing journey to the Grotto del

Cane on purpose to test its poisoning powers on a dog—got elaborately ready for the experiment, and then discovered that he had no dog. A wiser person would have kept such a thing discreetly to himself, but with this harmless creature everything comes out. He hurts his foot in a rut two thousand years old in exhumed Pompeii, and presently, when staring at one of the cinder-like corpses unearthed in the next square, conceives the idea that may be it is the remains of the ancient Street Commissioner, and straightway his horror softens down to a sort of chirpy contentment with the condition of things. In Damascus he visits the well of Ananias, three thousand years old, and is as surprised and delighted as a child to find that the water is 'as pure and fresh as if the well had been dug yesterday.' In the Holy Land he gags desperately at the hard Arabic and Hebrew Biblical names, and finally concludes to call them Baldwinsville, Williamsburgh, and so on, 'for convenience of spelling.'

"We have thus spoken freely of this man's stupefying simplicity and innocence, but we cannot deal similarly with his colossal ignorance. We do not know where to begin. And if we knew where to begin, we certainly would not know where to leave off. We will give one specimen, and one only. He did not know, until he got to Rome, that Michael Angelo was dead! And then, instead of crawling away and hiding his shameful ignorance somewhere, he proceeds to express a pious, grateful sort of satisfaction that he is gone and out of his troubles!

"No, the reader may seek out the author's exhibition of his uncultivation for himself. The book is absolutely dangerous, considering the magnitude and variety of its misstatements, and the convincing confidence with which they are made. And yet it is a text-book in the schools of America.

The poor blunderer mouses among the sublime crea-
tions of the Old Masters, trying to acquire the elegant
proficiency in art-knowledge, which he has a groping
sort of comprehension is a proper thing for the travelled
man to be able to display. But what is the manner of
his study? And what is the progress he achieves? To
what extent does he familiarize himself with the great
pictures of Italy, and what degree of appreciation does
he arrive at? Read:

"'When we see a monk going about with a lion and
looking up into heaven, we know that that is St. Mark.
When we see a monk with a book and a pen, looking
tranquilly up to heaven, trying to think of a word, we
know that that is St. Matthew. When we see a monk
sitting on a rock, looking tranquilly up to heaven, with
a human skull beside him, and without other baggage,
we know that that is St. Jerome. Because we know
that he always went flying light in the matter of baggage. When we see other monks looking tranquilly up
to heaven, but having no trade-mark, we always ask
who those parties are. We do this because we humbly
wish to learn.'

"He then enumerates the thousands and thousands
of copies of these several pictures which he has seen, and
adds with accustomed simplicity that he feels encouraged
to believe that when he has seen 'Some More' of each,
and had a larger experience, he will eventually 'begin
to take an absorbing interest in them'—the vulgar boor.

"That we have shown this to be a remarkable book,
we think no one will deny. That it is a pernicious book
to place in the hands of the confiding and uninformed, we
think we have also shown. That the book is a deliberate
and wicked creation of a diseased mind, is apparent upon
every page. Having placed our judgment thus upon
record, let us close with what charity we can, by re-
marking that even in this volume there is some good to

be found; for whenever the author talks of his own country and lets Europe alone, he never fails to make himself interesting, and not only interesting, but instructive. No one can read without benefit his occasional chapters and paragraphs, about life in the gold and silver mines of California and Nevada; about the Indians of the plains and deserts of the West, and their cannibalism; about the raising of vegetables in kegs of gunpowder by the aid of two or three teaspoonfuls of guano; about the moving of small farms from place to place at night in wheelbarrows to avoid taxes; and about a sort of cows and mules in the Humboldt mines, that climb down chimneys and disturb the people at night. These matters are not only new, but are well worth knowing. It is a pity the author did not put in more of the same kind. His book is well written and is exceedingly entertaining, and so it just barely escaped being quite valuable also."

*(One month later)*

Latterly I have received several letters, and see a number of newspaper paragraphs, all upon a certain subject, and all of about the same tenor. I here give honest specimens. One is from a New York paper, one is from a letter from an old friend, and one is from a letter from a New York publisher who is a stranger to me. I humbly endeavor to make these bits toothsome with the remark that the article they are praising (which appeared in the December *Galaxy*, and *pretended* to be a criticism from the London *Saturday Review* on my *Innocents Abroad*) *was written by myself, every line of it*:

"The *Herald* says the richest thing out is the 'serious critique' in the London *Saturday Review*, on Mark

Twain's *Innocents Abroad*.   We thought before we read
it that it must be 'serious,' as everybody said so, and
were even ready to shed a few tears; but since perusing
it, we are bound to confess that next to Mark Twain's
'Jumping Frog' it's the finest bit of humor and sarcasm
that we've come across in many a day."

(I do not get a compliment like that every day.)

"I used to think that your writings were pretty good,
but after reading the criticism in *The Galaxy* from the
*London Review*, have discovered what an ass I must
have been.   If suggestions are in order, mine is, that
you put that article in your next edition of the *Innocents*,
as an extra chapter, if you are not afraid to put your
own humor in competition with it.   It is as rich a thing
as I ever read."

(Which is strong commendation from a book publisher.)

"The London Reviewer, my friend, is not the stupid,
'serious' creature he pretends to be, *I* think; but, on
the contrary, has a keen appreciation and enjoyment of
your book.   As I read his article in *The Galaxy*, I could
imagine him giving vent to many a hearty laugh.   But
he is writing for Catholics and Established Church people, and high-toned, antiquated, conservative gentility,
whom it is a delight to him to help you shock, while he
pretends to shake his head with owlish density.   He is
a magnificent humorist himself."

(Now that is graceful and handsome.   I take off
my hat to my life-long friend and comrade, and with
my feet together and my fingers spread over my

heart, I say, in the language of Alabama, "You do me proud.")

I stand guilty of the authorship of the article, but I did not mean any harm. I saw by an item in the Boston *Advertiser* that a solemn, serious critique on the English edition of my book had appeared in the London *Saturday Review*, and the idea of *such* a literary breakfast by a stolid, ponderous British ogre of the quill was too much for a naturally weak virtue, and I went home and burlesqued it—revelled in it, I may say. I never saw a copy of the real *Saturday Review* criticism until after my burlesque was written and mailed to the printer. But when I did get hold of a copy, I found it to be vulgar, awkwardly written, ill-natured, and entirely serious and in earnest. The gentleman who wrote the newspaper paragraph above quoted had not been misled as to its character.

If any man doubts my word now, I will kill him. No, I will not kill him; I will win his money. I will bet him twenty to one, and let any New York publisher hold the stakes, that the statements I have above made as to the authorship of the article in question are entirely true. Perhaps I may get wealthy at this, for I am willing to take all the bets that offer; and if a man wants larger odds, I will give him all he requires. But he ought to find out whether I am betting on what is termed "a sure thing" or not before he ventures his money, and he can do that by going to a public library and examining the London *Saturday Review* of October 8th, which contains the real critique.

Bless me, some people thought that *I* was the "sold" person!

P. S.—I cannot resist the temptation to toss in this most savory thing of all—this easy, graceful, philosophical disquisition, with its happy, chirping confidence. It is from the Cincinnati *Enquirer*:

"Nothing is more uncertain than the value of a fine cigar. Nine smokers out of ten would prefer an ordinary domestic article, three for a quarter, to a fifty-cent Partaga, if kept in ignorance of the cost of the latter. The flavor of the Partaga is too delicate for palates that have been accustomed to Connecticut seed leaf. So it is with humor. The finer it is in quality, the more danger of its not being recognized at all. Even Mark Twain has been taken in by an English review of his *Innocents Abroad*. Mark Twain is by no means a coarse humorist, but the Englishman's humor is so much finer than his, that he mistakes it for solid earnest, and 'larfs most consumedly.'"

A man who cannot learn stands in his own light. Hereafter, when I write an article which I know to be good, but which I may have reason to fear will not, in some quarters, be considered to amount to much, coming from an American, I will aver that an Englishman wrote it and that it is copied from a London journal. And then I will occupy a back seat and enjoy the cordial applause.

*(Still later)*

"Mark Twain at last sees that the *Saturday Review's* criticism of his *Innocents Abroad* was not serious, and he is intensely mortified at the thought of having been so badly sold. He takes the only course left him, and in the last *Galaxy* claims that *he* wrote the criticism himself, and published it in *The Galaxy* to sell the public. This is ingenious, but unfortunately it is not true. If any of our readers will take the trouble to call at this office we will show them the original article in the *Saturday Review* of October 8th, which, on comparison, will be found to be identical with the one published in *The Galaxy*. The best thing for Mark to do will be to admit that he was sold, and say no more about it."

The above is from the Cincinnati *Enquirer*, and is a falsehood. Come to the proof. If the *Enquirer* people, through any agent, will produce at *The Galaxy* office a London *Saturday Review* of October 8th, containing an "article which, on comparison, will be found to be identical with the one published in *The Galaxy*, I will pay to that agent five hundred dollars cash. Moreover, if at any specified time I fail to produce at the same place a copy of the London *Saturday Review* of October 8th, containing a lengthy criticism upon the *Innocents Abroad*, entirely different, in every paragraph and sentence, from the one I published in *The Galaxy*, I will pay to the *Enquirer* agent another five hundred dollars cash. I offer Sheldon & Co., publishers, 500 Broadway, New York, as my "backers." Any one in New York, authorized by the *Enquirer*, will receive prompt attention. It is an easy and profitable way for the *Enquirer* people to prove that they have not uttered a pitiful, deliberate falsehood in the above paragraphs. Will they swallow that falsehood ignominiously, or will they send an agent to *The Galaxy* office? I think the Cincinnati *Enquirer* must be edited by children.

# A LETTER TO THE SECRETARY OF THE TREASURY

RIVERDALE-ON-THE-HUDSON,
*October 13, 1902.*

*The Hon. the Secretary of the Treasury, Washington,
D. C.:*

SIR, — Prices for the customary kinds of winter fuel having reached an altitude which puts them out of the reach of literary persons in straitened circumstances, I desire to place with you the following order:

Forty-five tons best old dry government bonds, suitable for furnace, gold 7 per cents., 1864, preferred.

Twelve tons early greenbacks, range size, suitable for cooking.

Eight barrels seasoned 25 and 50 cent postal currency, vintage of 1866, eligible for kindlings.

Please deliver with all convenient dispatch at my house in Riverdale at lowest rates for spot cash, and send bill to Your obliged servant,

MARK TWAIN,

who will be very grateful, and will vote right.

# AMENDED OBITUARIES

*To the Editor:*

SIR, — I am approaching seventy; it is in sight; it is only three years away. Necessarily, I must go soon. It is but matter-of-course wisdom, then, that I should begin to set my worldly house in order now, so that it may be done calmly and with thoroughness, in place of waiting until the last day, when, as we have often seen, the attempt to set both houses in order at the same time has been marred by the necessity for haste and by the confusion and waste of time arising from the inability of the notary and the ecclesiastic to work together harmoniously, taking turn about and giving each other friendly assistance —not perhaps in fielding, which could hardly be expected, but at least in the minor offices of keeping game and umpiring; by consequence of which conflict of interests and absence of harmonious action a draw has frequently resulted where this ill-fortune could not have happened if the houses had been set in order one at a time and hurry avoided by beginning in season, and giving to each the amount of time fairly and justly proper to it.

In setting my earthly house in order I find it of moment that I should attend in person to one or two matters which men in my position have long had the habit of leaving wholly to others, with consequences often most regrettable. I wish to speak of only one of these matters at this time: Obituaries. Of necessity, an Obituary is a thing which cannot be so judi-

Done by Tuf Maus

Mark Twain

N.B. I cannot make a good likeness, therefore leave it out, there is enough without it anyway.
Do with the best ink. M. T.

ciously edited by any hand as by that of the subject of it. In such a work it is not the Facts that are of chief importance, but the light which the obituarist shall throw upon them, the meanings which he shall dress them in, the conclusions which he shall draw from them, and the judgments which he shall deliver upon them.   The Verdicts, you understand: that is the danger-line.

In considering this matter, in view of my approaching change, it has seemed to me wise to take such measures as may be feasible, to acquire, by courtesy of the press, access to my standing obituaries, with the privilege—if this is not asking too much—of editing, not their Facts, but their Verdicts.   This, not for present profit, further than as concerns my family, but as a favorable influence usable on the Other Side, where there are some who are not friendly to me.

With this explanation of my motives, I will now ask you of your courtesy to make an appeal for me to the public press.   It is my desire that such journals and periodicals as have obituaries of me lying in their pigeon-holes, with a view to sudden use some day, will not wait longer, but will publish them now, and kindly send me a marked copy.   My address is simply New York city—I have no other that is permanent and not transient.

I will correct them—not the Facts, but the Verdicts —striking out such clauses as could have a deleterious influence on the Other Side, and replacing them with clauses of a more judicious character.   I should, of course, expect to pay double rates for both the omissions and the substitutions; and I should also expect to pay quadruple rates for all obituaries which proved to be rightly and wisely worded in the originals, thus requiring no emendations at all.

It is my desire to leave these Amended Obituaries

neatly bound behind me as a perennial consolation and entertainment to my family, and as an heirloom which shall have a mournful but definite commercial value for my remote posterity.

I beg, sir, that you will insert this Advertisement (1t-eow, agate, inside), and send the bill to

Yours very respectfully,

MARK TWAIN.

P. S.—For the best Obituary—one suitable for me to read in public, and calculated to inspire regret—I desire to offer a Prize, consisting of a Portrait of me done entirely by myself in pen and ink without previous instructions. The ink warranted to be the kind used by the very best artists.

16

# A MONUMENT TO ADAM

SOME one has revealed to the *Tribune* that I once suggested to Rev. Thomas K. Beecher, of Elmira, New York, that we get up a monument to Adam, and that Mr. Beecher favored the project. There is more to it than that. The matter started as a joke, but it came somewhat near to materializing.

It is long ago—thirty years. Mr. Darwin's *Descent of Man* had been in print five or six years, and the storm of indignation raised by it was still raging in pulpits and periodicals. In tracing the genesis of the human race back to its sources, Mr. Darwin had left Adam out altogether. We had monkeys, and "missing links," and plenty of other kinds of ancestors, but no Adam. Jesting with Mr. Beecher and other friends in Elmira, I said there seemed to be a likelihood that the world would discard Adam and accept the monkey, and that in the course of time Adam's very name would be forgotten in the earth; therefore this calamity ought to be averted; a monument would accomplish this, and Elmira ought not to waste this honorable opportunity to do Adam a favor and herself a credit.

Then the unexpected happened. Two bankers
came forward and took hold of the matter—not for
fun, not for sentiment, but because they saw in the
monument certain commercial advantages for the
town. The project had seemed gently humorous
before—it was more than that now, with this stern
business gravity injected into it. The bankers discussed the monument with me. We met several
times. They proposed an indestructible memorial,
to cost twenty-five thousand dollars. The insane
oddity of a monument set up in a village to preserve
a name that would outlast the hills and the rocks
without any such help, would advertise Elmira to the
ends of the earth—and draw custom. It would be
the only monument on the planet to Adam, and in
the matter of interest and impressiveness could never
have a rival until somebody should set up a monument to the Milky Way.

People would come from every corner of the globe
and stop off to look at it, no tour of the world would
be complete that left out Adam's monument. Elmira
would be a Mecca; there would be pilgrim ships at
pilgrim rates, pilgrim specials on the continent's railways; libraries would be written about the monument, every tourist would kodak it, models of it
would be for sale everywhere in the earth, its form
would become as familiar as the figure of Napoleon.

One of the bankers subscribed five thousand dollars,
and I think the other one subscribed half as much,
but I do not remember with certainty now whether

that was the figure or not. We got designs made—some of them came from Paris.

In the beginning—as a detail of the project when it was as yet a joke—I had framed a humble and beseeching and perfervid petition to Congress begging the government to build the monument, as a testimony of the Great Republic's gratitude to the Father of the Human Race and as a token of her loyalty to him in this dark day of his humiliation when his older children were doubting him and deserting him. It seemed to me that this petition ought to be presented, now—it would be widely and feelingly abused and ridiculed and cursed, and would advertise our scheme and make our ground-floor stock go off briskly. So I sent it to General Joseph R. Hawley, who was then in the House, and he said he would present it. But he did not do it. I think he explained that when he came to read it he was afraid of it: it was too serious, too gushy, too sentimental—the House might take it for earnest.

We ought to have carried out our monument scheme; we could have managed it without any great difficulty, and Elmira would now be the most celebrated town in the universe.

Very recently I began to build a book in which one of the minor characters touches incidentally upon a project for a monument to Adam, and now the *Tribune* has come upon a trace of the forgotten jest of thirty years ago. Apparently mental telegraphy is still in business. It is odd; but the freaks of mental telegraphy are usually odd.

# A HUMANE WORD FROM SATAN

[The following letter, signed by Satan and purporting to come from him, we have reason to believe was not written by him, but by Mark Twain.—EDITOR.]

*To the Editor of Harper's Weekly:*

DEAR SIR AND KINSMAN,—Let us have done with this frivolous talk. The American Board accepts contributions from me every year: then why shouldn't it from Mr. Rockefeller? In all the ages, three-fourths of the support of the great charities has been conscience-money, as my books will show: then what becomes of the sting when that term is applied to Mr. Rockefeller's gift? The American Board's trade is financed mainly from the graveyards. Bequests, you understand. Conscience-money. Confession of an old crime and deliberate perpetration of a new one; for deceased's contribution is a robbery of his heirs. Shall the Board decline bequests because they stand for one of these offences every time and generally for both?

Allow me to continue. The charge most persistently and resentfully and remorselessly dwelt upon is, that Mr. Rockefeller's contribution is incurably tainted by perjury—perjury proved against him in the courts. *It makes us smile*—down in my place! Because there isn't a rich man in your vast city who doesn't perjure himself every year before the tax board. They are all caked with perjury, many layers thick. Iron clad, so to speak. If there is one that isn't, I desire to acquire him for my museum, and will pay Dinosaur rates. Will you say it isn't infraction of law, but only annual evasion of it? Comfort yourselves with that nice distinction if you like—*for the present*. But by-and-by, when you arrive, I will show you something interesting: a whole hell-full of evaders! Sometimes a frank law-breaker turns up elsewhere, but I get those others every time.

To return to my muttons. I wish you to remember that my rich perjurers are contributing to the American Board with frequency: it is money filched from the sworn-off personal tax; therefore it is the wages of sin; therefore it is my money; therefore it is *I* that contribute it; and, finally, it is therefore as I have said: since the Board daily accepts contributions from me, why should it decline them from Mr. Rockefeller, who is as good as I am, let the courts say what they may?

　　　　　　　　　　　.. .. .. SATAN.

# INTRODUCTION TO "THE NEW GUIDE OF THE CONVERSATION IN PORTUGUESE AND ENGLISH"

BY PEDRO CAROLINO

IN this world of uncertainties, there is, at any rate, one thing which may be pretty confidently set down as a certainty: and that is, that this celebrated little phrase-book will never die while the English language lasts. Its delicious unconscious ridiculousness, and its enchanting naïveté, are as supreme and unapproachable, in their way, as are Shakespeare's sublimities. Whatsoever is perfect in its kind, in literature, is imperishable: nobody can add to the absurdity of this book, nobody can imitate it successfully, nobody can hope to produce its fellow; it is perfect, it must and will stand alone: its immortality is secure.

It is one of the smallest books in the world, but few big books have received such wide attention, and been so much pondered by the grave and the learned, and so much discussed and written about by the thoughtful, the thoughtless, the wise, and the foolish. Long notices of it have appeared, from time

to time, in the great English reviews, and in erudite
and authoritative philological periodicals; and it has
been laughed at, danced upon, and tossed in a blanket
by nearly every newspaper and magazine in the
English-speaking world. Every scribbler, almost,
has had his little fling at it, at one time or another;
I had mine fifteen years ago. The book gets out of
print, every now and then, and one ceases to hear of
it for a season; but presently the nations and near
and far colonies of our tongue and lineage call for it
once more, and once more it issues from some London
or Continental or American press, and runs a new
course around the globe, wafted on its way by the
wind of a world's laughter.

Many persons have believed that this book's mirac-
ulous stupidities were studied and disingenuous; but
no one can read the volume carefully through and
keep that opinion. It was written in serious good
faith and deep earnestness, by an honest and upright
idiot who believed he knew something of the English
language, and could impart his knowledge to others.
The amplest proof of this crops out somewhere or
other upon each and every page. There are sentences
in the book which could have been manufactured by
a man in his right mind, and with an intelligent and
deliberate purpose to seem innocently ignorant; but
there are other sentences, and paragraphs, which no
mere pretended ignorance could ever achieve—nor
yet even the most genuine and comprehensive ignorance, when unbacked by inspiration.

It is not a fraud who speaks in the following paragraph of the author's Preface, but a good man, an honest man, a man whose conscience is at rest, a man who believes he has done a high and worthy work for his nation and his generation, and is well pleased with his performance:

"We expect then, who the little book (for the care what we wrote him, and for her typographical correction) that may be worth the acceptation of the studious persons, and especialy of the Youth, at which we dedicate him particularly."

One cannot open this book anywhere and not find richness. To prove that this is true, I will open it at random and copy the page I happen to stumble upon. Here is the result:

## "DIALOGUE 16

### "FOR TO SEE THE TOWN

"Anthony, go to accompany they gentilsmen, do they see the town.

"We won't to see all that is it remarquable here.

"Come with me, if you please. I shall not folget nothing what can to merit your attention. Here we are near to cathedral; will you come in there?

"We will first to see him in oudside, after we shall go in there for to look the interior.

"Admire this master piece gothic architecture's.

"The chasing of all they figures is astonishing'indeed.

"The cupola and the nave are not less curious to see.

"What is this palace how I see youder?

"It is the town hall.

"And this tower here at this side?

"It is the Observatory.

"The bridge is very fine, it have ten archs, and is constructed of free stone.

"The streets are very layed out by line and too paved.

"What is the circuit of this town?

"Two leagues.

"There is it also hospitals here?

"It not fail them.

"What are then the edifices the worthest to have seen?

"It is the arsnehal, the spectacle's hall, the Cusiom-house, and the Purse.

"We are going too see the others monuments such that the public pawnbroker's office, the plants garden's, the money office's, the library.

"That it shall be for another day; we are tired."


"DIALOGUE 17

"TO INFORM ONE'SELF OF A PERSON

"How is that gentilman who you did speak by and by?

"Is a German.

"I did think him Englishman.

"He is of the Saxony side.

"He speak the french very well.

"Tough he is German, he speak so much well italyan, french, spanish and english, that among the Italyans, they believe him Italyan, he speak the frenche as the Frenches himselves. The Spanishesmen believe him

Spanishing, and the Englishes, Englisman. It is difficult to enjoy well so much several langages."

The last remark contains a general truth; but it ceases to be a truth when one contracts it and applies it to an individual—provided that that individual is the author of this book, Senhor Pedro Carolino. I am sure I should not find it difficult "to enjoy well so much several langages"—or even a thousand of them—if he did the translating for me from the originals into his ostensible English.

# ADVICE TO LITTLE GIRLS

GOOD little girls ought not to make mouths at their teachers for every trifling offence. This retaliation should only be resorted to under peculiarly aggravated circumstances.

If you have nothing but a rag-doll stuffed with sawdust, while one of your more fortunate little playmates has a costly China one, you should treat her with a show of kindness nevertheless. And you ought not to attempt to make a forcible swap with her unless your conscience would justify you in it, and you know you are able to do it.

You ought never to take your little brother's "chewing-gum" away from him by main force; it is better to rope him in with the promise of the first two dollars and a half you find floating down the river on a grindstone. In the artless simplicity natural to his time of life, he will regard it as a perfectly fair transaction. In all ages of the world this eminently plausible fiction has lured the obtuse infant to financial ruin and disaster.

If at any time you find it necessary to correct your brother, do not correct him with mud—never, on any account, throw mud at him, because it will spoil his clothes. It is better to scold him a little, for then you obtain desirable results. You secure his immediate attention to the lessons you are inculcating, and at the same time your hot water will have a tendency to move impurities from his person, and possibly the skin, in spots.

If your mother tells you to do a thing, it is wrong to reply that you won't. It is better and more becoming to intimate that you will do as she bids you, and then afterwards act quietly in the matter according to the dictates of your best judgment.

You should ever bear in mind that it is to your kind parents that you are indebted for your food, and your nice bed, and for your beautiful clothes, and for the privilege of staying home from school when you let on that you are sick. Therefore you ought to respect their little prejudices, and humor their little whims, and put up with their little foibles until they get to crowding you too much.

Good little girls always show marked deference for the aged. You ought never to "sass" old people unless they "sass" you first.

# POST-MORTEM POETRY[1]

IN Philadelphia they have a custom which it would be pleasant to see adopted throughout the land. It is that of appending to published death-notices a little verse or two of comforting poetry. Any one who is in the habit of reading the daily Philadelphia *Ledger*, must frequently be touched by these plaintive tributes to extinguished worth. In Philadelphia, the departure of a child is a circumstance which is not more surely followed by a burial than by the accustomed solacing poesy in the *Public Ledger*. In that city death loses half its terror because the knowledge of its presence comes thus disguised in the sweet drapery of verse. For instance, in a late *Ledger* I find the following (I change the surname):

### "DIED

"HAWKS.—On the 17th inst., Clara, the daughter of Ephraim and Laura Hawks, aged 21 months and 2 days.

> "That merry shout no more I hear,
>     No laughing child I see,
> No little arms are round my neck,
>     No feet upon my knee;

[1] Written in 1870.

> No kisses drop upon my cheek,
>   These lips are sealed to me.
> Dear Lord, how could I give Clara up
>   To any but to Thee?"

A child thus mourned could not die wholly discontented. From the *Ledger* of the same date I make the following extract, merely changing the surname, as before:

"BECKET.—On Sunday morning, 19th inst., John P., infant son of George and Julia Becket, aged 1 year, 6 months, and 15 days.

> "That merry shout no more I hear,
>   No laughing child I see,
> No little arms are round my neck,
>   No feet upon my knee;
> No kisses drop upon my cheek,
>   These lips are sealed to me.
> Dear Lord, how could I give Johnnie up
>   To any but to Thee?"

The similarity of the emotions as produced in the mourners in these two instances is remarkably evidenced by the singular similarity of thought which they experienced, and the surprising coincidence of language used by them to give it expression.

In the same journal, of the same date, I find the following (surname suppressed, as before):

"WAGNER.—On the 10th inst., Ferguson G., the son of William L. and Martha Theresa Wagner, aged 4 weeks and 1 day.

'That merry shout no more I hear,
 No laughing child I see,
No little arms are round my neck,
 No feet upon my knee;
No kisses drop upon my cheek,
 These lips are sealed to me.
Dear Lord, how could I give Ferguson up
 To any but to Thee?"


It is strange what power the reiteration of an essentially poetical thought has upon one's feelings. When we take up the *Ledger* and read the poetry about little Clara, we feel an unaccountable depression of the spirits. When we drift further down the column and read the poetry about little Johnnie, the depression of spirits acquires an added emphasis, and we experience tangible suffering. When we saunter along down the column further still and read the poetry about little Ferguson, the word torture but vaguely suggests the anguish that rends us.

In the *Ledger* (same copy referred to above) I find the following (I alter surname, as usual):


"WELCH.—On the 5th inst., Mary C. Welch, wife of William B. Welch, and daughter of Catharine and George W. Markland, in the 29th year of her age.


"A mother dear, a mother kind,
 Has gone and left us all behind.
Cease to weep, for tears are vain,
 Mother dear is out of pain.

"Farewell, husband, children dear,
　　Serve thy God with filial fear,
　　And meet me in the land above,
　　Where all is peace, and joy, and love."

What could be sweeter than that? No collection
of salient facts (without reduction to tabular form)
could be more succinctly stated than is done in the
first stanza by the surviving relatives, and no more
concise and comprehensive programme of farewells,
post-mortuary general orders, etc., could be framed
in any form than is done in verse by deceased in the
last stanza. These things insensibly make us wiser
and tenderer, and better. Another extract:

"BALL.—On the morning of the 15th inst, Mary E.,
daughter of John and Sarah F. Ball.

"'Tis sweet to rest in lively hope
　　That when my change shall come
　　Angels will hover round my bed,
　　To waft my spirit home."

The following is apparently the customary form for
heads of families:

"BURNS.—On the 20th inst., Michael Burns, aged 40
years.
　　"Dearest father, thou hast left us,
　　　Here thy loss we deeply feel;
　　　But 'tis God that has bereft us,
　　　He can all our sorrows heal.

"Funeral at 2 o'clock sharp."
17

There is something very simple and pleasant about the following, which, in Philadelphia, seems to be the usual form for consumptives of long standing. (It deplores four distinct cases in the single copy of the *Ledger* which lies on the Memoranda editorial table):

"BROMLEY.—On the 29th inst., of consumption, Philip Bromley, in the 50th year of his age.

"Affliction sore long time he bore,
    Physicians were in vain—
Till God at last did hear him mourn,
    And eased him of his pain.

"The friend whom death from us has torn,
    We did not think so soon to part;
An anxious care now sinks the thorn
    Still deeper in our bleeding heart."

This beautiful creation loses nothing by repetition. On the contrary, the oftener one sees it in the *Ledger*, the more grand and awe-inspiring it seems.

With one more extract I will close:

"DOBLE.—On the 4th inst., Samuel Peveril Worthington Doble, aged 4 days.

"Our little Sammy's gone,
    His tiny spirit's fled;
Our little boy we loved so dear
    Lies sleeping with the dead.

> " A tear within a father's eye,
>   A mother's aching heart,
> Can only tell the agony
>   How hard it is to part."

Could anything be more plaintive than that, without requiring further concessions of grammar? Could anything be likely to do more towards reconciling deceased to circumstances, and making him willing to go? Perhaps not. The power of song can hardly be estimated. There is an element about some poetry which is able to make even physical suffering and death cheerful things to contemplate and consummations to be desired. This element is present in the mortuary poetry of Philadelphia degree of development.

The custom I have been treating of is one that should be adopted in all the cities of the land.

It is said that once a man of small consequence died, and the Rev. T. K. Beecher was asked to preach the funeral sermon—a man who abhors the lauding of people, either dead or alive, except in dignified and simple language, and then only for merits which they actually possessed or possess, not merits which they merely ought to have possessed. The friends of the deceased got up a stately funeral. They must have had misgivings that the corpse might not be praised strongly enough, for they prepared some manuscript headings and notes in which nothing was left unsaid on that subject that a fervid imagination and an unabridged dictionary could compile, and these they handed to the minister as he entered the pulpit. They were merely intended as suggestions, and so the friends were filled with consternation when the minister stood up in the pulpit and proceeded to read off the curious odds and ends in ghastly detail and in a loud voice! And their consternation solidified to petrification when he paused at the end, contemplated the multitude reflectively, and then said, impressively:

"The man would be a fool who tried to add anything to that. Let us pray!"

And with the same strict adhesion to truth it can be said that the man would be a fool who tried to add anything to the following transcendent obituary poem. There is something so innocent, so guileless, so complacent, so unearthly serene and self-satisfied about this peerless "hogwash," that the man must be made of stone who can read it without a dulcet ecstasy creeping along his backbone and quivering in his marrow. There is no need to say that this poem is genuine and in earnest, for its proofs are written all over its face. An ingenious scribbler might imitate it after a fashion, but Shakespeare himself could not counterfeit it. It is noticeable that the country editor who published it did not know that it was a treasure and the most perfect thing of its kind that the storehouses and museums of literature could show. He did not dare to say no to the dread poet—for such a poet must have been something of an apparition—but he just shovelled it into his paper anywhere that came handy, and felt ashamed, and put that disgusted

"Published by Request" over it, and hoped that his subscribers would overlook it or not feel an impulse to read it:

"(*Published by request*)

"LINES

"Composed on the death of Samuel and Catharine Belknap's children

"BY M. A. GLAZE

"Friends and neighbors all draw near,
    And listen to what I have to say;
And never leave your children dear
    When they are small, and go away.

"But always think of that sad fate,
    That happened in year of '63;
Four children with a house did burn,
    Think of their awful agony.

"Their mother she had gone away,
    And left them there alone to stay;
The house took fire and down did burn,
    Before their mother did return.

"Their piteous cry the neighbors heard,
    And then the cry of fire was given;
But, ah! before they could them reach,
    Their little spirits had flown to heaven.

"Their father he to war had gone,
    And on the battle-field was slain;
But little did he think when he went away,
    But what on earth they would meet again.

"The neighbors often told his wife
    Not to leave his children there,
Unless she got someone to stay,
    And of the little ones take care.

"The oldest he was years not six,
    And the youngest only eleven months old
But often she had left them there alone,
    As, by the neighbors, I have been told.

"How can she bear to see the place.
    Where she so oft has left them there,
Without a single one to look to them,
    Or of the little ones to take good care.

"Oh, can she look upon the spot,
    Whereunder their little burnt bones lay,
But what she thinks she hears them say,
    ''Twas God had pity, and took us on high

"And there may she kneel down and pray,
    And ask God her to forgive;
And she may lead a different life
    While she on earth remains to live.

"Her husband and her children too,
    God has took from pain and woe.
May she reform and mend her ways,
    That she may also to them go.

"And when it is God's holy will,
    O, may she be prepared
To meet her God and friends in peace,
    And leave this world of care."

# A DECEPTION

YOU may remember that I lectured lately for the young gentlemen of the Clayonian Society? During the afternoon of that day I was talking with one of the young gentlemen referred to, and he said he had an uncle who, from some cause or other, seemed to have grown permanently bereft of all emotion. And with tears in his eyes this young man said:

"Oh, if I could only see him laugh once more! Oh, if I could only see him weep!"

I was touched. I could never withstand distress. I said:

"Bring him to my lecture. I'll start him for you."

"Oh, if you could but do it! If you could but do it, all our family would bless you for evermore; for he is very dear to us. Oh, my benefactor, can you make him laugh? Can you bring soothing tears to those parched orbs?"

I was profoundly moved. I said:

"My son, bring the old party round. I have got some jokes in my lecture that will make him laugh, if there is any laugh in him; and, if they miss fire, I have got some others that'll make him cry or kill him, one or the other."

Then the young man wept on my neck, and presently spread both hands on my head and looked up
towards heaven, mumbling something reverently;
and then he went after his uncle. He placed him in
full view, in the second row of benches, that night,
and I began on him. I tried him with mild jokes—
then with severe ones; I dosed him with bad jokes,
and riddled him with good ones; I fired old, stale jokes
on him, and peppered him fore and aft with red-hot
new ones. I warmed up to my work, and assaulted
him on the right and left, in front and behind; I
fumed, and charged, and ranted, till I was hoarse and
sick, and frantic and furious; but I never moved him
once — I never started a smile or a tear! Never a
ghost of a smile, and never a suspicion of moisture!
I was astounded. I closed the lecture at last with
one despairing shriek—with one wild burst of humor
—and hurled a joke of supernatural atrocity full at
him. It never phased him! Then I sat down be-
wildered and exhausted.

The president of the society came up and bathed
my head with cold water, and said:

"What made you carry on so towards the last?"

I said, "I was trying to make that confounded old
idiot laugh in the second row."

And he said, "Well, you were wasting your time;
because he is deaf and dumb, and as blind as a
badger."

Now was that any way for that old man's nephew
to impose on a stranger and an orphan like me?

# THE DANGER OF LYING IN BED

THE man in the ticket-office said:

"Have an accident insurance ticket, also?"

"No," I said, after studying the matter over a little. "No, I believe not; I am going to be travelling by rail all day to-day. However, to-morrow I don't travel. Give me one for to-morrow."

The man looked puzzled. He said:

"But it is for accident insurance, and if you are going to travel by rail—"

"If I am going to travel by rail I sha'n't need it. Lying at home in bed is the thing *I* am afraid of."

I had been looking into this matter. Last year I travelled twenty thousand miles, almost entirely by rail; the year before, I travelled over twenty-five thousand miles, half by sea and half by rail; and the year before that I travelled in the neighborhood of ten thousand miles, exclusively by rail. I suppose if I put in all the little odd journeys here and there, I may say I have travelled sixty thousand miles during the three years I have mentioned. *And never an accident.*

For a good while I said to myself every morning:

"Now I have escaped thus far, and so the chances are just that much increased that I shall catch it this time. I will be shrewd, and buy an accident ticket." And to a dead moral certainty I drew a blank, and went to bed that night without a joint started or a bone splintered. I got tired of that sort of daily bother, and fell to buying accident tickets that were good for a month. I said to myself, "A man *can't* buy thirty blanks in one bundle."

But I was mistaken. There was never a prize in the lot. I could read of railway accidents every day —the newspaper atmosphere was foggy with them; but somehow they never came my way. I found I had spent a good deal of money in the accident business, and had nothing to show for it. My suspicions were aroused, and I began to hunt around for somebody that had won in this lottery. I found plenty of people who had invested, but not an individual that had ever had an accident or made a cent. I stopped buying accident tickets and went to ciphering. The result was astounding. THE PERIL LAY NOT IN TRAVELLING, BUT IN STAYING AT HOME.

I hunted up statistics, and was amazed to find that after all the glaring newspaper headings concerning railroad disasters, less than *three hundred* people had really lost their lives by those disasters in the preceding twelve months. The Erie road was set down as the most murderous in the list. It had killed forty-six—or twenty-six, I do not exactly remember which, but I know the number was double that of any other road. But the fact straightway suggested itself that the Erie was an immensely long road, and did more business than any other line in the country; so the double number of killed ceased to be matter for surprise.

By further figuring, it appeared that between New York and Rochester the Erie ran eight passenger trains each way every day—sixteen altogether; and carried a daily average of 6000 persons. That is about a million in six months—the population of New York City. Well, the Erie kills from thirteen to twenty-three persons out of *its* million in six months; and in the same time 13,000 of New York's million die in their beds! My flesh crept, my hair stood on end. "This is appalling!" I said. "The danger isn't in travelling by rail, but in trusting to those deadly beds. I will never sleep in a bed again."

I had figured on considerably less than one-half the length of the Erie road. It was plain that the entire road must transport at least eleven or twelve thousand people every day. There are many short roads running out of Boston that do fully half as much; a great many such roads. There are many roads scattered about the Union that do a prodigious passenger business. Therefore it was fair to presume that an average of 2500 passengers a day for each road in the country would be about correct. There are 846 railway lines in our country, and 846 times 2500 are 2,115,000. So the railways of America move more than two millions of people every day; six hun-

dred and fifty millions of people a year, without
counting the Sundays. They do that, too—there is
no question about it; though where they get the raw
material is clear beyond the jurisdiction of my arith-
metic; for I have hunted the census through and
through, and I find that there are not that many
people in the United States, by a matter of six hundred and ten millions at the very least. They must
use some of the same people over again, likely.

San Francisco is one-eighth as populous as New
York; there are 60 deaths a week in the former and
500 a week in the latter—if they have luck. That is
3120 deaths a year in San Francisco, and eight times
as many in New York—say about 25,000 or 26,000.
The health of the two places is the same. So we will
let it stand as a fair presumption that this will hold
good all over the country, and that consequently
25,000 out of every million of people we have must
die every year. That amounts to one-fortieth of our
total population. One million of us, then, die an-
nually. Out of this million ten or twelve thousand
are stabbed, shot, drowned, hanged, poisoned, or
meet a similarly violent death in some other popular
way, such as perishing by kerosene lamp and hoop-
skirt conflagrations, getting buried in coal - mines,
falling off house - tops, breaking through church or
lecture-room floors, taking patent medicines, or com-
mitting suicide in other forms. The Erie railroad
kills from 23 to 46; the other 845 railroads kill an
average of one-third of a man each; and the rest of

that million, amounting in the aggregate to the appalling figure of nine hundred and eighty-seven thousand six hundred and thirty-one corpses, die naturally in their beds!

You will excuse me from taking any more chances on those beds. The railroads are good enough for me.

And my advice to all people is, Don't stay at home any more than you can help; but when you have *got* to stay at home a while, buy a package of those insurance tickets and sit up nights. You cannot be too cautious.

[One can see now why I answered that ticket-agent in the manner recorded at the top of this sketch.]

The moral of this composition is, that thoughtless people grumble more than is fair about railroad management in the United States. When we consider that every day and night of the year full fourteen thousand railway trains of various kinds, freighted with life and armed with death, go thundering over the land, the marvel is, *not* that they kill three hundred human beings in a twelvemonth, but that they do not kill three hundred times three hundred!

# PORTRAIT OF KING WILLIAM III

I NEVER can look at those periodical portraits in *The Galaxy* magazine without feeling a wild, tempestuous ambition to be an artist. I have seen thousands and thousands of pictures in my time—acres of them here and leagues of them in the galleries of Europe—but never any that moved me as these portraits do.

There is the portrait of Monsignore Capel in the November number, now *could* anything be sweeter than that? And there was Bismarck's, in the October number; who can look at that without being purer and stronger and nobler for it? And Thurlow Weed's picture in the September number; I would not have died without seeing that, no, not for anything this world can give. But look back still further and recall my own likeness as printed in the August number; if I had been in my grave a thousand years when that appeared, I would have got up and visited the artist.

I sleep with all these portraits under my pillow every night, so that I can go on studying them as soon as the day dawns in the morning. I know them all as thoroughly as if I had made them myself; I know

every line and mark about them.  Sometimes when
company are present I shuffle the portraits all up together, and then pick them out one by one and call
their names, without referring to the printing at the
bottom.  I seldom make a mistake—never, when I
am calm.

I have had the portraits framed for a long time,
waiting till my aunt gets everything ready for hanging them up in the parlor.  But first one thing and
then another interferes, and so the thing is delayed.
Once she said they would have more of the peculiar
kind of light they needed in the attic.  The old simpleton! it is as dark as a tomb up there.  But she does
not know anything about art, and so she has no
reverence for it.  When I showed her my "Map of
the Fortifications of Paris," she said it was rubbish.

Well, from nursing those portraits so long, I have
come at last to have a perfect infatuation for art.  I
have a teacher now, and my enthusiasm continually
and tumultuously grows, as I learn to use with more
and more facility the pencil, brush, and graver.  I
am studying under De Mellville, the house and portrait
painter.  [His name was Smith when he lived West.]
He does any kind of artist work a body wants, having
a genius that is universal, like Michael Angelo.  Resembles that great artist, in fact.  The back of his
head is like his, and he wears his hat-brim tilted down
on his nose to expose it.

I have been studying under De Mellville several

months now. The first month I painted fences, and gave general satisfaction. The next month I whitewashed a barn. The third, I was doing tin roofs; the fourth, common signs; the fifth, statuary to stand before cigar shops. This present month is only the sixth, and I am already in portraits!

The humble offering which accompanies these remarks — the portrait of his Majesty William III., King of Prussia—is my fifth attempt in portraits, and my greatest success. It has received unbounded praise from all classes of the community, but that which gratifies me most is the frequent and cordial verdict that it resembles the *Galaxy* portraits. Those were my first love, my earliest admiration, the original source and incentive of my art-ambition. Whatever I am in Art to-day, I owe to these portraits. I ask no credit for myself—I deserve none. And I never take any, either. Many a stranger has come to my exhibition (for I have had my portrait of King William on exhibition at one dollar a ticket), and would have gone away blessing *me*, if I had let him, but I never did. I always stated where I got the idea.

King William wears large bushy side-whiskers, and some critics have thought that this portrait would be more complete if they were added. But it was not possible. There was not room for side-whiskers and epaulettes both, and so I let the whiskers go, and put in the epaulettes, for the sake of style. That thing on his hat is an eagle. The Prussian eagle—it is a national emblem. When I say hat I mean helmet;

WILLIAM III.,
King of Prussia.

but it seems impossible to make a picture or a helmet that a body can have confidence in.

I wish kind friends everywhere would aid me in my endeavor to attract a little attention to the *Galaxy* portraits. I feel persuaded it can be accomplished, if the course to be pursued be chosen with judgment. I write for that magazine all the time, and so do many abler men, and if I can get these portraits into universal favor, it is all I ask; the reading matter will take care of itself.

## COMMENDATIONS OF THE PORTRAIT

There is nothing like it in the Vatican.    Pius IX.

It has none of that vagueness, that dreamy spirituality about it, which many of the first critics of Arkansas have objected to in the Murillo school of Art.

RUSKIN.

The expression is very interesting.   J. W. TITIAN.

(Keeps a macaroni store in Venice, at the old family stand.)

It is the neatest thing in still life I have seen for years.                          ROSA BONHEUR.

The smile may be almost called unique.  BISMARCK.

I never saw such character portrayed in a pictured face before.                          DE MELLVILLE.

There is a benignant simplicity about the execution of this work which warms the heart towards it as much, full as much, as it fascinates the eye.   LANDSEER.

One cannot see it without longing to contemplate the artist.          FREDERICK WILLIAM.

Send me the entire edition—together with the plate and the original portrait—and name your own price. And—would you like to come over and stay a while with Napoleon at Wilhelmshöhe? It shall not cost you a cent.          WILLIAM III.

# DOES THE RACE OF MAN LOVE A LORD?

*Often a quite assified remark becomes sanctified by use and petrified by custom; it is then a permanency, its term of activity a geologic period.*

THE day after the arrival of Prince Henry I met an English friend, and he rubbed his hands and broke out with a remark that was charged to the brim with joy—joy that was evidently a pleasant salve to an old sore place:

"Many a time I've had to listen without retort to an old saying that is irritatingly true, and until now seemed to offer no chance for a return jibe: 'An Englishman does dearly love a lord'; but after this I shall talk back, and say 'How about the Americans?'"

It is a curious thing, the currency that an idiotic saying can get. The man that first says it thinks he has made a discovery. The man he says it to, thinks the same. It departs on its travels, is received everywhere with admiring acceptance, and not only as a piece of rare and acute observation, but as being exhaustively true and profoundly wise; and so it

presently takes its place in the world's list of recognized and established wisdoms, and after that no
one thinks of examining it to see whether it is really
entitled to its high honors or not. I call to mind
instances of this in two well-established proverbs,
whose dulness is not surpassed by the one about the
Englishman and his love for a lord: one of them
records the American's Adoration of the Almighty
Dollar, the other the American millionaire-girl's ambition to trade cash for a title, with a husband
thrown in.

It isn't merely the American that adores the Almighty Dollar, it is the human race. The human
race has always adored the hatful of shells, or the
bale of calico, or the half-bushel of brass rings, or
the handful of steel fish-hooks, or the houseful of
black wives, or the zareba full of cattle, or the two
score camels and asses, or the factory, or the farm,
or the block of buildings, or the railroad bonds, or
the bank stock, or the hoarded cash, or—anything
that stands for wealth and consideration and independence, and can secure to the possessor that most
precious of all things, another man's envy. It was
a dull person that invented the idea that the American's devotion to the dollar is more strenuous than
another's.

Rich American girls do buy titles, but they did not
invent that idea; it had been worn threadbare several
hundred centuries before America was discovered.
European girls still exploit it as briskly as ever; and,

when a title is not to be had for the money in hand, they buy the husband without it. They must put up the "dot," or there is no trade. The commercialization of brides is substantially universal, except in America. It exists with us, to some little extent, but in no degree approaching a custom.

"The Englishman dearly loves a lord."

What is the soul and source of his love? I think the thing could be more correctly worded:

"The human race dearly envies a lord."

That is to say, it envies the lord's place. Why? On two accounts, I think: its Power and its Conspicuousness.

Where Conspicuousness carries with it a Power which, by the light of our own observation and experience, we are able to measure and comprehend, I think our envy of the possessor is as deep and as passionate as is that of any other nation. No one can care less for a lord than the backwoodsman, who has had no personal contact with lords and has seldom heard them spoken of; but I will not allow that any Englishman has a profounder envy of a lord than has the average American who has lived long years in a European capital and fully learned how immense is the position the lord occupies.

Of any ten thousand Americans who eagerly gather, at vast inconvenience, to get a glimpse of Prince Henry, all but a couple of hundred will be there out of an immense curiosity; they are burning up with desire to see a personage who is so much talked about.

They envy him; but it is Conspicuousness they envy mainly, not the Power that is lodged in his royal quality and position, for they have but a vague and spectral knowledge and appreciation of that; through their environment and associations they have been accustomed to regard such things lightly, and as not being very real; consequently, they are not able to value them enough to consumingly envy them.

But, whenever an American (or other human being) is in the presence, for the first time, of a combination of great Power and Conspicuousness which he thoroughly understands and appreciates, his eager curiosity and pleasure will be well-sodden with that other passion—envy—whether he suspect it or not. At any time, on any day, in any part of America, you can confer a happiness upon any passing stranger by calling his attention to any other passing stranger and saying:

"Do you see that gentleman going along there? It is Mr. Rockefeller."

Watch his eye. It is a combination of power and conspicuousness which the man understands.

When we understand rank, we always like to rub against it. When a man is conspicuous, we always want to see him. Also, if he will pay us an attention we will manage to remember it. Also, we will mention it now and then, casually; sometimes to a friend, or if a friend is not handy, we will make out with a stranger.

Well, then, what is rank, and what is conspicuousness? At once we think of kings and aristocracies, and of world-wide celebrities in soldiership, the arts, letters, etc., and we stop there. But that is a mistake. Rank holds its court and receives its homage on every round of the ladder, from the emperor down to the rat-catcher; and distinction, also, exists on every round of the ladder, and commands its due of deference and envy.

To worship rank and distinction is the dear and valued privilege of all the human race, and it is freely and joyfully exercised in democracies as well as in monarchies—and even, to some extent, among those creatures whom we impertinently call the Lower Animals. For even they have some poor little vanities and foibles, though in this matter they are paupers as compared to us.

A Chinese Emperor has the worship of his four hundred millions of subjects, but the rest of the world is indifferent to him. A Christian Emperor has the worship of his subjects and of a large part of the Christian world outside of his dominions; but he is a matter of indifference to all China. A king, class A, has an extensive worship; a king, class B, has a less extensive worship; class C, class D, class E get a steadily diminishing share of worship; class L (Sultan of Zanzibar), class P (Sultan of Sulu), and class W (half-king of Samoa), get no worship at all outside their own little patch of sovereignty.

Take the distinguished people along down. Each has his group of homage-payers. In the navy, there are many groups; they start with the Secretary and the Admiral, and go down to the quartermaster—and below; for there will be groups among the sailors, and each of these groups will have a tar who is distinguished for his battles, or his strength, or his daring, or his profanity, and is admired and envied by his group. The same with the army; the same with the literary and journalistic craft; the publishing craft; the cod-fishery craft; Standard Oil; U. S. Steel; the class A hotel—and the rest of the alphabet in that line; the class A prize-fighter—and the rest of the alphabet in his line—clear down to the lowest and obscurest six-boy gang of little gamins, with its one boy that can thrash the rest, and to whom he is king of Samoa, bottom of the royal race, but looked up to with a most ardent admiration and envy.

There is something pathetic, and funny, and pretty, about this human race's fondness for contact with power and distinction, and for the reflected glory it gets out of it. The king, class A, is happy in the state banquet and the military show which the emperor provides for him, and he goes home and gathers the queen and the princelings around him in the privacy of the spare room, and tells them all about it, and says:

"His Imperial Majesty put his hand on my shoulder in the most friendly way—just as friendly and familiar, oh, you can't imagine it!—and everybody *seeing* him do it; charming, perfectly charming!"

The king, class G, is happy in the cold collation

and the police-parade provided for him by the king, class B, and goes home and tells the family all about it, and says:

"And His Majesty took me into his own private cabinet for a smoke and a chat, and there we sat just as sociable, and talking away and laughing and chatting, just the same as if we had been born in the same bunk; and all the servants in the anteroom could see us doing it! Oh, it was too lovely for anything!"

The king, class Q, is happy in the modest entertainment furnished him by the king, class M, and goes home and tells the household about it, and is as grateful and joyful over it as were his predecessors in the gaudier attentions that had fallen to their larger lot.

Emperors, kings, artisans, peasants, big people, little people—at bottom we are all alike and all the same; all just alike on the inside, and when our clothes are off, nobody can tell which of us is which. We are unanimous in the pride we take in good and genuine compliments paid us, in distinctions conferred upon us, in attentions shown us. There is not one of us, from the emperor down, but is made like that. Do I mean attentions shown us by the great? No, I mean simply flattering attentions, let them come whence they may. We despise no source that can pay us a pleasing attention—there is no source that is humble enough for that. You have heard a dear little girl say of a frowzy and disreputable dog: "He

came right to me and let me pat him on the head, and
he wouldn't let the others touch him!" and you have
seen her eyes dance with pride in that high distinction. You have often seen that. If the child were
a princess, would that random dog be able to confer
the like glory upon her with his pretty compliment?
Yes; and even in her mature life and seated upon a
throne, she would still remember it, still recall it, still
speak of it with frank satisfaction. That charming
and lovable German princess and poet, Carmen Sylva,
Queen of Roumania, remembers yet that the flowers
of the woods and fields "talked to her" when she was
a girl, and she sets it down in her latest book; and
that the squirrels conferred upon her and her father
the valued compliment of not being afraid of them;
and "once one of them, holding a nut between its
sharp little teeth, ran right up against my father"—
it has the very note of "He came right to me and let
me pat him on the head"—"and when it saw itself
reflected in his boot it was very much surprised, and
stopped for a long time to contemplate itself in the
polished leather"—then it went its way. And the
birds! she still remembers with pride that "they
came boldly into my room," when she had neglected
her "duty" and put no food on the window-sill for
them; she knew all the wild birds, and forgets the
royal crown on her head to remember with pride that
they knew her; also that the wasp and the bee were
personal friends of hers, and never forgot that gracious
relationship to her injury: "never have I been stung

by a wasp or a bee." And here is that proud note
again that sings in that little child's elation in being
singled out, among all the company of children, for
the random dog's honor-conferring attentions. "Even
in the very worst summer for wasps, when, in lunching
out-of-doors, our table was covered with them and
every one else was stung, they never hurt me."

When a queen whose qualities of mind and heart
and character are able to add distinction to so distinguished a place as a throne, remembers with grateful exultation, after thirty years, honors and distinctions conferred upon her by the humble, wild creatures
of the forest, we are helped to realize that complimen-
tary attentions, homage, distinctions, are of no caste,
but are above all caste — that they are a nobility-
conferring power apart.

We all like these things. When the gate-guard at the
railway station passes me through unchallenged and
examines other people's tickets, I feel as the king, class
A, felt when the emperor put the imperial hand on
his shoulder, "everybody seeing him do it"; and as
the child felt when the random dog allowed her to
pat his head and ostracized the others; and as the
princess felt when the wasps spared her and stung
the rest; and I felt just so, four years ago in Vienna
(and remember it yet), when the helmeted police shut
me off, with fifty others, from a street which the
Emperor was to pass through, and the captain of the
squad turned and saw the situation and said indignantly to that guard:

"Can't you see it is the Herr Mark Twain? Let him through!"

It was four years ago; but it will be four hundred before I forget the wind of self-complacency that rose in me, and strained my buttons when I marked the deference for me evoked in the faces of my fellow-rabble, and noted, mingled with it, a puzzled and resentful expression which said, as plainly as speech could have worded it: "And who in the nation is the Herr Mark Twain *um Gotteswillen?*"

How many times in your life have you heard this boastful remark:

"I stood as close to him as I am to you; I could have put out my hand and touched him."

We have all heard it many and many a time. It was a proud distinction to be able to say those words. It brought envy to the speaker, a kind of glory; and he basked in it and was happy through all his veins. And who was it he stood so close to? The answer would cover all the grades. Sometimes it was a king; sometimes it was a renowned highwayman; sometimes it was an unknown man killed in an extraordinary way and made suddenly famous by it; always it was a person who was for the moment the subject of public interest—the public interest of a nation, maybe only the public interest of a village.

"I was there, and I saw it myself." That is a common and envy-compelling remark. It can refer to a battle; to a hanging; to a coronation, to the killing of Jumbo by the railway train; to the arrival

of Jenny Lind at the Battery; to the meeting of the
President and Prince Henry; to the chase of a murderous maniac; to the disaster in the tunnel; to the
explosion in the subway; to a remarkable dog-fight;
to a village church struck by lightning.  It will be
said, more or less casually, by everybody in America
who has seen Prince Henry do anything, or try to.
The man who was absent and didn't see him do anything, will scoff.   It is his privilege; and he can make
capital out of it, too; he will seem, even to himself,
to be different from other Americans, and better.
As his opinion of his superior Americanism grows, and
swells, and concentrates and coagulates, he will go
further and try to belittle the distinction of those
that saw the Prince do things, and will spoil their
pleasure in it if he can.   My life has been embittered
by that kind of persons.   If you are able to tell of a
special distinction that has fallen to your lot, it
gravels them; they cannot bear it; and they try to
make believe that the thing you took for a special
distinction was nothing of the kind and was meant
in quite another way.   Once I was received in private
audience by an emperor.   Last week I was telling a
jealous person about it, and I could see him wince
under it, see it bite, see him suffer.   I revealed the
whole episode to him with considerable elaboration
and nice attention to detail.   When I was through,
he asked me what had impressed me most.   I said:

"His Majesty's delicacy.   They told me to be sure
and back out from the presence, and find the door-

knob as best I could; it was not allowable to face around. Now the Emperor knew it would be a difficult ordeal for me, because of lack of practice; and so, when it was time to part, he turned, with exceeding delicacy, and pretended to fumble with things on his desk, so that I could get out in my own way, without his seeing me."

It went home! It was vitriol! I saw the envy and disgruntlement rise in the man's face; he couldn't keep it down. I saw him trying to fix up something in his mind to take the bloom off that distinction. I enjoyed that, for I judged that he had his work cut out for him. He struggled along inwardly for quite a while; then he said, with the manner of a person who has to say something and hasn't anything relevant to say:

"You said he had a handful of special-brand cigars lying on the table?"

"Yes: I never saw anything to match them."

I had him again. He had to fumble around in his mind as much as another minute before he could play; then he said in as mean a way as I ever heard a person say anything:

"He could have been counting the cigars, you know."

I cannot endure a man like that. It is nothing to him how unkind he is, so long as he takes the bloom off. It is all he cares for.

"An Englishman (or other human being) does dearly love a lord," (or other conspicuous person).

It includes us all. We love to be noticed by the conspicuous person; we love to be associated with such, or with a conspicuous event, even in a seventh-rate fashion, even in a forty-seventh, if we cannot do better. This accounts for some of our curious tastes in mementos. It accounts for the large private trade in the Prince of Wales's hair, which chambermaids were able to drive in that article of commerce when the Prince made the tour of the world in the long ago —hair which probably did not always come from his brush, since enough of it was marketed to refurnish a bald comet; it accounts for the fact that the rope which lynches a negro in the presence of ten thousand Christian spectators is saleable five minutes later at two dollars an inch; it accounts for the mournful fact that a royal personage does not venture to wear buttons on his coat in public.

We do love a lord—and by that term I mean any person whose situation is higher than our own. The lord of a group, for instance: a group of peers, a group of millionaires, a group of hoodlums, a group of sailors, a group of newsboys, a group of saloon politicians, a group of college girls. No royal person has ever been the object of a more delirious loyalty and slavish adoration than is paid by the vast Tammany herd to its squalid idol of Wantage. There is not a bifurcated animal in that menagerie that would not be proud to appear in a newspaper-picture in his company. At the same time, there are some in that organization who would scoff at the people who have been daily pictured in company with Prince Henry, and would say vigorously that *they* would not consent to be photographed with him — a statement which would not be true in any instance. There are hundreds of people in America who would frankly say to you that they would not be proud to be photographed in a group with the Prince, if invited; and some of these unthinking people would believe it when they said it; yet in no instance would it be true. We have a large population, but we have not a large enough one, by several millions, to furnish that man. He has not yet been begotten, and in fact he is not begettable.

You may take any of the printed groups, and there isn't a person in it who isn't visibly glad to be there; there isn't a person in the dim background who isn't visibly trying to be vivid; if it is a crowd of ten thousand — ten thousand proud, untamed democrats, horny-handed sons of toil and of politics, and fliers of the eagle—there isn't one who isn't conscious of the camera, there isn't one who is trying to keep out of range, there isn't one who isn't plainly meditating a purchase of the paper in the morning, with the intention of hunting himself out in the picture and of framing and keeping it if he shall find so much of his person in it as his starboard ear.

We all love to get some of the drippings of Conspicuousness, and we will put up with a single, humble drip, if we can't get any more. We may pretend otherwise, in conversation; but we can't pretend it

19

to ourselves privately—and we don't. We do confess in public that we are the noblest work of God, being moved to it by long habit, and teaching, and superstition; but deep down in the secret places of our souls we recognize that, if we *are* the noblest work, the less said about it the better.

We of the North poke fun at the South for its fondness for titles—a fondness for titles pure and simple, regardless of whether they are genuine or pinchbeck. We forget that whatever a Southerner likes the rest of the human race likes, and that there is no law of predilection lodged in one people that is absent from another people. There is no variety in the human race. We are all children, all children of the one Adam, and we love toys. We can soon acquire that Southern disease if some one will give it a start. It already has a start, in fact. I have been personally acquainted with over eighty-four thousand persons who, at one time or another in their lives, have served for a year or two on the staffs of our multitudinous governors, and through that fatality have been generals temporarily, and colonels temporarily, and judge-advocates temporarily; but I have known only nine among them who could be hired to let the title go when it ceased to be legitimate. I know thousands and thousands of governors who ceased to be governors away back in the last century; but I am acquainted with only three who would answer your letter if you failed to call them "Governor" in it. I know acres and acres of men who have done time in a legislature in prehistoric days, but among them is not half an acre whose resentment you would not raise if you addressed them as "Mr." instead of "Hon." The first thing a legislature does is to convene in an impressive legislative attitude, and get itself photographed. Each member frames his copy and takes it to the woods and hangs it up in the most aggressively conspicuous place in his house; and if you visit the house and fail to inquire what that accumulation is, the conversation will be brought around to it by that aforetime legislator, and he will show you a figure in it which in the course of years he has almost obliterated with the smut of his finger-marks, and say with a solemn joy, "It's me!"

Have you ever seen a country Congressman enter the hotel breakfast-room in Washington with his letters?—and sit at his table and let on to read them? —and wrinkle his brows and frown statesman-like?— keeping a furtive watch-out over his glasses all the while to see if he is being observed and admired?— those same old letters which he fetches in every morning? Have you seen it? Have you seen him show off? It is *the* sight of the national capital. Except one; a pathetic one. That is the ex-Congressman: the poor fellow whose life has been ruined by a two-year taste of glory and of fictitious consequence; who has been superseded, and ought to take his heartbreak home and hide it, but cannot tear himself away from the scene of his lost little grandeur; and so he lingers, and still lingers, year after year, unconsidered, sometimes snubbed, ashamed of his fallen estate, and valiantly trying to look otherwise; dreary and depressed, but counterfeiting breeziness and gayety, hailing with chummy familiarity, which is not always welcomed, the more-fortunates who are still in place and were once his mates. Have you seen him? He clings piteously to the one little shred that is left of his departed distinction—the "privilege of the floor"; and works it hard and gets what he can out of it. That is the saddest figure I know of.

Yes, we do so love our little distinctions! And then we loftily scoff at a Prince for enjoying his larger ones; forgetting that if we only had his chance—ah! "Senator" is not a legitimate title. A Senator has no more right to be addressed by it than have you or I; but, in the several State capitals and in Washington, there are five thousand Senators who take very kindly to that fiction, and who purr gratefully when you call them by it—which you may do quite unrebuked. Then those same Senators smile at the self-constructed majors and generals and judges of the South!

Indeed, we do love our distinctions, get them how we may. And we work them for all they are worth. In prayer we call ourselves "worms of the dust," but it is only on a sort of tacit understanding that the remark shall not be taken at par. *We*—worms of the dust! Oh, no, we are not that. Except in fact; and we do not deal much in fact when we are contemplating ourselves.

As a race, we do certainly love a lord—let him be

Croker, or a duke, or a prize-fighter, or whatever other personage shall chance to be the head of our group. Many years ago, I saw a greasy youth in overalls standing by the *Herald* office, with an expectant look in his face. Soon a large man passed out, and gave him a pat on the shoulder. That was what the boy was waiting for—the large man's notice. The pat made him proud and happy, and the exultation inside of him shone out through his eyes; and his mates were there to see the pat and envy it and wish they could have that glory. The boy belonged down cellar in the press-room, the large man was king of the upper floors, foreman of the composing-room. The light in the boy's face was worship, the foreman was his lord, head of his group. The pat was an accolade. It was as precious to the boy as it would have been if he had been an aristocrat's son and the accolade had been delivered by his sovereign with a sword. The quintessence of the honor was all there; there was no difference in values; in truth there was no difference present except an artificial one—clothes.

All the human race loves a lord—that is, it loves to look upon or be noticed by the possessor of Power or Conspicuousness; and sometimes animals, born to better things and higher ideals, descend to man's level in this matter. In the Jardin des Plantes I have seen a cat that was so vain of being the personal friend of an elephant that I was ashamed of her.

# EVE'S DIARY

TRANSLATED FROM THE ORIGINAL

SATURDAY.—I am almost a whole day old, now. I arrived yesterday. That is as it seems to me. And it must be so, for if there was a day-before-yesterday I was not there when it happened, or I should remember it. It could be, of course, that it did happen, and that I was not noticing. Very well; I will be very watchful, now, and if any day-before-yesterdays happen I will make a note of it. It will be best to start right and not let the record get confused, for some instinct tells me that these details are going to be important to the historian some day. For I feel like an experiment, I feel exactly like an experiment; it would be impossible for a person to feel more like an experiment than I do, and so I am coming to feel convinced that that is what I *am*—an experiment; just an experiment, and nothing more.

Then if I am an experiment, am I the whole of it? No, I think not; I think the rest of it is part of it. I am the main part of it, but I think the rest of it has its share in the matter. Is my position assured, or do I have to watch it and take care of it? The latter, perhaps. Some instinct tells me that eternal vigilance is the price of supremacy. [That is a good phrase, I think, for one so young.]

Everything looks better to-day than it did yesterday. In the rush of finishing up yesterday, the mountains were left in a ragged condition, and some of the plains were so cluttered with rubbish and remnants that the aspects were quite distressing. Noble and beautiful works of art should not be subjected to haste; and this majestic new world is indeed a most noble and beautiful work. And certainly marvellously near to being perfect, notwithstanding the shortness of the time. There are too many stars in some places and not enough in others, but that can be remedied presently, no doubt. The moon got loose last night, and slid down and fell out of the scheme—a very great loss; it breaks my heart to think of it. There isn't another thing among the ornaments and decorations that is comparable to it for beauty and finish. It should have been fastened better. If we can only get it back again—

But of course there is no telling where it went to. And besides, whoever gets it will hide it; I know it because I would do it myself. I believe I can be honest in all other matters, but I already begin to realize that the core and centre of my nature is love of the beautiful, a passion for the beautiful, and that it would not be safe to trust me with a moon that

belonged to another person and that person didn't
know I had it. I could give up a moon that I found
in the daytime, because I should be afraid some one
was looking; but if I found it in the dark, I am sure
I should find some kind of an excuse for not saying
anything about it. For I do love moons, they are
so pretty and so romantic. I wish we had five or
six; I would never go to bed; I should never get
tired lying on the moss-bank and looking up at them.

Stars are good, too. I wish I could get some to
put in my hair. But I suppose I never can. You
would be surprised to find how far off they are, for
they do not look it. When they first showed, last
night, I tried to knock some down with a pole, but it
didn't reach, which astonished me; then I tried clods
till I was all tired out, but I never got one. It was
because I am left-handed and cannot throw good.
Even when I aimed at the one I wasn't after I
couldn't hit the other one, though I did make some
close shots, for I saw the black blot of the clod sail
right into the midst of the golden clusters forty or fifty
times, just barely missing them, and if I could have
held out a little longer maybe I could have got one.

So I cried a little, which was natural, I suppose,
for one of my age, and after I was rested I got a
basket and started for a place on the extreme rim of
the circle, where the stars were close to the ground
and I could get them with my hands, which would
be better, anyway, because I could gather them ten-
derly then, and not break them. But it was farther

than I thought, and at last I had to give it up; I was so tired I couldn't drag my feet another step; and besides, they were sore and hurt me very much.

I couldn't get back home; it was too far and turning cold; but I found some tigers and nestled in among them and was most adorably comfortable, and their breath was sweet and pleasant, because they live on strawberries. I had never seen a tiger before, but I knew them in a minute by the stripes. If I could have one of those skins, it would make a lovely gown.

To-day I am getting better ideas about distances. I was so eager to get hold of every pretty thing that I giddily grabbed for it, sometimes when it was too far off, and sometimes when it was but six inches away but seemed a foot—alas, with thorns between! I learned a lesson; also I made an axiom, all out of my own head—my very first one: *The scratched Experiment shuns the thorn.* I think it is a very good one for one so young.

I followed the other Experiment around, yesterday afternoon, at a distance, to see what it might be for, if I could. But I was not able to make out. I think it is a man. I had never seen a man, but it looked like one, and I feel sure that that is what it is. I realize that I feel more curiosity about it than about any of the other reptiles. If it is a reptile, and I suppose it is; for it has frowsy hair and blue eyes, and looks like a reptile. It has no hips; it tapers like a carrot; when it stands, it spreads itself apart like a derrick; so I think it is a reptile, though it may be architecture.

I was afraid of it at first, and started to run every time it turned around, for I thought it was going to chase me; but by-and-by I found it was only trying to get away, so after that I was not timid any more, but tracked it along, several hours, about twenty yards behind, which made it nervous and unhappy. At last it was a good deal worried, and climbed a tree. I waited a good while, then gave it up and went home.

To-day the same thing over. I've got it up the tree again.

*Sunday.*—It is up there yet. Resting, apparently. But that is a subterfuge: Sunday isn't the day of rest; Saturday is appointed for that. It looks to me like a creature that is more interested in resting than in anything else. It would tire me to rest so much. It tires me just to sit around and watch the tree. I do wonder what it is for; I never see it do anything.

They returned the moon last night, and I was *so* happy! I think it is very honest of them. It slid down and fell off again, but I was not distressed; there is no need to worry when one has that kind of neighbors; they will fetch it back. I wish I could do something to show my appreciation. I would like to send them some stars, for we have more than we can use. I mean I, not we, for I can see that the reptile cares nothing for such things.

It has low tastes, and is not kind. When I went there yesterday evening in the gloaming it had crept down and was trying to catch the little speckled fishes that play in the pool, and I had to clod it to make it go up the tree again and let them alone. I wonder if *that* is what it is for? Hasn't it any heart? Hasn't it any compassion for those little creatures? Can it be that it was designed and manufactured for such ungentle work? It has the look of it. One of the clods took it back of the ear, and it used language. It gave me a thrill, for it was the first time I had ever heard speech, except my own. I did not understand the words, but they seemed expressive.

When I found it could talk I felt a new interest in it, for I love to talk; I talk, all day, and in my sleep, too, and I am very interesting, but if I had another to talk to I could be twice as interesting, and would never stop, if desired.

If this reptile is a man, it isn't an *it*, is it? That wouldn't be grammatical, would it? I think it would be *he*. I think so. In that case one would parse it thus: nominative, *he;* dative, *him;* possessive, *his'n.* Well, I will consider it a man and call it he until it turns out to be something else. This will be handier than having so many uncertainties.

*Next week Sunday.*—All the week I tagged around after him and tried to get acquainted. I had to do the talking, because he was shy, but I didn't mind it. He seemed pleased to have me around, and I

used the sociable "we" a good deal, because it
seemed to flatter him to be included.

*Wednesday.*—We are getting along very well indeed, now, and getting better and better acquainted.
He does not try to avoid me any more, which is a
good sign, and shows that he likes to have me with
him.  That pleases me, and I study to be useful to
him in every way I can, so as to increase his regard.
During the last day or two I have taken all the work
of naming things off his hands, and this has been a
great relief to him, for he has no gift in that line, and
is evidently very grateful.  He can't think of a rational name to save him, but I do not let him see
that I am aware of his defect.  Whenever a new
creature comes along I name it before he has time
to expose himself by an awkward silence.  In this
way I have saved him many embarrassments.  I
have no defect like his.  The minute I set eyes on
an animal I know what it is.  I don't have to reflect
a moment; the right name comes out instantly, just
as if it were an inspiration, as no doubt it is, for I
am sure it wasn't in me half a minute before.  I
seem to know just by the shape of the creature and
the way it acts what animal it is.

When the dodo came along he thought it was a
wild-cat—I saw it in his eye.  But I saved him.
And I was careful not to do it in a way that could
hurt his pride.  I just spoke up in a quite natural
way of pleased surprise, and not as if I was dreaming

of conveying information, and said, "Well, I do declare, if there isn't the dodo!" I explained—without seeming to be explaining—how I knew it for a dodo, and although I thought maybe he was a little piqued that I knew the creature when he didn't, it was quite evident that he admired me. That was very agreeable, and I thought of it more than once with gratification before I slept. How little a thing can make us happy when we feel that we have earned it.

*Thursday.*—My first sorrow. Yesterday he avoided me and seemed to wish I would not talk to him. I could not believe it, and thought there was some mistake, for I loved to be with him, and loved to hear him talk, and so how could it be that he could feel unkind towards me when I had not done anything? But at last it seemed true, so I went away and sat lonely in the place where I first saw him the morning that we were made and I did not know what he was and was indifferent about him; but now it was a mournful place, and every little thing spoke of him, and my heart was very sore. I did not know why very clearly, for it was a new feeling; I had not experienced it before, and it was all a mystery, and I could not make it out.

But when night came I could not bear the lonesomeness, and went to the new shelter which he has built, to ask him what I had done that was wrong and how I could mend it and get back his kindness again; but he put me out in the rain, and it was my first sorrow.

*Sunday.*—It is pleasant again, now, and I am happy; but those were heavy days; I do not think of them when I can help it.

I tried to get him some of those apples, but I cannot learn to throw straight. I failed, but I think the good intention pleased him. They are forbidden, and he says I shall come to harm; but so I come to harm through pleasing him, why shall I care for that harm?

*Monday.*—This morning I told him my name, hoping it would interest him. But he did not care for it. It is strange. If he should tell me his name, I would care. I think it would be pleasanter in my ears than any other sound.

He talks very little. Perhaps it is because he is not bright, and is sensitive about it and wishes to conceal it. It is such a pity that he should feel so, for brightness is nothing; it is in the heart that the values lie. I wish I could make him understand that a loving good heart is riches, and riches enough, and that without it intellect is poverty.

Although he talks so little he has quite a considerable vocabulary. This morning he used a surprisingly good word. He evidently recognized, himself, that it was a good one, for he worked it in twice afterwards, casually. It was not good casual art, still it showed that he possesses a certain quality of perception. Without a doubt that seed can be made to grow, if cultivated.

Where did he get that word? I do not think I have ever used it.

No, he took no interest in my name. I tried to hide my disappointment, but I suppose I did not succeed. I went away and sat on the moss-bank with my feet in the water. It is where I go when I hunger for companionship, some one to look at, some one to talk to. It is not enough—that lovely white body painted there in the pool—but it is something, and something is better than utter loneliness. It talks when I talk; it is sad when I am sad; it comforts me with its sympathy; it says, "Do not be downhearted, you poor friendless girl; I will be your friend." It *is* a good friend to me, and my only one; it is my sister.

That first time that she forsook me! ah, I shall never forget that—never, never. My heart was lead in my body! I said, "She was all I had, and now she is gone!" In my despair I said, "Break, my heart; I cannot bear my life any more!" and hid my face in my hands, and there was no solace for me. And when I took them away, after a little, there she was again, white and shining and beautiful, and I sprang into her arms!

That was perfect happiness; I had known happiness before, but it was not like this, which was ecstasy. I never doubted her afterwards. Sometimes she stayed away—maybe an hour, maybe almost the whole day, but I waited and did not doubt; I said, "She is busy, or she is gone a journey, but she will come." And it was so: she always did. At night she would not come if it was dark, for she was a timid little thing; but if there was a moon she would come. I am not afraid of the dark, but she is younger than I am; she was born after I was. Many and many are the visits I have paid her; she is my comfort and my refuge when my life is hard—and it is mainly that.

*Tuesday.*—All the morning I was at work improving the estate; and I purposely kept away from him in the hope that he would get lonely and come. But he did not.

At noon I stopped for the day and took my recreation by flitting all about with the bees and the butterflies and revelling in the flowers, those beautiful creatures that catch the smile of God out of the sky and preserve it! I gathered them, and made them into wreaths and garlands and clothed myself in them while I ate my luncheon — apples, of course; then I sat in the shade and wished and waited. But he did not come.

But no matter. Nothing would have come of it, for he does not care for flowers. He calls them rubbish, and cannot tell one from another, and thinks it is superior to feel like that. He does not care for me, he does not care for flowers, he does not care for the painted sky at eventide—is there anything

he does care for, except building shacks to coop himself up in from the good clean rain, and thumping
the melons, and sampling the grapes, and fingering
the fruit on the trees, to see how those properties
are coming along?

I laid a dry stick on the ground and tried to bore
a hole in it with another one, in order to carry out a
scheme that I had, and soon I got an awful fright.
A thin, transparent bluish film rose out of the hole,
and I dropped everything and ran! I thought it
was a spirit, and I *was* so frightened! But I looked
back, and it was not coming; so I leaned against a
rock and rested and panted, and let my limbs go on
trembling until they got steady again; then I crept
warily back, alert, watching, and ready to fly if there
was occasion; and when I was come near, I parted
the branches of a rose-bush and peeped through—
wishing the man was about, I was looking so cunning and pretty—but the sprite was gone. I went
there, and there was a pinch of delicate pink dust in
the hole. I put my finger in, to feel it, and said
*ouch!* and took it out again. It was a cruel pain. I
put my finger in my mouth; and by standing first
on one foot and then the other, and grunting, I presently eased my misery; then I was full of interest,
and began to examine.

I was curious to know what the pink dust was.
Suddenly the name of it occurred to me, though I
had never heard of it before. It was *fire!* I was
as certain of it as a person could be of anything in

the world.   So without hesitation I named it that—
fire.

I had created something that didn't exist before;
I had added a new thing to the world's uncountable
properties; I realized this, and was proud of my
achievement, and was going to run and find him and
tell him about it, thinking to raise myself in his
esteem—but I reflected, and did not do it.   No—he
would not care for it.   He would ask what it was
good for, and what could I answer? for if it was
not *good* for something, but only beautiful, merely
beautiful—

So I sighed, and did not go.   For it wasn't good
for anything; it could not build a shack, it could not
improve melons, it could not hurry a fruit crop; it
was useless, it was a foolishness and a vanity; he
would despise it and say cutting words.   But to me
it was not despicable; I said, "Oh, you fire, I love
you, you dainty pink creature, for you are *beautiful*
—and that is enough!" and was going to gather it
to my breast.   But refrained.   Then I made another maxim out of my own head, though it was so
nearly like the first one that I was afraid it was
only a plagiarism: "*The burnt Experiment shuns the
fire.*"

I wrought again; and when I had made a good
deal of fire-dust I emptied it into a handful of dry
brown grass, intending to carry it home and keep it
always and play with it; but the wind struck it and
it sprayed up and spat out at me fiercely, and I

dropped it and ran. When I looked back the blue spirit was towering up and stretching and rolling away like a cloud, and instantly I thought of the name of it—*smoke!*—though, upon my word, I had never heard of smoke before.

Soon, brilliant yellow - and - red flares shot up through the smoke, and I named them in an instant —*flames!*—and I was right, too, though these were the very first flames that had ever been in the world. They climbed the trees, they flashed splendidly in and out of the vast and increasing volume of tumbling smoke, and I had to clap my hands and laugh and dance in my rapture, it was so new and strange and so wonderful and so beautiful!

He came running, and stopped and gazed, and said not a word for many minutes. Then he asked what it was. Ah, it was too bad that he should ask such a direct question. I had to answer it, of course, and I did. I said it was fire. If it annoyed him that I should know and he must ask, that was not my fault; I had no desire to annoy him. After a pause he asked:

"How did it come?"

Another direct question, and it also had to have a direct answer.

"I made it."

The fire was travelling farther and farther off. He went to the edge of the burned place and stood looking down, and said:

"What are these?"

"Fire-coals."

He picked up one to examine it, but changed his mind and put it down again. Then he went away. *Nothing* interests him.

But I was interested. There were ashes, gray and soft and delicate and pretty — I knew what they were at once. And the embers; I knew the embers, too. I found my apples, and raked them out, and was glad; for I am very young and my appetite is active. But I was disappointed; they were all burst open and spoiled. Spoiled apparently; but it was not so; they were better than raw ones. Fire is beautiful; some day it will be useful, I think.

*Friday.*—I saw him again, for a moment, last Monday at nightfall, but only for a moment. I was hoping he would praise me for trying to improve the estate, for I had meant well and had worked hard. But he was not pleased, and turned away and left me. He was also displeased on another account: I tried once more to persuade him to stop going over the Falls. That was because the fire had revealed to me a new passion—quite new, and distinctly different from love, grief, and those others which I had already discovered — *fear*. And it is horrible! — I wish I had never discovered it; it gives me dark moments, it spoils my happiness, it makes me shiver and tremble and shudder. But I could not persuade him, for he has not discovered fear yet, and so he could not understand me.

## Extract from Adam's Diary

*Perhaps I ought to remember that she is very young, a mere girl, and make allowances. She is all interest, eagerness, vivacity, the world is to her a charm, a wonder, a mystery, a joy; she can't speak for delight when she finds a new flower, she must pet it and caress it and smell it and talk to it, and pour out endearing names upon it. And she is color-mad: brown rocks, yellow sand, gray moss, green foliage, blue sky; the pearl of the dawn, the purple shadows on the mountains, the golden islands floating in crimson seas at sunset, the pallid moon sailing through the shredded cloud-rack, the star-jewels glittering in the wastes of space—none of them is of any practical value, so far as I can see, but because they have color and majesty, that is enough for her, and she loses her mind over them. If she could quiet down and keep still a couple of minutes at a time, it would be a reposeful spectacle. In that case I think I could enjoy looking at her; indeed I am sure I could, for I am coming to realize that she is a quite remarkably comely creature — lithe, slender, trim, rounded, shapely, nimble, graceful; and once when she was standing marble-white and sun-drenched on a bowlder, with her young head tilted back and her hand shading her eyes, watching the flight of a bird in the sky, I recognized that she was beautiful.*

*Monday noon.—If there is anything on the planet that she is not interested in it is not in my list. There are animals that I am indifferent to, but it is not so with her. She has no discrimination, she takes to all of them, she thinks they are all treasures, every new one is welcome.*

*When the mighty brontosaurus came striding into camp, she regarded it as an acquisition. I considered it a calamity; that is a good sample of the lack of harmony that prevails in our views of things. She wanted to domesticate it, I wanted to make it a present of the homestead and move out. She believed it could be tamed by kind treatment and would be a good pet; I said a pet twenty-one feet high and eighty-four feet long would be no proper thing to have about the place, because, even with the best intentions and without meaning any harm, it could sit down on the house and mash it, for any one could see by the look of its eye that it was absent-minded.*

*Still, her heart was set upon having that monster, and she couldn't give it up. She thought we could start a dairy with it, and wanted me to help her milk it; but I wouldn't; it was too risky. The sex wasn't right, and we hadn't any ladder anyway. Then she wanted to ride it, and look at the scenery. Thirty or forty feet of its tail was lying on the ground, like a fallen tree, and she thought she could climb it, but she was mistaken; when she got to the steep place it was too slick and down she came, and would have hurt herself but for me.*

*Was she satisfied now? No. Nothing ever satisfies her but demonstration; untested theories are not in her line, and she won't have them. It is the right spirit, I concede it; it attracts me; I feel the influence of it; if I were with her more I think I should take it up myself. Well, she had one theory remaining about this colossus: she thought that if we could tame him and make him friendly we could stand him in the river and use him for a bridge. It turned out that he was already plenty tame enough—at least as far as she was concerned—so she tried her theory, but it failed: every time she got him properly placed in the river and went ashore to cross over on him, he came out and followed her around like a pet mountain. Like the other animals. They all do that.*

*Friday.*—Tuesday—Wednesday—Thursday—and to-day: all without seeing him. It is a long time to be alone; still, it is better to be alone than unwelcome.

I *had* to have company—I was made for it, I think—so I made friends with the animals. They are just charming, and they have the kindest disposition and the politest ways; they never look sour, they never let you feel that you are intruding, they smile at you and wag their tail, if they've got one, and they are always ready for a romp or an excursion or anything you want to propose. I think they are perfect gentlemen. All these days we have had such good times, and it hasn't been lonesome for me, ever. Lonesome! No, I should say not. Why, there's always a swarm of them around—sometimes as much as four or five acres—you can't count them; and when you stand on a rock in the midst and look out over the furry expanse it is so mottled and splashed and gay with color and frisking sheen and sun-flash, and so rippled with stripes, that you might think it was a lake, only you know it isn't; and there's storms of sociable birds, and hurricanes of whirring wings; and when the sun strikes all that feathery commotion, you have a blazing up of all the colors you can think of, enough to put your eyes out.

We have made long excursions, and I have seen a

great deal of the world; almost all of it, I think; and
so I am the first traveller, and the only one. When
we are on the march, it is an imposing sight—there's
nothing like it anywhere. For comfort I ride a tiger
or a leopard, because it is soft and has a round back
that fits me, and because they are such pretty animals; but for long distance or for scenery I ride the
elephant. He hoists me up with his trunk, but I
can get off myself; when we are ready to camp, he
sits and I slide down the back way.

The birds and animals are all friendly to each
other, and there are no disputes about anything.
They all talk, and they all talk to me, but it must be
a foreign language, for I cannot make out a word
they say; yet they often understand me when I talk
back, particularly the dog and the elephant. It
makes me ashamed. It shows that they are brighter
than I am, and are therefore my superiors. It an-
noys me, for I want to be the principal Experiment
myself—and I intend to be, too.

I have learned a number of things, and am educated, now, but I wasn't at first. I was ignorant at
first. At first it used to vex me because, with all
my watching, I was never smart enough to be
around when the water was running up-hill; but
now I do not mind it. I have experimented and
experimented until now I know it never does run up-
hill, except in the dark. I know it does in the dark,
because the pool never goes dry; which it would, of
course, if the water didn't come back in the night.

It is best to prove things by actual experiment; then you *know;* whereas if you depend on guessing and supposing and conjecturing, you will never get educated.

Some things you *can't* find out; but you will never know you can't by guessing and supposing: no, you have to be patient and go on experimenting until you find out that you can't find out. And it is delightful to have it that way, it makes the world so interesting. If there wasn't anything to find out, it would be dull. Even trying to find out and not finding out is just as interesting as trying to find out and finding out, and I don't know but more so. The secret of the water was a treasure until I *got* it; then the excitement all went away, and I recognized a sense of loss.

By experiment I know that wood swims, and dry leaves, and feathers, and plenty of other things; therefore by all that cumulative evidence you know that a rock will swim; but you have to put up with simply knowing it, for there isn't any way to prove it—up to now. But I shall find a way—then *that* excitement will go. Such things make me sad; because by-and-by when I have found out everything there won't be any more excitements, and I do love excitements so! The other night I couldn't sleep for thinking about it.

At first I couldn't make out what I was made for, but now I think it was to search out the secrets of this wonderful world and be happy and thank the Giver of it all for devising it. I think there **are**

many things to learn yet—I hope so; and by econo-
mizing and not hurrying too fast I think they will
last weeks and weeks. I hope so. When you cast
up a feather it sails away on the air and goes out of
sight; then you throw up a clod and it doesn't. It
comes down, every time. I have tried it and tried
it, and it is always so. I wonder why it is? Of
course it *doesn't* come down, but why should it *seem*
to? I suppose it is an optical illusion. I mean, one
of them is. I don't know which one. It may be
the feather, it may be the clod; I can't prove which
it is, I can only demonstrate that one or the other is
a fake, and let a person take his choice.

By watching, I know that the stars are not going
to last. I have seen some of the best ones melt and
run down the sky. Since one can melt, they can all
melt; since they can all melt, they can all melt the
same night. That sorrow will come—I know it. I
mean to sit up every night and look at them as long as
I can keep awake; and I will impress those sparkling
fields on my memory, so that by-and-by when they
are taken away I can by my fancy restore those lovely
myriads to the black sky and make them sparkle
again, and double them by the blur of my tears.

### AFTER THE FALL

When I look back, the Garden is a dream to me.
It was beautiful, surpassingly beautiful, enchant-
ingly beautiful; and now it is lost, and I shall not see
it any more.

The Garden is lost, but I have found *him*, and am content. He loves me as well as he can; I love him with all the strength of my passionate nature, and this, I think, is proper to my youth and sex. If I ask myself why I love him, I find I do not know, and do not really much care to know; so I suppose that this kind of love is not a product of reasoning and statistics, like one's love for other reptiles and animals. I think that this must be so. I love certain birds because of their song; but I do not love Adam on account of his singing—no, it is not that; the more he sings the more I do not get reconciled to it. Yet I ask him to sing, because I wish to learn to like everything he is interested in. I am sure I can learn, because at first I could not stand it, but now I can. It sours the milk, but it doesn't matter; I can get used to that kind of milk.

It is not on account of his brightness that I love him—no, it is not that. He is not to blame for his brightness, such as it is, for he did not make it himself; he is as God made him, and that is sufficient. There was a wise purpose in it, *that* I know. In time it will develop, though I think it will not be sudden; and besides, there is no hurry; he is well enough just as he is.

It is not on account of his gracious and considerate ways and his delicacy that I love him. No, he has lacks in these regards, but he is well enough just so, and is improving.

It is not on account of his industry that I love

him—no, it is not that. I think he has it in him, and I do not know why he conceals it from me. It is my only pain. Otherwise he is frank and open with me, now. I am sure he keeps nothing from me but this. It grieves me that he should have a secret from me, and sometimes it spoils my sleep, thinking of it, but I will put it out of my mind; it shall not trouble my happiness, which is otherwise full to overflowing.

It is not on account of his education that I love him—no, it is not that. He is self-educated, and does really know a multitude of things, but they are not so.

It is not on account of his chivalry that I love him—no, it is not that. He told on me, but I do not blame him; it is a peculiarity of sex, I think, and he did not make his sex. Of course I would not have told on him, I would have perished first; but that is a peculiarity of sex, too, and I do not take credit for it, for I did not make my sex.

Then why is it that I love him? *Merely because he is masculine*, I think.

At bottom he is good, and I love him for that, but I could love him without it. If he should beat me and abuse me, I should go on loving him. I know it. It is a matter of sex, I think.

He is strong and handsome, and I love him for that, and I admire him and am proud of him, but I could love him without those qualities. If he were plain, I should love him; if he were a wreck, I should love him; and I would work for him, and slave over him, and pray for him, and watch by his bedside until I died.

Yes, I think I love him merely because he is *mine* and is *masculine*. There is no other reason, I suppose. And so I think it is as I first said: that this kind of love is not a product of reasonings and statistics. It just *comes* — none knows whence — and cannot explain itself. And doesn't need to.

It is what I think. But I am only a girl, and the first that has examined this matter, and it may turn out that in my ignorance and inexperience I have not got it right.

### FORTY YEARS LATER

It is my prayer, it is my longing, that we may pass from this life together—a longing which shall never perish from the earth, but shall have place in the heart of every wife that loves, until the end of time; and it shall be called by my name.

But if one of us must go first, it is my prayer that it shall be I; for he is strong, I am weak, I am not so necessary to him as he is to me—life without him would not be life; how could I endure it? This prayer is also immortal, and will not cease from being offered up while my race continues. I am the first wife; and in the last wife I shall be repeated.

### AT EVE'S GRAVE

ADAM: Wheresoever she was, *there* was Eden.

## Date Loaned

| | | | |
|---|---|---|---|
| NOV 2 5 | 1942 | *Edith Taylor* | |
| JAN 1 9 | 1944 | *Mrs. Lowrey* | N JM |
| | | | |
| | | | |
| | | | |
| | | | |
| | | | |
| | | | |
| | | | |
| | | | |
| | | | |
| | | | |
| | | | |
| | | | |
| | | | |
| | | | |
| | | | |
| | | | |
| | | | |
| | | | |
| | | | |
| | | | |